He took her breath away...

He had the high cheekbones and dark, burning eyes of a desert warrior. He looked as though he'd ridden out of every woman's fantasy...and into Cathy's hotel lobby.

"I would like the bridal suite," he said.

Cathy was annoyed to feel a twinge of loss. She smothered it instantly. "May I have your name, please, and how many are in your party?"

"I am Sheikh Kedar Bahram...and I am alone, but the Secret Service will catch up to me eventually."

"The Secret Service!" Cathy swallowed hard. "Are you expecting any trouble?"

"Nothing I cannot handle."

"You aren't planning to kidnap this bride, are you?"

"It should not be necessary. We have been betrothed since she was a month old."
Sheikh Kedar Bahram gave Cathy a slight bow.
"I wish to greet you formally and to beg your forgiveness for any offense. You are Catherine Maxwell...and you are about to become a mother-in-law. My betrothed is your three-year-old daughter."

Dear Reader,

Thanks so much for your wonderful response to the
HOW TO MARRY... trilogy we brought you last year.
You loved those romances and told us you wanted
more. And we listened.

We're happy to bring you another fun-filled
HOW TO MARRY... book—this time it's
A Real-Live Sheikh. Like his predecessors, this
sheikh is sexy, sensuous and sure to make your toes
curl. You'll delight in how he teaches our heroine a
thing or two about real passion.

After living in Italy and traveling in many countries,
Jacqueline Diamond has developed a strong
appreciation for other cultures. Marakite can't be
found on any map, but it is based in part on several
Arabian lands. Jackie hopes readers will share her
fascination with and respect for its warmhearted and
courageous people.

Happy reading!

Regards,

Debra Matteucci
Senior Editor & Editorial Coordinator
Harlequin Books
300 East 42nd Street
New York, NY 10017

HOW TO MARRY...

A Real-Live Sheikh

JACQUELINE DIAMOND

Harlequin Books

TORONTO • NEW YORK • LONDON
AMSTERDAM • PARIS • SYDNEY • HAMBURG
STOCKHOLM • ATHENS • TOKYO • MILAN
MADRID • WARSAW • BUDAPEST • AUCKLAND

To Lynn Gunzberg

ISBN 0-373-16716-4

A REAL-LIVE SHEIKH

Copyright © 1998 by Jackie Hyman.

Chapter One

As she came out of the courthouse, Cathy Maxwell paused to let the June sunlight warm her face. She took a deep breath and let herself enjoy a profound sense of happiness.

Little Yasmin's hand shifted in hers, but there was none of the eager tugging one might expect from a child a month shy of her fourth birthday. Since infancy, Cathy's daughter had regarded the world through calm, dark eyes that seemed to brim with ancient wisdom.

"Miss Maxwell?" A woman with chin-length brown hair and a pink designer suit hurried up the courthouse steps, followed by a photographer. "Sorry we're late. Did the adoption go through?"

This must be the reporter from the *Los Angeles Globe* who'd called yesterday. Cathy hadn't expected her to actually show up, since her paper was based in downtown L.A., some forty miles away.

The *Globe* had run a brief article when Yasmin was abandoned three and a half years ago, and done a few follow-ups about Cathy's battle to keep her. But it wasn't an important enough story to merit major coverage.

"Yasmin's all mine, forever and ever," she said. "My

lawyer can give you the details. He should be out in a minute, if you'd like to speak to him."

"I will," the reporter said. "But this is such a heart-warming story. Do you feel it was fate that led you to find Yasmin?"

Cathy sighed. "I didn't find her, she was given to me. Her mother put her in my arms and said, 'Take good care of her.' I feel that she made me the guardian."

"Is that why you've been fighting so hard for the baby?"

"No." Cathy smiled down at her daughter, and heard the whirr of the camera's lens. "I've been fighting for her because I love her."

Standing straight in her velvet-edged tweed coat, Yasmin looked as regal as a princess. Dark curls tumbled around her heart-shaped face, and the only sign of impatience was the way she fingered one of her tiny half-moon earrings.

The reporter crouched down. "Honey, what do you think of all this?"

"I think I'd like some ice cream," Yasmin said. "Mommy promised me some if I was good."

The reporter chuckled, then straightened. "Well, Cathy, congratulations. But tell me, don't you ever wonder where Yasmin's real mother is today?"

In a level voice, Cathy said, "I'm her real mother now."

"Of course." The woman jotted a note.

Cathy didn't stick around for any more questions. Yasmin's self-control had given way, and the little girl was dragging her toward the car.

"SAW YOUR PICTURE in the paper today," Bert Lowie, manager of the Laguna Sand and Stars Hotel, told Cathy late the next morning. With one minor crisis following another, it was the first chance her boss had had to speak to her about anything personal.

"Really? I missed it." She'd been so tired after yesterday's excitement, she'd overslept and barely made it to work on time.

"I'll bring you a copy." Bert ran his fingers through his thinning brown hair. Seven years ago, when Cathy first came to work at the hotel, he'd been stiff and formal, but he'd since lightened up and they'd become friends. "To tell you the truth, I never thought you'd pull it off."

"The adoption? Sometimes I didn't, either." Now that it was over, Cathy could admit the truth. "If Mom hadn't put a lawyer on the case right away, the social workers would have taken Yasmin."

"What will you do now?" Bert glanced across the lobby from where they stood at the concierge's desk. A couple with two teenagers was checking out, being handled efficiently by the desk clerk. Other than that, the place was mercifully quiet after a flurry of early arrivals and mixed-up reservations.

Everything about the Sand and Stars was low-key, from the unassuming lobby to the scatter of palm trees and bird-of-paradise plants around the grounds. Ocean vistas, Laguna Beach's art shows and a short commute to Disneyland drew guests. But Cathy rarely saw crisp business types or self-absorbed socialites, just ordinary vacationers.

"What will I do now?" she echoed. "Bert, I don't expect any big changes. Mostly I'll keep working and supporting my child."

He shook his head. "You used to be ambitious. You never intended to spend your whole life being the assistant manager of a hotel. Having to work all that overtime to pay the lawyers put you offtrack, but I imagine you'll be going for that M.B.A. soon.''

"Maybe someday." Cathy shrugged. "Mostly I want to spend as much time as possible with Yasmin."

"I admire you," Bert said, "but I also know you. You want the best for her, and your mother may not always be around to help out. In the old days, people would have said you needed a husband."

"In the old days, if my fiancé had let me help put him through medical school and then run out on me, some male relative of mine would have gone after him with a shotgun," Cathy flared with more ferocity than she'd intended. "Bert, a man is the last thing I need."

He hesitated as if about to say more, but a call came in for Cathy about booking a wedding. While she was on the phone, a guest arrived in the lobby clad in nothing but a bath towel, shouting that he couldn't get any hot water in his room. Bert hurriedly ushered the man out of sight.

Cathy went through her wedding checklist, making sure enough space was reserved for overnight guests plus changing rooms for the bridal party. The catering manager took over the details of the reception, and Cathy retreated into her office for a bite of homemade lunch.

She didn't want to think about her M.B.A. She just wanted to relish the fact that for the first time ever, she didn't have to worry about losing her daughter.

Three and a half years ago, Cathy had been the front-desk clerk on a rainy night when a young woman hurried into the lobby with a baby in her arms. The woman had huddled into her raincoat and scarf, her young face tense.

"Is someone chasing you?" Cathy had asked. "I can call for help."

"No, no." The woman had a thick accent, one that Cathy couldn't place. "It is nothing like that."

"Do you need a room?"

Two smoky eyes had bored into Cathy's. "No, I must leave. But..." With sudden determination she thrust the baby into Cathy's arms. "You are a kind woman. Take good care of her." With that, she fled into the night.

"Wait!" There hadn't been anyone else around, and Cathy didn't dare set the baby down. By the time she reached the door, still gingerly holding her charge, the woman had vanished.

Cathy's first thought was to call the authorities. At twenty-three, she'd known nothing about babies and hadn't planned on ever having any.

Her youthful fantasies of being swept away by love had ended a year earlier when her fiancé, Ralph, dumped her right after receiving his medical degree. She'd gotten over being angry and hurt, but the worst damage had run deeper. She'd lost her ability to dream about anything except succeeding in the tough, impersonal world of business.

Until, that is, she felt the baby's little fingers touch her wrist. She had glanced down into its alert, inquisitive face, and fallen head over heels in love, hopelessly and forever.

The only clues to the child's identity were the half-moon earrings that pierced her tiny lobes, and a silver bracelet inscribed with the name Yasmin. For a time after the information appeared in the local paper, Cathy had feared relatives might appear to claim the baby, but no one ever turned up.

Now the child was hers. Warmth spread through her as she downed her brown-bagged corned beef sandwich. She could plan Yasmin's fourth birthday party without having to worry that someone, somehow, would disrupt everything.

She was cleaning up the remains of lunch when she heard the desk clerk call, "Wow! You'd better come see this!"

On arriving in the lobby, Cathy discovered she wasn't the only one who had heard his words. Several members of the staff plus a half-dozen guests had assembled to stare out the glass front.

The longest limousine she had ever seen was trying to angle down a slope from the busy Pacific Coast Highway into the narrow turnaround in front of the hotel. The sleek white vehicle almost made the corner—almost, but not quite. Now it was well and truly stuck.

The only possible escape was to back up, but she doubted the driver could see very well uphill. Besides, trying to back up onto the highway was a hair-raising prospect even for a normal-size car.

"Were we expecting someone important?" asked the gaping desk clerk.

"All our guests are important!" Cathy snapped. "I'd better go help."

She strode out of the lobby, trying not to feel self-conscious as the watchers' eyes followed her. Where was the doorman, anyway?

To make matters worse, a brisk offshore breeze whipped her skirt around her thighs and flapped her blazer away from the form-fitting white blouse. Cathy felt as if her clothes were molded to her body, revealing the feminine curves she tried to disguise when she was working. Thank goodness her sandy hair was cut in a thick wedge; it, at least, would fall docilely back into place.

She had just cleared the portico and was approaching the limousine when a tall, white-robed figure emerged from the rear compartment. As he turned to close his door, she noticed a snowy cloth cascading from the top of his head, anchored by a coiled black band.

What was a sheikh doing at the Sand and Stars without advance notice? A wealthy foreign guest might have tastes and needs that required special preparation, and usually the staff was given ample warning.

Yet Cathy's reaction to the man had little to do with her duties as assistant manager. Although, from the back, the visitor was completely covered by his robe save for a pair of burnished Italian loafers, she couldn't help noticing the width of his shoulders and the decisiveness with which he swung around, as if he were accustomed to command.

Then she got a good look at his face, and could only hope the sound of the wind covered her sharp intake of breath.

The sun-bronzed hardness of his face bore no resemblance to the easy tans of Southern California surfers. The man had the high cheekbones and dark, burning eyes of a desert warrior. Cathy could picture him astride an Arabian stallion, leading a charge against impossible odds.

She gritted her teeth, annoyed at being distracted by a fantasy. No bold and tender man would ever sweep through her life, only self-absorbed tricksters like her former fiancé.

"Can I help you?" she asked.

The man surveyed her with no hint of disrespect, yet there was an intimacy in his gaze that made Cathy feel as if he noted every exposed inch of her legs. "My driver will need to back out."

To her surprise, the man spoke English with scarcely a trace of an accent. Only the arrogant tilt of his head and his unusual costume revealed that he came from another world.

"I'm Cathy Maxwell, the assistant manager. If you'll get back in the car, I'd be glad to help."

"Get back in the car?" One eyebrow lifted imperiously.

"For insurance purposes, pedestrians aren't allowed in the driveway," she explained. "Don't worry. This isn't the first time something like this has happened. I know how to run interference."

A front window unrolled in the limo and the uniformed driver poked his head out. "If one of you would watch traffic for me, I'll stop blocking your entrance."

"Of course." Cathy gestured toward the rear door. "Sir? If you would be so good as to..."

Instead of complying, the tall figure strode up the driveway toward the road, his robes flapping in the wind. The sight reminded Cathy of a scene from *Lawrence of Arabia*.

This was no movie, however. She couldn't let a guest expose himself to risk when it was the hotel's driveway that fell short of optimum design. Most limousine drivers paid close enough attention to angle their cars safely, but it took only a slight misjudgment to get stuck.

"Sir!" She ran after the man so fast, her high heels kept slipping on the concrete. "Sir, I can't allow you to do this!"

At the sidewalk, he turned to stare at her. The angle made him seem even taller than he was. "Allow me?" he repeated in a deep voice. "No one allows me to do anything, Miss Maxwell. Or prevents me from it, either."

Cathy could feel her temper heating up. Couldn't the man see that his insistence on acting macho might get her in trouble?

"This isn't my choice," she snapped as she reached the sidewalk. Her breath came fast, but Cathy tried not to show it. "Our insurance requires that only hotel personnel or law-enforcement officers assist with traffic."

Amusement glinted in his dark eyes. "Let me see exactly how you 'assist with traffic,' then."

On previous occasions, Cathy had simply waited a few seconds for a traffic break and then signaled the driver to back up. Today, however, the cars flowed seamlessly along the highway.

To make matters worse, motorists in both directions kept slowing to gape at the sheikh, who stood like an exotic icon with his arms folded. They would be here for a long time if they waited for the traffic to let up, and in the meantime no cars could enter the hotel driveway.

Cathy drew herself up, trying to ignore the way the sea breeze kept snapping her skirt and blazer. Stepping toward the curb lane, she waved her arms in overlapping arcs.

No one stopped. What was wrong with those idiots?

Actually, she knew what was wrong. Just before it reached the hotel, the highway curved, blocking the sight lines so that drivers couldn't grasp the situation until they were nearly on top of her. Furthermore, she was so short that truck drivers might not even notice her.

His Lordship stood watching, his lips curving into a smile. She couldn't back down.

Finally Cathy spotted a slight break in the flow. As two cars passed, she stepped into the nearest lane and resumed her semicircular waving. There was only a panel truck heading this way, and it had time to stop, although just barely.

From the corner of her eye, she caught a blur of white, and then two powerful arms lifted her off her feet. She felt herself pressed against a hard body as the man swung her onto the sidewalk.

He handled her with an ease that further ruffled Cathy's dignity. She wasn't some child to be picked up and set aside!

Biting back angry words, she watched the sheikh take her place on the highway. The truck had stopped, and the white-robed man held the rest of the oncoming traffic at bay while the limo backed, straightened and pulled beneath the hotel's portico. Turning on his heel as if the waiting vehicles didn't exist, the sheikh joined Cathy on the sidewalk.

"That wasn't necessary." She knew she shouldn't use such an angry tone on a guest, but his behavior had been outrageous. "I had everything under control."

"Possibly," said the man. "However, I cannot allow a woman to endanger herself on my behalf."

"I'm not a woman, I'm the assistant manager of this hotel!" she flared. "Your chivalry on my behalf is sorely misplaced, sir!"

Without waiting for his response, Cathy stalked down the slope toward the lobby. As she did, the missing doorman appeared from a side entrance.

"Where have you been?" Cathy demanded, unable to contain her annoyance.

He ducked his head. "I'm sorry, Miss Maxwell. Something I ate for lunch disagreed with me."

He did look pale, and the doorman was usually reliable. "Very well," she said. "Take care of this gentleman's bags, will you, please?"

"Don't bother. My driver will get them." The sheikh strode ahead of Cathy and held the heavy glass door for her.

His action was courteous, she supposed, but it riled her

further. In business situations, men didn't behave toward each other as if they were at a tea party, and they shouldn't behave that way toward women, either.

Restraining her impulse to rebuke him, Cathy marched to the front desk. The employees and guests had dispersed, and the clerk moved aside to let her take charge.

"Do you have a reservation, sir?" she asked crisply.

"No." He leaned on the desk, his face disturbingly close to hers. The heat of his skin and the almost subliminal scent of exotic spices threatened to disrupt her concentration. "Is that a problem?"

"Not in June," she said. "But if this were July, after the arts festivals open, you'd be out of luck. What kind of accommodations did you wish?"

"The bridal suite would be appropriate," he said.

So the man was a newlywed. She hadn't noticed a woman in the limo, but then, the windows were darkened.

"We don't have a bridal suite as such, but there's a large unit available right above the beach," she said. "Would you like us to have flowers delivered for your wife?"

"I have not married her yet," the man said. "And I doubt she would be interested in flowers."

"I see." She didn't, actually, but her guest's private life was none of Cathy's business. "May I have your name, sir?"

"I am Sheikh Kedar Bahram." He announced his title in a booming voice that must have carried all the way to the hotel restaurant.

He handed over a diplomatic passport, and she copied his name into the computer. "How many are in your party, sir?"

"At present, one, but the Secret Service will catch up

with me sooner or later," he said. "They will take care of their own accommodations, I presume."

"The Secret Service?" she said.

"I am the foreign minister of the Emirate of Marakite," he announced in stentorian tones.

Cathy swallowed hard. She had assumed the man was some sort of dignitary, but she hadn't expected him to be a highly placed government official, even of a tiny kingdom. If he required Secret Service protection, that might mean there was some danger. "Are you expecting any trouble?"

"Nothing I cannot handle." He looked as if he might actually enjoy mixing it up.

"You're not planning to kidnap this bride or anything, are you?" The words slipped out before it occurred to Cathy he might not realize she was joking.

Sheikh Kedar Bahram fixed her with a gaze that would have felled a lesser woman. "It should not be necessary. We have been betrothed since she was a month old."

His passport gave his age as twenty-nine. That meant that either his bride had been waiting a long time, or she was much younger. Still, it seemed odd that she should live here. "You're sure she's in Laguna Beach?"

"Positive." He drew a newspaper clipping from a pocket inside his robe. "You are Miss Catherine Maxwell, are you not?"

She nodded curtly. "I believe I introduced myself outside." What on earth was this man up to, some kind of scam?

The sheikh gave a slight bow. "I wish to greet you formally and beg your forgiveness for any offense I have given. It seems we are going to be related."

"I don't think so." She wondered if she should call Bert to run interference with this kook. Yet if he really *was* the foreign minister of Marakite, she didn't want to do anything that might insult him.

"My dear Miss Maxwell, you are about to become my mother-in-law," he said. "My betrothed is Yasmin Al-Haroum and she is, I believe, your daughter."

Chapter Two

Now Cathy knew this had to be a joke. "Of all the sick ideas! I don't know who you are—"

"Of course you do. You have my passport." The man didn't flinch. Apparently he'd been expecting this kind of reaction.

She glanced down at the dark vinyl-covered booklet. She had no idea what a passport from the Emirate of Marakite was supposed to look like. "Obviously you got hold of that newspaper clipping and thought you could blackmail me. Well, I'm sorry to disappoint you, but I don't have any money."

"Fortunately, I do." The sheikh was still leaning on the counter, his dark, dramatic face wearing the same calm expression. "My wife will be a very wealthy woman."

"The operative word here is *woman*," Cathy snapped. "You're trying to tell me you're engaged to a three-year-old? I'm not buying it."

"You are right to be cautious," said the sheikh, or whatever he was. "I would suggest you place a telephone call to my country's consulate in Los Angeles. They will verify that I am here to claim my bride."

After a moment's hesitation, she rang Information for

the number, and dialed it. To her amazement, the consul took her call personally and confirmed that yes, his country's esteemed foreign minister, Sheikh Kedar Bahram, had left the consulate an hour ago for Laguna Beach.

To claim his bride? Oh, yes, yes, a young girl from the Al-Haroum family. A very prominent family, she must know. Really, the whole situation was most delicate. Please to accommodate the sheikh in any way that she could; he was a cousin and adviser to the emir himself.

Maybe it was her exertions of a few minutes earlier, or perhaps it was the effort to absorb this fantastic story, but as soon as she hung up, Cathy felt her head whirl. She must have wavered visibly, because the sheikh reached over and caught her arm.

His grasp was firm, just enough to steady her. "You should sit down, Miss Maxwell."

The desk clerk had been watching them anxiously. "Should I call Bert?"

Cathy nodded. "Tell him I'm taking a break, okay?" Everything around her seemed so normal: the limousine driver carrying in expensive leather suitcases, the tourist family heading out the door with Donald Duck hats on their heads. This man standing in front of her couldn't really expect to marry three-year-old Yasmin.

"There is a restaurant on the premises?" asked the sheikh. "We shall go there and have coffee."

His suggestion reminded Cathy that she'd skipped her usual midmorning cup. That must be why she wasn't feeling quite herself. "All right."

They walked down a carpeted hallway lined with seascape paintings. It seemed to her as if the floor had tilted and the lights glared more than usual. She definitely needed coffee.

A lunch crowd jammed the restaurant, but because of the brisk breeze, no one was sitting on the deck. Sheikh Bahram escorted Cathy outside and held a chair for her at one of the half-dozen tables.

A waitress appeared at once. Cathy guessed that gossip had spread quickly among the hotel staff about their lordly arrival, because the service was speedy even for the Sand and Stars. Before she knew it, they had been presented with mugs filled with black steaming liquid.

"I think we'd better run through this again," she told the sheikh when they were alone. "With names, addresses and serial numbers. You claim you know my daughter's birth family, Mr. Bahram?"

"You must call me Dar. I attended university in your country and went to graduate school in Britain. I am accustomed to the use of first names."

He took his time, choosing his words carefully and discreetly, like a man accustomed to handling complex diplomatic situations. Someone this sophisticated was new to her experience, and she no longer felt so certain she could hold her own.

But Cathy had the home court advantage, she told herself. She was fighting for her child. "I will call you by any name you like, but I will never call you my son-in-law."

The sheikh held out the clipping, which featured a photo of Cathy smiling down at Yasmin. "You see the unusual earrings? She was given those by her grandmother."

Cathy swallowed. She had always known that somewhere Yasmin must have relatives, but the reality hit hard.

Adoptions were supposed to be final. Still, during the past few years, Cathy had read every horror story in the newspapers about birth parents changing their minds, and she knew that nothing was carved in stone.

Particularly if an official from a foreign government was involved. The law might still take her side, but paying lawyers to get this far had nearly broken her. She couldn't afford to battle some rich family.

"Also, we have footprints and fingerprints taken at birth," the sheikh went on. "I am certain we can make a positive identification."

Cathy swallowed a gulp of coffee. "Her mother gave her to me."

"That was not her mother." Dar spoke softly, the arrogance gone from his face. "That was her nanny."

Cathy felt as if the deck had dropped from beneath her and she were free-falling down the cliff onto the sand. Never once had she questioned the assumption that the woman who bequeathed her Yasmin was the child's mother.

Had the girl been kidnapped? It would be unthinkable to withhold her from distraught parents. Yet Dar hadn't said he was here to take Yasmin home, but to marry her.

"I don't understand," she said. "Where are her parents?"

His jaw tightened. "Dead."

"What happened?"

"They were killed in a plane crash when she was six months old," he said. "They were on a trade mission to this country. It was believed the baby and the nanny died with them."

The story sounded logical, but there were still holes in it. "Why would the nanny abandon her?"

Dar stretched in his chair. He moved with such grace that it was easy to forget how solid the man was.

"She believed the child to be cursed," he said. "She

blamed that curse for the plane crash. Only last year did we hear reports that the nanny had been seen alive, but we have not been able to find her.''

"And you just happened to be in Los Angeles the day the photograph ran?''

"I visit here frequently on behalf of my country's pharmaceutical industry. There is no oil in Marakite, but we are located on the ancient frankincense trail. We have discovered another sort of riches in our medicinal plants.''

When he talked about business, Dar sounded rational and Western. A few minutes earlier, when he'd mentioned a curse, he had seemed to Cathy like a figure from Arabian folklore.

"Look, I'm not entirely ignorant,'' she said. "I realize people in other parts of the world have different customs from ours. But I've never heard of men marrying three-year-olds, even in Marakite. Under the laws of our country, I'm Yasmin's mother now, and there is no way I would even consider allowing such a thing.''

"I have not explained myself well.'' Impatiently Dar waved away the waitress's attempt to refill his cup. "I am not talking about anything that would give you cause for concern. This would be a mere formality until Yasmin is grown. There is a great deal that rides on this marriage. It must take place.''

"No!'' Cathy stood so abruptly, she bumped the table. Thank goodness their cups were nearly empty. "It's outrageous. It's disgusting. I can't believe you seriously expect me to entertain such an idea!''

The sheikh also rose. A shaft of afternoon sunlight gleamed on his hawklike face. "You have no idea how many have died already!''

"How many have died...? Are you threatening me?''

Below on the beach, people were sunbathing and playing volleyball. Inside, visible through the glass, a roomful of diners chattered blithely.

But standing here alone with this menacing figure, Cathy felt suddenly vulnerable. The man could pitch her over the railing, or pull out a dagger, and what would happen to Yasmin then?

He made no move toward her, however. "You are frightened. I did not mean to alarm you. I assure you, Cathy, you are in no danger from me."

His deep voice pronounced her name with a romantic lilt. She stood transfixed by the intensity with which he studied her. Her fear had vanished; for some reason, she wanted to trust him. But trust him to do what?

Doors at either end of the deck flew open with a crash that sent Cathy's heart racing. Men in gray suits ran out, their hands thrust inside their coats as if clutching guns. One appeared to be talking into his sleeve.

"Sheikh Bahram?" said the leader. "Are you all right, sir?"

For a moment, Cathy had thought they were being attacked by terrorists. Now she realized these must be the Secret Service agents Dar had mentioned.

"Impeccable timing," he muttered before responding more clearly, "Yes, I am fine. Miss Maxwell presents no threat to me, I assure you. In fact, gentlemen, you are speaking to my future mother-in-law."

Surprise registered on several faces before the men resumed their impassive expressions. "Excuse us, Miss Maxwell," said one who appeared to be the agent in charge.

"If you gentlemen will inquire at the desk, I am sure rooms can be arranged." Cathy headed for the inner door but couldn't help adding, "However, any future relationship between Sheikh Bahram and me exists purely in his imagination.''

She left the deck with her head high, proud of her exit line until she remembered Dar's reference to people dying.

What on earth had he been talking about?

As soon as he was alone in his room overlooking the beach, Dar removed his headdress and shrugged out of his robes. As usual, he wore a Western-style business suit beneath it.

As he yanked a brush through his hair, he silently swore at the Secret Service agents who had barged into his conversation. How could he ever make his case to Cathy Maxwell without privacy?

On the other hand, honesty compelled him to admit that he had had ample time to lay out his case but had done a poor job of it. For reasons he didn't understand, he had found himself distracted by her concerns for her daughter, and by something more—by the woman herself.

He had read honesty and forthrightness in her face, but also a deep-seated anger. That sort of underlying emotion usually sprang from a tragic loss or betrayal. Who had hurt this woman, and why should it matter to him?

Restlessly he picked up the phone and placed an international call. It would be very late in Marakite, but Ezzat had a habit of reading into the small hours, when the palace lay quiet.

The private line rang only twice before it was answered. "Yes, my friend?" Ezzat Al-Aziz sounded faintly puzzled, which was in character. He often seemed to be lost in deep thought, and surprised to awaken in the modern world.

"It is I—Dar."

"Ah. Have you found the child?"

"I have found her adoptive mother." Dar hesitated. It was his duty to report to the emir, but the emir also happened to be his cousin and his best friend. How much should he tell, and how much should he leave until matters became clearer? "We are in negotiations."

"She wants money?" Ezzat asked.

"Not exactly."

"What does she want, then?"

"I believe she wants me to scatter myself on the four winds and never trouble her again."

His cousin laughed. It was a merry sound—unrestrained and genuine. "I did not expect she would cooperate easily. We must be patient."

"Fasad Al-Haroum will not be patient." Distressed, Dar ran his hand through his hair, undoing the brush's work. "The other rebels will not be, either."

"Does she understand that she need not give up the child?" Ezzat pressed.

"Are you so sure of that?" Dar knew the urgency of his marrying Yasmin, but it went against everything he believed to lie to Cathy. "Do you really think Fasad will leave his granddaughter in America?"

"The mother could come to Marakite with her."

"The mother is an American woman with a career. She is not going to give that up. Nor will she sit quietly in the background while her daughter's future is shaped by other people."

"It sounds as if you admire her," Ezzat said softly. "Be careful, my cousin. I have never known you to show such weakness."

"Is it weakness, what you feel for Leila?" Dar bit off the words when he realized what he'd said. Leila was

Ezzat's wife. Cathy Maxwell was a stranger, an outsider and, at present, an obstacle to the welfare of his country. "I apologize. I spoke out of turn."

"I can see you are troubled." Ezzat could be firm when necessary, but he also possessed keen insight into the people close to him. "You believe that, no matter what you do, you will bring pain to this woman."

He had clarified the situation perfectly. "Either she must agree to something I know she can never accept, or we will be forced to act against her with whatever means are necessary. Ezzat, will you do me one favor?"

"Certainly," said his cousin.

"Will you consult the Three-Eyed Woman? Perhaps there is another way than for me to marry this child."

Ezzat clicked his tongue. "In three and a half years, do you not think I have asked this question?"

Dar knew the chances were slim that the prophecy would be altered, but he could not proceed in good conscience without making sure.

"Sometimes a change in external circumstances will bring a broader vision to the oracle," he reminded the emir. "It might offer us some new approach."

"You believe that having located this Maxwell woman presents such a change in circumstances?" Skepticism colored his cousin's voice.

"Not the mere fact that we have found her, but that yesterday, under the laws of her country, she became Yasmin's mother," Dar said. "That is something new, is it not?"

There was a long silence. Dar took it to mean his cousin was considering the suggestion.

"Prophesying is hard on the Three-Eyed Woman," the emir said at last. "However, it is my obligation to present the Council of Elders with this information. I cannot guarantee a swift response, however."

"I know you will do your best," Dar said.

They exchanged wishes of good health, and cut the connection.

Dar remained where he stood by the bed, staring out the sliding glass doors at the Pacific Ocean. True to its name, it lapped quietly at the beach, a contrast to his own turbulent thoughts.

Never before had he been so sharply aware of living in two worlds. He had not imagined he could find himself so strongly attracted to an American woman, nor had he considered, in his quest to find Yasmin, that he might entertain second thoughts about marrying her.

The marriage was a matter of duty, and would exist in name only until either it could be dissolved, or Yasmin came of age and agreed to the union of her free will. Under the laws of Marakite, such an arrangement would not prevent Dar from taking a second wife, but he had absorbed enough of Western culture to find the idea distasteful.

But his strongest reservations sprang from his unexpected feelings about Cathy. He sensed in her a reservoir of strength and dignity that he rarely encountered.

What he felt for the blond woman, he conceded silently, was also partly physical. She moved with a fresh, healthy vigor that hinted at natural sensuality. He even liked the defiant way her wedge-cut hair flew in the wind and then fell stubbornly into place.

But what future could there be for them? Ultimately Dar owed both his loyalty and his life to Marakite and to Ezzat.

If not for his cousin, Dar would still live a nomadic life with the tribe into which he had been born. Although they were as likely to drive pickup trucks as to ride camels, in many ways his people still lived as their ancestors had for thousands of years, herding sheep and goats.

After his father died when he was twelve, Dar had assumed the leadership of his tribe. He had enjoyed taking command, but had worried about the future of his people in a land that lived in the shadow of change.

At fifteen, he had met his cousin during a festival. Ezzat, then twenty-one, was being groomed for the position of emir during the long illness of his father, and had been seeking loyal, intelligent men on whom he could rely once he took power.

It was he who had seen the potential in the rough boy. He had arranged for tutoring to augment Dar's informal education, then paid for him to attend Harvard University and the London School of Economics.

At twenty-nine, Dar still considered himself primarily a man of the desert. His reaction to Cathy, however, was forcing him to face how deeply ingrained the ways of the West had become. Such a woman could not possibly feel comfortable in his homeland and yet...

There could be no "and yet." Unless there were a change in the prophecy, he must marry Yasmin.

Resolutely Dar lifted the phone and put in a series of calls. He must waste no time in winning Cathy's consent to the union.

"I'VE HAD HIM checked out. He's an impressive man, this Sheikh Bahram."

Mary Maxwell set a bowl of homemade spaghetti sauce on the table. Beside her, Yasmin laid one crookedly folded napkin at each of the three places.

"Well, I knew he was the foreign minister of Marakite," Cathy said dubiously. "But it *is* a small country."

She wanted to find some reason to cut off all contact with the arrogant Kedar Bahram. The way his eyes assessed her with each glance was disturbing. And she hated remembering the feel of his powerful arms as he lifted her from the pavement.

She hated it because she kept wishing she could feel his warmth again, and wondering how his hard mouth would taste against hers. These wayward and, for her, highly unusual speculations were driving her crazy.

"He's held in high respect in financial circles," Mary informed her as they went into the kitchen. "I understand he's played a key role in international economic negotiations, although he tends to stay behind the scenes."

If Cathy's mother stated the information with such confidence, it must be true. Despite her air of grandmotherly indulgence as she showed Yasmin how to arrange the forks and spoons, Mary could be a hard-driving businesswoman, and she always got her facts straight.

As a young widow, Cathy's mother had struggled to found a cosmetics company. When it became established, she had branched into holistic beauty preparations.

Her empire had grown slowly, at first because she wanted to stay close to home for her daughter's sake. Then, only a few years after Cathy's college graduation, along had come Yasmin. Since then, Mary had funneled much of her revenue into the legal battle to adopt her granddaughter.

It was she who had enabled Cathy to triumph where social workers advised there was little chance of succeeding. Usually, they had warned, abandoned children became wards of the state and then were given to pre-screened couples.

But Mary always seemed able to dig up an extra fact or a fresh approach or a few more dollars for attorneys' fees. At the same time, she had finally brought her business to the brink of a major expansion. She was the most competent person Cathy knew and, if she said Dar was an important figure on the world scene, it must be true.

"This whole business about the marriage, though. It's preposterous." Cathy had told her mother the story earlier, while Yasmin was playing in the other room.

"Well, of course. Out of the question. Fortunately, in this case the law is on our side." Mary handed unbreakable plates to Yasmin, who carried them solemnly to the table.

Hardly noticing what she was doing, Cathy opened a bag of prepared salad and poured it into a glass bowl. She tossed in some cherry tomatoes and a sprinkling of croutons, which were Yasmin's favorite part.

"Something else is bothering you," her mother said as she retrieved a loaf of French bread from the oven and placed it on a cutting board.

There was no point in trying to hide anything. "The man is gorgeous," Cathy admitted. "I guess I've been alone too long. I have to be careful."

Her mother's mouth pursed thoughtfully as she carried the bread into the dining room. "I'd like to meet this fellow."

"He's like something out of an old movie," Cathy admitted, following her with the salad. Yasmin, eager to help as always, ran to get the salad dressing from the refrigerator.

"That movie wouldn't be *The Sheik,* would it?" teased her mother.

"What's a sheikh?" Yasmin plopped into her chair.

"He's the leader of an Arab tribe." That wouldn't mean much to a three-year-old, so Cathy added, "He wears long robes and a headdress and comes from the East."

"Like the Three Wise Men in the Bible!" piped her daughter. "Is he burying gifts?"

"That's *bearing*," Mary said with a smile, and began serving the food. "It means carrying."

"Oh," Yasmin said solemnly. "I wondered why they buried them."

The women chuckled and exchanged glances. Like all fond mothers and grandmothers, they cherished each childish misstatement.

Then they fell silent, busy eating dinner, and Cathy's thoughts returned to the subject of the Middle East, specifically Marakite. It seemed very far from this small dining alcove.

Through the window, she gazed over the rooftops of neighboring cottages, which lay below them on a steep hill, and out to sea. Long ago, Mary had made the choice to live in a small house near the ocean rather than spend the same money on a larger home inland.

The beach dwellers created a world of their own, funkier and friendlier than could be found elsewhere in the area. Cathy was glad she'd had a chance to grow up in this environment, and she wanted the same for her daughter.

But was it in Yasmin's best interest to have neither a father nor a grandfather? Surely a girl needed some masculine guidance.

Well, perhaps someday Cathy would meet the right man to marry. She had no idea what he might be like; since Ralph left, she had instinctively avoided entanglements. That must be why she felt so susceptible to Dar's masculine presence.

Her jaw tightened instinctively. What tactic would he try next?

She could scarcely bear the prospect of facing another battalion of lawyers. Still, it was unthinkable that any judge would give custody of a little girl to a grown man who intended to marry her.

In front of their cottage, a vehicle jounced to a halt. "Sounds like a delivery truck." Mary frowned. "They should know to take my orders to the warehouse."

Yasmin ran to the living room and climbed onto the couch so she could see out the window. "Come and look, Mommy! The man has flowers. And balloons!"

"Oh, really?" Cathy joined her daughter in the living room. She had a sneaking idea where the gifts came from, but hoped she was wrong.

When she opened the door, the driver staggered inside beneath an enormous arrangement of exotic flowers, roses and Mylar balloons. "Miss Yasmin Maxwell?"

"That's me!" The little girl hopped up and down. "They're for me?"

"There's more." The driver set the arrangement on the coffee table and returned to his truck. The street outside was little wider than an alley, and he was blocking it, but fortunately there was no traffic at the moment.

The deliveryman made three more trips into the house. He brought a basket of stuffed animals: teddy bears, and Sesame Street characters, and Disney figures. Then came a tray of flowering plants, from African violets to orchidlike cyclamens.

By the time he delivered the final offering of Godiva chocolates, fancy cookies and imported tins of caviar and oysters, Yasmin was arranging stuffed animals on every square inch of seating space in the living room.

Cathy tried to tip the man, but he refused. "It's been

taken care of," he said cheerfully. "I'd better go unblock your street before I get a ticket."

She thanked him again and then steered her daughter back to the dinner table. "You'd better finish your meal if you expect to eat any of that chocolate."

Yasmin made a face but didn't argue. Cathy had often thanked her stars for landing such an agreeable child. With the emotional tightrope she'd walked these past few years, it was a blessing not to have to put up with tantrums.

On the other hand, she felt a special obligation to make sure she and others didn't take advantage of Yasmin's good nature. Being a parent meant looking out for her daughter's best interests in a thousand unforeseen ways, Cathy reflected as she finished a slice of French bread.

Few cars used their street, since it served only a handful of houses, so her ears perked up minutes later at the approach of another vehicle. This one was smoother than the delivery truck, but it, too, stopped directly outside.

Abandoning her still-unfinished meal, Yasmin raced for the window again. She climbed onto the couch between the stuffed animals and peered out, her little rear end quivering with excitement. "Mommy, it's the longest car I ever saw!"

Mary placed a reassuring hand atop her daughter's. "It's a good sign if he's come here."

"It is?"

"He wants to talk, not strong-arm you," she said. "Perhaps the man will listen to reason."

"I can't believe you're advising me to meet with him!" Cathy hadn't realized how agitated she felt until she heard her own shrillness. "Mom, have you forgotten what he wants?"

"No." Her mother's strong face, lined from too much

sun and too many worries, mirrored Cathy's conflict.
"But he's held in high regard by people I respect. There
must be a rational explanation for such a bizarre proposal."

"Well, I guess I don't have much choice about receiving him, do I?" Cathy grumbled, ashamed of being so
childish but unable to stop the words. "If I slam the door
in his face, it could create an international incident."

"And if you don't learn the whole story, it wouldn't
be fair to Yasmin," said her mother. "We aren't the only
people who care about her."

The comment felt like cold water thrown in Cathy's
face. She'd been trying not to think about the discovery
that her daughter had foreign grandparents, and perhaps
aunts and uncles and cousins, too.

Maybe I am *being selfish,* she thought. *Yasmin has a
right to know the rest of her family, at least.*

The doorbell rang. A glance out the window confirmed
that Sheikh Kedar Bahram of Marakite had come to call.

Chapter Three

Framed by the modest doorway, the sheikh loomed like a medieval invader. He wore robes of a finer silken weave than earlier, and the snowy richness of the cloth heightened his dramatic coloring.

He leveled a keen gaze at Cathy. Standing only a few feet away, she found herself struck by his intensity as he turned to study the little girl on the couch.

Yasmin returned his interest. "Are you one of the Three Wise Men?"

Dar chuckled. "Not very wise, I do not think."

"Did you send me all these presents?" Her heart-shaped face shone with innocent acquisitiveness. "I haven't had any chocolate yet. Do I really have to finish my dinner?"

"That is up to your mother," Dar said politely. "Are the gifts to your liking?"

The little girl nodded. "Especially Elmo." She indicated a bright red Muppet. "And all the teddy bears!"

"I don't think she's going to eat any more dinner," Cathy conceded. "She's too excited. All right, sweetie, you can have two pieces of candy. Eat them at the table, please."

"Thanks, Mommy!" Yasmin snatched up one of the Godiva boxes and hurried off with it.

Mary, who had sat quietly through this exchange, helped her granddaughter open the box and then came to stand in the archway of the dining alcove. "You must be Sheikh Bahram."

"Please call me Dar. And you are Mrs. Maxwell?"

Cathy watched in fascination as the older woman and the tall man shook hands and locked gazes. There was a self-possessed wariness to their stances that seemed oddly alike.

Into the silence, she said, "What happened to your Secret Service escort?"

Dar released Mary's hand. "I have been forced to give them the slip again. I do appreciate their concern, but at times it becomes inconvenient."

"Are you in danger?" Mary asked.

"There are always rumors of conspiracies." Dar shrugged. "The situation in my country has been unstable for some time. But to my knowledge I have not been singled out as a target."

Here was a threat that hadn't occurred to Cathy. "You mean you're trying to drag my daughter into some sort of political mess?"

"Actually, I am trying to resolve one." Dar glanced through the archway at the little girl, who stared back with wide eyes above a chocolate-smeared mouth. "It might be best if we continued this conversation elsewhere. Perhaps we could walk on the beach."

It was nearly dark outside, but in the small town of Laguna, Cathy felt safer on the beach at night than on some Los Angeles streets in full daylight. "All right. Just let me get my shoes."

"Also, if we do not wish the Secret Service to spot us, I should remove my outer clothing," Dar said.

"You're going to get undressed?" Yasmin asked. "Can I see your underpants?"

The sheikh gave her a startled look.

"She's wondering if they have cartoon characters on them. That is...I think that's what she means." Cathy felt herself blushing. How dared she stand here with this dignitary, discussing his underwear?

A smile creased Dar's face. "In truth," he said, "I wear clothes beneath my robes."

"Feel free to use a bedroom if you'd like a little privacy," Mary said, motioning to a closed door.

"Thank you. I gladly accept your offer." With a bow, he disappeared down the hallway.

"Wow!" said Yasmin. "He's neat!"

"You were right," Mary added in a low voice. "He's gorgeous."

Restlessly Cathy began collecting dishes. "I shouldn't stick you with the cleanup. You've taken care of Yasmin all day."

"You can hardly expect His Eminence to stand around while you wash dishes," her mother said.

"Well, he's busy right now." Cathy stacked three plates and topped them with flatware.

"I'll help!" The little girl hopped up and began collecting small items. "Can I take Elmo to bed tonight?"

"Of course," Cathy responded automatically, her mind whirling as she marched into the kitchen.

"And the bears, too?"

"A couple of them. Otherwise there won't be room for you." She could barely concentrate on what she was saying. Her mind was too full, trying to absorb the reality of Dar's presence in her own home.

Seeing him here made him seem more human, some-how. It also made her feel vulnerable. His sumptuous gifts might have charmed her daughter, but they re-minded Cathy that she could never provide the luxuries that Yasmin's birth family offered.

Most people paid lip service to the importance of real values over materialism. But Dar's lawyers wouldn't ar-gue in terms of stuffed animals or designer candy.

They would talk about the cost of an education and the need for financial security. On that level, Cathy couldn't hope to compete.

Furthermore, she doubted Dar, or whoever might seek custody, would be foolish enough to tell an American judge that they intended to marry off a preschooler. They would describe a family bereft of their granddaughter and a nanny who had had no right to relinquish the baby.

On those grounds, they might win. The prospect set Cathy's stomach churning.

She scrubbed the dishes with unusual vigor, slamming them into the drainer so hard, they rattled. It was a good thing the Maxwells used the unbreakable kind.

"You need to calm down." Mary came up behind her and massaged her shoulders. "Otherwise, you won't be able to keep your wits about you."

"I thought we were finally safe!" Cathy swallowed against a lump in her throat. "Why did this have to hap-pen?"

"Just hear him out," Mary said. "Negotiations always go more smoothly when all parties have been listened to and respected."

Negotiations? Cathy wished she could take her mother's objective view. Still, Mary couldn't be any more thrilled about the developments than she was.

Dar entered, wearing a blue-gray tailored suit that

skimmed the contours of his well-developed shoulders and chest, and emphasized the leanness of his hips. Beneath the jacket, he wore a maroon-and-gray-striped tie over a pale blue shirt.

Freed from the headdress, his skillfully cut dark hair was just long enough to give him the tousled air of a man freshly arisen from bed. The effect was startlingly sexy.

"May I dry?" he said.

"Here!" Eager to help, Yasmin snatched a clean towel from a drawer and handed it to him. "Be careful with the glasses! And if you drop a fork, you have to wash it again."

"I will do that." Dar took his place at the drainboard and began meticulously erasing water spots from the dishes. He had sturdy hands, Cathy noticed, and the fingers were deft.

She could imagine him stroking her back as Mary had done moments before. But if Dar were touching her, she doubted she would relax. The thought of his caress sent heat tingling across her skin.

"Yasmin and I can finish up," her mother said. "You two go have that talk. Better take a jacket—it's chilly out." To Dar, she said, "It may be summer, but June is a cool month around here."

"I know," he said. "I come to Los Angeles often."

Reluctantly Cathy surrendered her position and dried her hands. She wished she felt in full possession of her wits.

From the hall closet, she snatched a blazer. "Coming?" she called, and led the way out the door.

THEY DESCENDED A FLIGHT of wooden steps to the beach. Stars were coming out and, along the cliffs, house lights glimmered.

The shoreline curved smoothly in the deepening twilight and the ocean murmured as if ready for sleep. A couple of dark figures broke the water. Probably die-hard surfers, Dar decided.

Other than that, the cool evening was shared only by a woman walking a dog and an older couple in jogging suits double-timing it along the sand.

No one paid Dar any attention. What a relief it was to be anonymous!

He took pride in his native dress, and it served to distinguish him while conducting official duties. At other times, however, it marked him as an object of curiosity.

Now, although his business suit was a bit formal for the surroundings, he and Cathy might almost have been an ordinary couple taking a stroll. For some reason, Dar found the idea pleasing.

As he had told Ezzat, he knew that she wished he would disappear. Yet he had noticed little things like a glance at his hands while he dried the dishes, and an indrawn breath when he came near, that hinted at a feminine response.

It wasn't surprising, given his own masculine reaction to her. Dar was well schooled in self-control, but Cathy intrigued him.

As they walked, her face was turned partly away, yet he could picture clearly how she had looked when he arrived at the house. Her animated features had been remarkably expressive, the eyes shining blue, the lips soft, the chin stubborn.

There had been no difficulty in reading her chief emotion: dismay. The curious part was that Dar kept wanting to protect her, even from himself.

He had never been accused of oversensitivity to others' feelings. In fact, he had had to work to overcome a tendency, born of his early coming to power in the desert, to skewer others with his will.

It was Ezzat who had taught him, by low-key example, how to accommodate the wishes of others where possible. Also how to persuade them to accept his dominance while reserving hard-core tactics for a last resort.

This time, however, Dar needed no tutoring. He did not want to run roughshod over Cathy. He did not want to see pain and rage and bitterness in her face.

Her voice broke into his reflections. "This afternoon, you referred to people dying. What did you mean?"

"There is a civil war in my country," Dar explained. "It has been going on for ten years, since the old emir died. There is much destruction, and many deaths."

"I've seen something about it on television, although I never paid much attention," she admitted. "But what does this have to do with Yasmin?"

A crisp breeze brought the scents of seaweed and salt air, reminding him of his homeland on the Arabian Sea. "Yasmin is the granddaughter of Sheikh Fasad Al-Haroum, half brother to the old emir and the patriarch of a large and powerful family," Dar said. "When the emir died, Fasad believed he should rule in place of the emir's only son, who is a scholar, not a soldier."

It had not seemed an unreasonable belief at the time. Ezzat was untested, and in the view of many patriots too much attuned to the West.

Dar himself might have sided with Fasad had he not come to know his canny and dedicated cousin. Also, having had a worldly education, Dar could see the importance of developing Marakite's international ties and establishing a solid economy.

"Couldn't they share power in some way?" Cathy asked.

"Perhaps if it were only a question of two men, they could have reached an agreement," Dar said. "But each had advisers who said they must be decisive, or others would call them weak and refuse to follow."

"Men," she grumbled. "Too much testosterone."

"And too much pride." Although he had been raised in the tradition of desert warriors, Dar had seen enough bloodshed these past ten years to teach him the value of diplomatic solutions. "The emir's son, Ezzat Al-Aziz, took power and was recognized by foreign governments. But many sheikhs sided with the Al-Haroums."

They had passed Cathy's hotel, the Sand and Stars, and reached the boardwalk that marked the city's central beach. From a nearby restaurant wafted the tantalizing scents of dinner on the broil.

"So you sided with the emir," Cathy summarized. "The consul described you as his adviser."

"We are good friends as well as cousins," Dar said. "He has seen to my education and been kind to me. But more than that, I respect and honor the man. He is a great leader, even if he is not by nature a warrior."

Without his saying another word, she made the connection between the story of the emir and Dar's reason for intruding into her life. "And you think marrying Yasmin will end this civil war by uniting the two factions? I find that hard to believe. For one thing, why should you be the groom? Why not the emir himself?"

"He is already married," Dar said. "A position as second wife would not be acceptable to Yasmin's family. Not to mention what Ezzat's wife would have to say about it."

"And this rebel leader, Yasmin's grandfather, he would go along with this marriage and a peace treaty? I should think he would object."

"He did, once," Dar admitted. "But no longer."

"Why?"

Here was the crux of the story, Dar reflected as they reached the end of the park and turned back. He answered in measured tones, as if retelling an old legend, which was indeed how it felt.

"Yasmin was the first child born to Ali, the oldest son of Sheikh Al-Haroum. She was born under unusual astrological signs, and her family sought the meaning.

"In Marakite, it is the responsibility of a Council of Elders to rule on matters of significance, whether they be the adoption of Western technology, or how to interpret supernatural occurrences," he said. "We wish to remain true to our beliefs and our traditions, but not to reject automatically all new things."

"So this council told you what the astrological signs meant?" Cathy said.

"They asked the Three-Eyed Woman to prophesy," he said.

"A woman with three eyes?"

"The third eye is hidden," he said. "It is believed to lie beneath the forehead. With it, there are people who can see what is veiled from the rest of us. Such a family lives in Marakite. For centuries, one woman of each generation has served as an oracle."

"You've been educated in the West," she said. "Don't you find this kind of bizarre?"

"It is not so unusual," Dar pointed out. "For more than a thousand years, the Greeks and other people of the ancient world consulted an oracle at Delphi. Even kings made the journey."

"I've heard of that," Cathy conceded. "But I'm not sure I can buy it, at least, not in a modern context."

"It is not important whether you believe in what the

Three-Eyed Woman prophesies." They were passing the Sand and Stars again, which reminded Dar that it wouldn't take the Secret Service long to realize he was missing and to follow his trail. He could not afford to waste time. "What matters is that others believe it with all their souls."

"Do you?" she demanded.

He did his best to answer truthfully. "I believe in doing whatever is best for my country. Some of our rebel tribes place great faith in prophecies. If the marriage takes place, they will stop fighting. Therefore, I accept the prophecy."

Moonlight touched Cathy's face with an almost magical luminescence. She had a way of listening that reverberated, as if she took his words to heart and weighed them on a scale of truth.

"I presume this has something to do with you marrying Yasmin," she said. "Was that what the astrological signs meant?"

"The Three-Eyed Woman, who is called Zahira, said they indicated that the child would bring peace to our kingdom," Dar said. "To do this, she was to be wed as soon as possible to a prince of the emir's family. I was away at college at the time, but Ezzat suggested me. He knew that I would do anything he asked, and that I would treat the child kindly."

"Yesterday, you mentioned a curse. Was that part of the prophecy, too?"

He nodded. "The oracle said that anyone who prevented the marriage would die."

"That's a pretty heavy curse," Cathy said. "Why didn't the marriage take place then?"

"Yasmin's father, Ali, was horrified at the idea of marrying off his baby daughter. He did not accept the old ways."

"What about Yasmin's grandfather?" Cathy asked.

"Fasad was unwilling to give up his claim to the throne, and inclined to respect his son's wishes," Dar said. "There was fear that someone might kidnap Yasmin and marry her off secretly, so he sent his son and daughter-in-law to America with the child, on a goodwill tour to raise money for the rebellion among Marakite expatriates."

"And they died in a plane crash." She pressed her lips together as she considered this turn of events. "Now you think Sheikh Al-Haroum has changed his mind about marrying off his granddaughter. Did the crash make him believe in the curse?"

"Difficult to say. He is an intelligent man, and not superstitious," Dar said. "But he has seen the death and destruction that come from the rebellion.

"I believe he has also realized that his nephew Ezzat is the leader our country needs. It is said that there are no more undeveloped countries, only mismanaged ones. Our emir is an excellent manager."

Cathy's smile lit up her face. "My mother said you had a good reputation in the international business community. I can see why. You think like a chief executive."

The praise pleased him. To be admired by Cathy and her mother seemed important to Dar, and he knew it wasn't only because he needed their cooperation.

He had known women as friends and as business associates and as lovers. However, he sensed something new in his experience with Cathy.

There was chemistry, of course, and an awareness that her intellect could stimulate and challenge his own. More than that, he felt in her a centered quality and an understanding of what really mattered.

The first priority for her was obviously Yasmin, for whom she had sacrificed much these past three and a half years. This woman would never stop fighting for what she believed in, he reflected, and wondered if she realized how much she had in common with his countrymen.

"Fasad wishes to end the rebellion," Dar went on. "Ezzat offered to make him prime minister, and he is willing to accept the role. But there are young hotheads who cannot accept compromise."

"How can you be certain they would lay down their arms even if you marry Yasmin?" Cathy said. "Will they really accept the prophecy?"

"We must hope so," Dar said. He stopped short of admitting that he himself had doubts on the subject. "Otherwise, one side or the other must win by force, and the cost in lives will be terrible."

They had returned to their starting point. In Cathy's downturned face and fisted hands, he read her resistance.

"It would be a marriage in name only, as I have said," Dar assured her. "By the time Yasmin comes of age, I believe peace will be so well established that we can obtain a divorce without creating problems."

"Don't you want a real wife? And children?" she asked.

"Someday." Dar did not dwell on his personal wishes. In fact, he was not sure what they were, so intertwined had his life and his work become. "I am only twenty-nine. There will be time for me to marry and have children later."

They climbed the stairs to the street, Cathy leading the way. She moved with easy grace, as if she scaled these steps often, which she probably did.

For a moment, Dar allowed himself to picture this strong-willed American woman in his homeland. His world would be new to her, and through her eyes he would see it afresh, as well.

He would take her to the marketplace, and show her the stalls filled with goods from every corner of the earth. The air would be fragrant with coffee and cinnamon, frankincense and attar of roses.

They would wander like Aladdin and his princess through hanging gardens of gold necklaces and prayer beads, past baskets of polished jade and amber and lapis lazuli. He imagined her fingers tracing the sensual surfaces of leather goods, and her lips curving as she tasted a cup of mint tea.

When she reached the top of the steps, Cathy wavered for a moment, perhaps thrown off balance by the disorienting effects of shadow and moonlight. Dar caught her wrist and steadied her.

He could feel energy thrumming along her arm. Cathy's vitality seemed coiled, tightly contained. He disliked pressing her, but he must seize upon every angle to win her consent.

"Have you thought about what it would mean, if Yasmin regained her heritage?" he asked as he escorted Cathy along the street. "I assure you, as my wife she would be welcome to live here with you, and there would be a generous trust fund for her education and upbringing."

"She has everything she needs," Cathy said tightly.

How could he make her understand, without insulting her pride? "You provide for her well, but it takes its toll on you," Dar persisted. "With a trust fund, you would not need to work, if you did not wish. You could stay home with your daughter. Take her on trips. Further *your* education, as well as hers.''

Cathy stopped dead on the sidewalk, her stance defiant. ''The one thing she wouldn't have, and neither would I, is freedom. We'd always be beholden to someone else. To her grandfather, and to you.''

''At least consider the possibility,'' Dar urged. ''Perhaps I have not made the stakes clear. There is a war raging in my country. People are dying, including children like Yasmin.''

''I wish I could help. But handing a three-year-old over to a husband is just plain wrong.'' He saw sadness in her eyes, and it troubled him. But it was not he who had created this terrible situation.

He had done his best to win her by honest argument. Now, Dar reflected unhappily, he might have to use different tactics.

Chapter Four

After her momentary light-headedness at the top of the stairs, Cathy wondered if she might be coming down with the flu. Certainly the heat radiating from within her had blotted out the chill of the sea breeze.

And despite the fact that she and Dar had been talking about matters essential to her daughter's future, she'd had a hard time concentrating. Her mind kept wandering into the depths of his dark eyes.

Who was she kidding? Cathy demanded silently. What she had wasn't the flu, it was a case of raging hormones. Her own body was proving a traitor in its longing to be held and touched by the most virile man she'd ever met.

Dar's appeal went far beyond the physical, although there was no denying that he did more to fill out a suit than any other man she'd met. She was also drawn by his keen intelligence and an air of mystery, the duality of coming from two worlds.

Even the way he walked along the sidewalk beside her was different from other men. He didn't so much walk as pace, like a panther.

Well, she had no intention of becoming his prey. And just in case she weakened, thank goodness her mother would be home.

They turned onto the narrow lane that led to Cathy's house. Every detail was familiar, even in the misty glow of lamplights.

She knew these shake-shingled cottages, shoehorned between small apartment buildings. She knew the beat-up Volkswagen Beetle parked, as always, in the same tiny reserved space, and the planter box where a perpetually scraggly lemon tree struggled to survive the salty air.

The fact was, she admitted silently, that she knew them a little too well. Quick as she'd been to reject Dar's offer of a trust fund, his mention of travel and education had been more tantalizing than she wanted to admit.

Once, she had felt a keen hunger for adventure. Going off to college had been a part of it, and making career plans, and falling in love.

Well, she'd done all those things. But the love part had ended unhappily, the career plans had gotten stuck and the adventuring, in retrospect, had been only a timid move that hadn't even taken her out of Southern California.

The mention of prophecies and a civil war alarmed her, but Dar had also referred to an ancient spice trail and desert tribes. His words conjured in Cathy an image of a rich culture with the flavor of biblical times.

She wanted to walk along narrow, ancient streets and to smell exotic fragrances like those that had perfumed the Queen of Sheba. At the same time, Dar's comfortable manners and easy grasp of her own perspective made Cathy feel that their worlds couldn't be so far apart.

If circumstances had been different, she would have had no hesitation about visiting Marakite. But despite Dar's assurances, she couldn't imagine allowing little Yasmin to be married off, even if it were in name only.

They stopped in front of her house. The limo had departed, as per Dar's instructions, before they left on their walk.

"I'm sorry I can't help you," she said.

"You understand that this will not end here." His expression was sober in the diffuse light from a street lamp. Fog had begun rolling in from the ocean, stealing the sharp edges from their surroundings. "For the sake of my country, I must persist, whatever my personal wishes might be."

"I'll fight you," she said. "If you take me to court, I'll go to the press. I don't want to insult your country, Dar, but can you imagine what people will think when they learn a little girl is expected to marry a grown man?"

To her surprise, he chuckled. "I promise never to underestimate you, Cathy."

"Then give up now." She spoke with more confidence than she felt. She was by no means sure that adverse publicity would be enough to combat the huge resources Marakite could muster. All his people needed to do was find one sympathetic judge, and Yasmin would vanish beyond any hope of recovery.

Cathy shuddered. Catching her shoulder, Dar guided her toward the house. "I have kept you out too long. That blazer is not warm enough."

"I'm fine." But she wasn't, not when the battle she'd thought she'd won had just resumed, with the odds stacked against her.

Mary waited inside the door. Yasmin would be in bed by now, and Cathy's first instinct was to go check on her. But it was obvious her mother had something to say.

"You got a phone call while you were gone," Mary told Dar. "Or rather, Yasmin did."

"What do you mean?" Cathy scarcely noticed the warm air that enveloped her, but she stopped shivering.

"Yasmin's grandfather called," Mary said. "He asked to speak to her on the phone."

"But she doesn't even know she has a grandfather!" Cathy protested.

Her mother helped remove her blazer and turned to hang it in the front closet. "You know I always refer to older people as grandmas and grandpas around Yasmin, so she won't be sensitive about only having me. She didn't think it was odd."

"You let her talk to him?" Cathy wondered if her mother had taken leave of her senses.

"I didn't see that it could hurt. I listened on the extension," Mary said. "He asked if she was happy and she told him about her new Elmo and the bears. I don't think he had a clue what she was talking about, but he seemed satisfied."

Cathy struggled to absorb this new development. It hadn't occurred to her that Fasad Al-Haroum would take it on himself to play the doting grandfather. "He shouldn't have called here."

"Why not?" Mary leveled a quelling gaze at her daughter. "Cathy, you have to admit, the man's been through a lot. From what you told me, he lost his son and daughter-in-law tragically, and he's only just discovered that his grandchild is alive. How do you expect him to react?"

Cathy couldn't formulate an answer. Here was another issue that had to be dealt with. Even if she were able to forestall this preposterous marriage, she couldn't in good conscience exclude Yasmin's relatives from her life.

They could afford not only to phone but to travel here.

She would have to reach some accommodation with them.

Distressed, Cathy plopped onto the couch with as much grace as a grumpy teenager, then remembered that Dar was watching. She tried to straighten her posture without being too obvious.

"Perhaps a cup of coffee would be a good idea," he told her mother quietly. "Cathy may have caught a chill."

"I'll fix some decaf for everyone." Mary brushed her hand across her daughter's hair. "I know this is hard to accept, but as a grandmother myself, I can sympathize with Mr. Al-Haroum and his wife."

Dar sat nearby on the sofa, his breathing taking on a restrained, watchful quality. She could almost hear him thinking, and wished she could read those thoughts.

He seemed so accessible, but was he? She'd been wrong before, and Ralph hadn't even come from a foreign culture.

If only she could believe that Dar was what he seemed—a kind man dedicated to his country and concerned for Yasmin's well-being. Maybe some compromise would be possible, but what kind?

A cold feeling in the pit of her stomach warned that not only were her legal rights at stake, but perhaps, in some ways, Yasmin's values. What if grandparents who offered splendid toys and other treats proved more alluring than an overworked mother on a tight budget?

"It might help if you could voice your concerns. I'd like to hear them." Dar spoke in a soothing tone. The man was indeed a master at diplomacy, Cathy thought.

"I'm concerned about a tug-of-war over Yasmin, even if there isn't a custody battle," she admitted. "What if the Al-Haroums try to buy her affection? I want my daughter to know what's important in life, but how can I guide her if other people interfere?''

Dar's hands rested on his thighs, the fingers slightly spread in an appeasing manner. She noticed a scar running across the back of the left hand, and wondered what had caused it.

''I have a certain standing in this matter,'' he said. ''As Yasmin's betrothed, my wishes will be heeded. And despite my rather gaudy attempt at gift-giving earlier this evening, I can promise that the child will not be spoiled. Your views in that regard, and in every other way, will be respected.''

Despite his apparent sincerity, Dar's words failed to reassure Cathy. His promise was only worth as much as his character, and for all she knew he might be just another Ralph in sheikh's clothing.

Instead of pursuing the matter, she yielded to her curiosity. ''How did you get that scar?''

Surprised, he glanced at his hand. ''This one? It is hardly anything.''

''Compared to what?'' Cathy rejoined, her natural sense of humor bubbling to the surface. ''Are you implying you've got a first-rate collection hidden away? 'Come up and see my etchings'?''

His deep laughter rolled through the room. ''I am sorry to disappoint you, but all I have hidden is an ordinary appendix scar.''

''What about your hand?'' she asked, and found herself reaching out instinctively to trace the thin line. ''It looks like a knife cut.''

''It is,'' Dar said. ''Someone tried to kill Ezzat during majlis.''

''Majlis? What's that?'' Mary came into the room carrying a tray with her best tea service and a plate of lemon cookies.

Cathy plucked her hand away quickly. She didn't know why she'd reached out to Dar, or how she'd dared to tease the man. Fortunately, he'd turned out to be the sort who could take a joke.

She wondered what other traits lay hidden beneath his self-possessed surface. It seemed unlikely she would ever have an opportunity find out, and she was surprised to realize she regretted that.

"Majlis is a traditional audience with the royal family in which anyone can ask for help or bring a request," Dar said. "They are held several times a week."

"Can anyone approach the emir? Women, too?" Cathy asked.

"Indeed, yes, although they rarely come." Dar thanked Mary as he accepted a cup of coffee, black. "Women are better at finding their own solutions than men, I think. Most of the men who come really do not need help anyway. They only want reassurance that, if they fail to get a loan or scholarship or job, the emir will help."

"And does he?" Mary finished serving the decaf and cookies, and settled into her favorite chair.

"If he can, yes," Dar said. "He uses his influence where it seems appropriate. Also, he refers matters of justice to the proper authorities."

"But you said someone attacked the emir during one of these sessions," Cathy noted. "Don't the visitors have to go through a metal detector?"

"That would be an insult." Dar balanced his delicate cup with ease, a skill Cathy doubted he'd acquired in the desert. It must be part of his diplomatic training. "More than twenty years ago, the king of Saudi Arabia was murdered during a majlis. Still, their petitioners are not searched, nor are ours."

"Was your emir badly hurt?" Mary asked.

"Thankfully, no." Dar's expression grew distant as if he were visualizing that long-ago scene. "I happened to be nearby, and saw the glint of the knife. I leapt forward and caught the attacker before he could harm the emir."

"But he hurt you." Although Cathy had no idea what the room or the other man had looked like, she could imagine Dar in his robes struggling with an attacker, and see the wicked blade slice across his hand. Involuntarily she quivered.

"You are too sensitive," Dar said, but he didn't sound disapproving. "For a sheikh, such an injury is nothing."

"It wouldn't be nothing if he'd cut deeply enough to do nerve damage," Mary responded tartly. "We're impressed by your courage, but not your bravado."

Dar threw back his head and laughed. "I see this family has two feisty women."

"Three," said Mary with a nod toward the bedroom, but she was smiling, too.

"And so we return to the subject that brings us together," Dar observed. "When Fasad Al-Haroum telephoned, did he say where he was calling from?"

"Where?" Mary repeated as if she didn't quite understand the question. "I presumed he was in Marakite, but he didn't say."

"As it happens, my visit to Los Angeles at this time was not entirely on business," Dar said. "The Al-Haroums' youngest daughter has graduated from the University of Southern California. It is a festive occasion."

"They're here?" Cathy's breath caught in her throat, and she could barely choke out the words. "Yasmin's grandparents are in L.A.?"

"Not precisely in L.A.," he said. "As you know, there are a number of small islands off the coast, some of them privately owned. One of our sheikhs owns the island of Los Olivos and has loaned it to the Al-Harooms. They are much more comfortable and private in his hacienda than in a hotel."

"They just popped over from this island to attend their daughter's graduation ceremony?" Cathy couldn't grasp the sense of it. "It must be an enormous hassle."

"Not when you have the use of a small airplane and several helicopters," Dar said. "Also two jets. But those are only used on long trips, of course."

"Of course," repeated Mary, her dazed expression mirroring Cathy's reaction. It was hard to imagine such wealth.

"I myself spoke to Fasad today," Dar went on. "He asked me to invite Cathy and Yasmin to visit the island and meet the family. I did not feel the time was right to mention this earlier, but perhaps now you will agree to let Yasmin spend some time with her other grandparents. In your presence, naturally."

"Is there a ferryboat?" Cathy asked.

"I am afraid not. The island is very private." Dar set his cup aside. "I can fly you there. You need not fear—I am qualified to fly many types of aircraft, including a jet, although that will not be necessary this time."

"You're a man of many talents," Mary observed dryly. "What else are you hiding up those sleeves?"

Dar pretended to examine his tailored suit sleeves. "Only my shirt, I fear, but my robes are more capacious. They can cover a Skorpion if necessary, although not in your country."

"We don't have anything worse than spiders around here." From the twist of his mouth, Cathy realized she'd misunderstood. "You weren't referring to bugs, were you?"

"A Skorpion is a submachine gun." Dar shot Mary an apologetic expression. "I was only joking. It is not my custom to carry weapons even in my own country, except under special circumstances."

Cathy decided not to ask what those circumstances were. Talk of civil wars and high-powered weapons only increased her apprehension about what Yasmin might be getting involved in. "Please tell Mr. Al-Haroum that he's welcome to visit Yasmin here."

"A sheikh with his family and entourage?" Dar said. "The limousines would block the entire neighborhood. It would make quite a spectacle. Besides, how would they all fit in the house?"

Cathy searched for another excuse. "Dar, I can't take Yasmin to Los Olivos for a long visit. I have to work."

"I could help you arrange some leave."

"I don't think..." A whimper from the other room sent Cathy flying to her feet. "I have to see to Yasmin," she said, grateful for the interruption, and hurried out.

The little girl was stirring in her sleep. Dark eyelashes fluttered against a creamy cheek as she lay with one of her new bears nestled in her arms.

Cathy pulled the quilt tighter over her daughter. Although it was clear her daughter didn't need any further attention, she lingered at the bedside, stroking an errant curl and relishing the velvety softness of her daughter's skin. Regular breathing made the covers cling intermittently, highlighting the shape of the little body.

How could such a sweet innocent baby be the focus of so many people's designs? None of the Marakites even knew Yasmin as a person.

On a bulletin board near the door were posted Yasmin's drawings from day care, glimpses into her world. The latest was a sketch of her with her best friend, the two stick-figure girls holding hands as they skimmed down a slide.

Beside it, a crayon scene depicted the seashore. In the waxy blue sky, a seagull spread its wings just as, in a sense, Yasmin would do someday. Cathy's heart constricted. She refused to let anyone take those unlimited horizons away from her daughter.

In the back of her mind, she knew she wasn't being fair. The Al-Haroums' youngest daughter had the freedom to attend USC, and the financial support, as well. Would Cathy be able to provide as well for Yasmin?

At last she returned to the living room. Although she wished she could simply refuse Dar's request and go back to living as before, she knew things would never be that simple again.

He waited on the couch with no hint of impatience. Mary, too, sat quietly, although normally she would be bustling about collecting the china. They seemed to have been put on hold during Cathy's absence.

"I need time to think about the invitation," she told Dar. "If you talk to Mr. Al-Haroum, please tell him I hope he understands that I know Yasmin better than anyone and I'm only trying to decide what's best for her."

"I will do that." Retrieving a cell phone from his pocket, Dar placed a call to summon his driver, then said, "I will contact you in the morning."

"Since you're staying at my hotel, I'm sure we'll have no trouble finding each other," she answered.

"I must finish dressing before I depart. We would not want the Secret Service to discover the secret to my walking on the beach undetected." He slipped from the room.

"He's quite a man." There was a glimmer in Mary's

eyes, as if she were remembering the romantic dreams of her own youth.

"This isn't about him and me," Cathy reminded her. "It's about Yasmin."

"At some point, it could become about you and him," her mother warned. "I've seen the way he looks at you. There's real chemistry there, whether you like it or not."

When Dar strode into the room a few minutes later, swathed in white, he resembled a conqueror from a by-gone age far more than the cautious negotiator who had sipped coffee with them. There were so many sides to him, how could she be sure which was his true self?

"Good night to you both, and thank you for your hospitality," he murmured, and then he was gone.

THE OLD MOVIE on television seemed to absorb her mother, but Cathy was so busy replaying the days' events that she couldn't begin to follow the plot. Finally she gave up and went to bed.

After checking on Yasmin, she retreated to her own room, which she had occupied since childhood. It was small, with barely space for a double bed, a dresser and a refinished thrift-shop desk.

While she was away at college, her mother had removed her tattered high-school posters and repainted the wall a pinky beige. The only decorations were two framed photographs of the Arizona desert, and a bed-spread in Southwestern colors.

There was something different about the room tonight, she realized as she began unbuttoning her blouse. Something in the air.

It was a spicy scent mixed with an almost subliminal masculine aroma. This was where Dar had disrobed. In just those few minutes, he seemed to have made a permanent imprint on the atmosphere.

She felt as if some part of him remained here, watching her without being intrusive. His presence lingered so strongly that she couldn't continue undressing. Although she knew it was foolish, Cathy went to the bathroom to change.

By the time she returned, her head had cleared a little. Something specific had been bothering her, and she had finally identified it.

Despite Dar's apparent openness and candor, she had sensed all evening that he was in some way manipulating her. Not tricking her, exactly, but approaching her with a deliberate strategy.

First, at the hotel, he'd used logic, describing the Al-Haroum family's terrible loss of their son and daughter-in-law, and pointing out that the nanny had no right to relinquish the baby.

Then he'd sent gifts, followed by an attempt to play on Cathy's emotions by citing the civil war in his country. Of course, she wished she could stop the war and save innocent lives.

But she couldn't believe men would lay down their arms simply because a sheikh married a three-year-old. A three-year-old whose most profound thought to date had been to ask, "Mommy, when I was born, did you make a birthday cake with no candles on it?"

Now he was inviting her to bring Yasmin to meet her grandparents on an island from which there would be no easy escape. How could she trust him? But how could she refuse without appearing unreasonable?

The man had maneuvered her into a difficult position. The fact that she found him physically attractive made it that much more difficult to resist.

As Cathy slipped beneath the covers, she caught another whiff of Dar's essence, almost as if he slept beside her. Despite the size of the bed, she knew that if he curved around her, the two of them would fit. Not just into the bed, but into each other, too.

A pure, hot blast of desire sent tears stinging into her eyes. Her yearning for Dar wrenched up painful emotions from long ago: anger and need, and something new—a sense that life was passing her by.

She lay awake for a long time, wondering what might have happened had she met Dar under other circumstances. And realizing that, one way or another, her hopes and dreams would never again be quite the same.

Chapter Five

As she sleepily buttered toast for Yasmin, Cathy's head was no clearer than it had been the night before. Her normal morning stiffness and drowsiness, however, mercifully chased away any sensual thoughts of Dar.

She must give him an answer today about the trip to Los Olivos. Most likely, Cathy reflected with a twinge of relief, she wouldn't be able to go.

Since the hotel's acquisition six months earlier by a multinational chain, staffing had been pared to a minimum. With the busiest season of the year about to begin, it was unlikely Bert could grant her any leave.

Soft eastern light from the window fell across Yasmin's face. The little girl was studying the weather forecast, her favorite part of the newspaper.

She couldn't read yet, but the paper printed a five-day forecast illustrated by a cartoon character. He carried an umbrella for rain and wore sunglasses for hot days.

"What's this mean?" Yasmin pointed to a picture of the little man flying a kite.

"Windy." Glancing at the front section of the paper, Cathy added, "Here's some new photographs from the space probe. Look, honey." She showed her daughter a full-color shot of Saturn and its rings.

Yasmin bit her lip as she studied it. Finally she said, "Mommy, why is the universe in outer space?"

Cathy was still trying to answer that question when Mary entered. "Isn't it time for you to leave? I'll take Yasmin to day care."

Although the center was excellent, Cathy wished she or Mary could stay with the little girl every day. Unwillingly, she remembered what Dar had said about a trust fund that would let her devote herself full-time to her daughter.

But the price, marrying off her child, was out of the question.

"Thanks, Mom." Cathy hugged Mary, then gave her daughter a kiss. "Be good, sweetie."

"Can I take Elmo with me?" Yasmin asked.

The center allowed children to bring a favorite toy. "That should be okay." As always on a workday morning, Cathy tried to ignore a wrench in her heart and forced herself to leave.

The Sand and Stars was busy that morning, with callers trying to cajole last-minute reservations for the booked-up months of July and August, and a group of Australian tourists arriving sans luggage. Arrangements had to be made for the airline to deliver the missing suitcases as quickly as possible.

From the corner of her eye, Cathy kept checking for a hint of white robes whisking by. The only indication that Dar was still in residence came when she noticed a gray-suited man walking through the lobby with such self-effacing blandness that he had to be Secret Service. He picked up one of the hotel's complimentary newspapers and disappeared back into the corridor.

At midday came the usual crush of guests checking out and new arrivals checking in. Cathy's duties included assisting the desk clerk when he got overloaded, and today that happened often.

She was about to snatch some lunch when Bert called her into his office. Hoping it wasn't bad news about the still-missing luggage, Cathy hurried in.

Bert's small, cluttered office lay upstairs overlooking the pool. On the desk, she noticed a new photo of his son, grinning with pride in his high-school graduation gown and tasseled mortarboard.

"Please, sit down." Bert waved her toward the only spare chair.

Since Cathy rarely had time to sit during the day, and almost never in her boss's office, she knew something serious must be in the offing. Gingerly she edged onto the chair. "What is it?"

"I just got a call from the CEO of IHRC." Mentally Cathy translated the initials. That would be the chief executive officer of International Hotel and Resort Corporation, the conglomerate that owned the Sand and Stars. "He seems to think you want to take two weeks' leave."

"What?" She'd never met, spoken to or even thought about the CEO of IHRC. For all she knew, the company might be run by a baboon.

"He's instructed me to grant you leave with pay." Bert looked slightly stunned. "In the interest of international relations."

Now Cathy got the picture. "This wouldn't have anything to do with a certain sheikh who's staying here, would it?"

"I have no idea." Her boss shoved his bifocals higher on his thin nose. He was adept at dealing with fuming men in towels and guests who refused to believe that EPCOT Center was at Disney World, not Disneyland.

This situation, however, obviously lay outside his experience. "Care to tell me what's going on?"

Cathy explained briefly about Yasmin's background and the Al-Haroums. "It seems they're bringing some pressure to bear."

"No one can force you to do anything you don't want to," Bert said. "But when the CEO takes a personal interest…"

"You think it could hurt my career if I don't go?"

"Let's just say it could help your career if you do." Quickly Bert added, "I'm not suggesting you go through with this cockamamy wedding idea. But apparently Yasmin comes from an important family with high-up connections."

Cathy could feel herself bristling. All families were equally important in her mind, although they certainly didn't all have high-up connections. Furthermore, she resented being manipulated by whoever had called the CEO.

But had Dar, or Fasad Al-Haroum, meant to corner her? Ensuring that she could take two weeks' leave with pay wasn't exactly doing her a disservice, was it?

Sooner or later, she was going to have to face Yasmin's grandparents. Perhaps if she showed that she was willing to be reasonable, there might be no need for a court fight.

Her mother had once said that, while an independent mind is a powerful thing, when all signs point to Rome, sometimes it makes sense to go to Rome.

In this case, at least, Rome wasn't far away. No more than a short hop in an airplane.

"I'll consider it," she said.

Bert, who knew her almost as well as she knew herself,

gave Cathy a sympathetic grin. "Your leave starts tomorrow."

"THE WHOLE WORLD'S a dollhouse!" cried Yasmin. "Mommy, look down there!"

"It's not really small. It just looks that way because we're high up," Cathy said from where she sat belted into the rear seat of the small plane.

A lot too high up, in her opinion. She'd only flown a few times before, and then it had been in commercial jets.

A small plane was another matter entirely, skimming on the air currents like a bird—or a runaway kite. The combination of nerves and occasional blasts of strong wind was making her stomach churn.

Cathy had read explanations of how planes could fly, about the shape of the wings, the thrust of the engine and the variations in air pressure. Nevertheless, it had always seemed like hocus-pocus to her.

She was trusting her life, and Yasmin's, to Dar. Oddly, she felt more confidence in him than in the airplane, as if it was the force of his will rather than anything mechanical that held them aloft.

He was certainly an unusual man. Being in his company was turning out to be an ongoing adventure.

Into her mind popped a memory of the scene at John Wayne Airport when they'd arrived at the small-craft terminal for departure. As Dar marched through the lobby in his sweeping robes, heads had turned, and one woman missed her step and had to perform an impromptu cha-cha to keep from stumbling.

Through it all, Yasmin had skipped with pure delight. She'd been thrilled from the moment she learned they were going to meet some new relatives.

"Do I have cousins?" she had asked Cathy last night as they packed. "How old are they? What are their names?"

Cathy had grown tired of saying, "You'll have to wait and see." She wished she knew the answers, not only for Yasmin's sake but for her own. Exactly how big *was* the Al-Haroum family?

When she'd informed Dar yesterday that they were accepting the invitation, she hadn't had time to gather much information. There'd been too many duties at the hotel, and she'd worked late to help Bert prepare for her absence.

He was bringing in a retired former manager to help out, so losing her for a week or two shouldn't pose any major problems. Still, she felt as if she were leaving him in the lurch.

At this point, Cathy wasn't even sure she wanted to further her career. Success with an international hotel chain would mean moving wherever she was assigned.

She and Yasmin depended on Mary's help, and that meant staying in Laguna. Having a child required giving up a lot, but it was worth it.

The airplane bucked, and her hands clamped on to the edges of her seat. Dar steadied the aircraft almost immediately. "It is just an air pocket," he said. "Nothing to worry about."

"It's fun!" cried Yasmin. "Make it go up and down again, Dar!"

He grinned at the little girl. "I'm not sure if you are fearless or just too young to know caution."

"Too young," said Cathy.

"My bears like looking out the window," her daughter announced. "Oh, no! Where did the houses go?"

Peering down, Cathy saw that they had left the land

and were heading north over water. "That's the ocean, honey. It's the Pacific. Remember the globe? On the other side are China and Japan."

Wiggling in her seat, Yasmin said, "I thought you had to dig to get to China."

"That's a joke." It was a silly story that children told each other on playgrounds when they were shoveling holes in the sand, Cathy thought, but in a way it epitomized her daughter's sheltered upbringing.

To Yasmin, and at some level to Cathy, the East was a place of legends rather than real flesh-and-blood people. China was a place you could dig a hole to, India resembled a scene from *The Jungle Book,* and Aladdin flew through Arabia on his magic carpet.

But there was nothing make-believe about Marakite, or about Dar, either. He filled the pilot's seat as if born to fly, handling the controls with skilled attentiveness.

His solid, commanding presence made other men seem drab. If only an awareness of him as a virile man didn't keep clouding her mind!

Her skin itched to brush against his, and his half-familiar, half-exotic scent tantalized her like a caress. Cathy had to restrain the impulse to reach out and straighten a crumpled fold of his headdress.

What could she be thinking? The man was a stranger with his own agenda and, if she ever let him close, sooner or later she would get hurt.

"Can I call you Daddy?" Yasmin asked suddenly. Cathy hadn't been paying attention to the little girl's chatter, but the words jumped out at her.

"I fear I am not your daddy, but I would like to be your friend," Dar said gravely.

"Why don't I have a daddy?" Yasmin asked.

"Honey, I told you last night about your first mommy

and daddy.'' Cathy leaned forward to make sure her daughter could hear. She had explained everything, but a three-year-old couldn't be expected to grasp such a complex situation. "They died and went to heaven.''

"Up there?'' Yasmin pointed at the sky. "Are we getting close? Can I see them?''

"We can't see people when they're in heaven,'' Cathy said.

"Unless they're angels!'' Yasmin said. "I've seen angels on TV. Mommy! Is that an angel?''

Out of the sun came wheeling a crescent of birds. For an instant, in the blue-and-gold glare, they did look like enchanted creatures. "They're geese, I think.''

Yasmin held her stuffed animals up to the window. "Look! Geese!''

Thank goodness the birds had taken her daughter's mind off her birth parents, Cathy thought as she sank back in the seat. The last thing she wanted was for Yasmin to remember that they'd died in a plane crash. She herself might feel nervous, but she didn't want to pass on her fears.

Over his shoulder, Dar shot her a quick glance and nodded as if to express approval of how she'd handled the situation. Cathy had to admit his good opinion pleased her.

By the time the birds vanished, they were passing near Los Angeles Harbor, where Dar pointed out a huge cargo ship heading for port. Even from this height, its size was astounding.

"That is how many manufactured goods are transported to your country from Asia,'' he told Yasmin. "They even bring cars on those vessels.''

"Cool,'' she said.

North of L.A., they turned west. A lump in Cathy's

throat warned that they were heading for terra incognita, just like sailors in ancient times.

"Is that the island?" Yasmin peered into the brightness. Following her gaze, Cathy made out a solid thrust of land. It hardly looked large enough to land on.

"I told you we would be there for lunch," Dar said. The nose of the plane dipped and they began their descent.

Cathy's stomach began to grind with tension. She hoped the Al-Haroums wouldn't be offended if she didn't have much of an appetite.

DAR TAXIED TO A STOP on the small strip. Although it lacked a control tower, it was flawlessly maintained.

Beyond the landing strip lay a lush sweep of lawn. Jacaranda and palm trees, huge bird-of-paradise plants and other non-native landscaping added splendor to what would otherwise have been a scrubby island.

Up a rise lay the hacienda-style mansion, barely visible behind a colorful circus-style tent. Only a few nights earlier, it had been filled with notables and USC classmates brought by helicopter to celebrate Maha Al-Haroum's graduation.

The plane's wheels had barely stopped rolling before a flock of people streamed from the sidelines. Most wore traditional flowing garments.

Here came Fasad's wife, Faiza, in the lead, her head scarf flapping as she outran younger relatives. Who could blame her for being eager to see her lost grandchild?

Behind, but not by much, trailed the rest of the family: Fasad, his younger son Khalid, his two daughters, his daughter-in-law and a clutch of children.

Dar jumped down from his seat and went around to help Yasmin and Cathy. Faiza was already pulling on the passenger door, trying to reach the little girl.

"Be careful. You don't want to frighten her," he warned through the closed door.

"She is beautiful! Just like her father! And her mother a little, too." Although only in her mid-fifties, Faiza had a face deeply etched with lines, as if she had seen centuries of trouble.

It was the loss of her son that had aged her, Dar believed. But now, regaining her granddaughter, Faiza was bursting with youthful energy.

Opening the door, he swung Yasmin onto his shoulders to keep her from being frightened by all the new people. Faiza stroked her granddaughter's arm and called her endearments, and the little girl didn't seem to mind.

Moving slowly through the cluster of well-wishers, he introduced the child to her new family one at a time. Judging by her wiggles of excitement, it was the other children who fascinated Yasmin.

The oldest, Ahmed, was seven. There were also two girls, Sara and Mona, and a two-year-old, Salman.

Yasmin showed Elmo to them. "I got him two days ago!"

"Here! This is his friend!" Sara, who was four, waved her Big Bird in response. Like all the children, she had been spoken to in English, as well as Arabic, from an early age.

Dar turned back toward the plane. Unaided, Cathy had descended and now stood alone, looking lost.

He reproached himself for not staying by her side, but it had been important to satisfy everyone's eagerness to meet Yasmin.

In the short time he had known her, Dar had become surprisingly attuned to Cathy. Now, in her eyes, he saw a touch of envy for the Al-Haroum family's obvious closeness, and uncertainty about her role here.

Many things were happening quickly, or so it must

seem to her, he thought. She had no idea how long the wait for Yasmin's arrival had seemed to everyone else.

"My friends," Dar said loudly enough that the throng quieted. "Please allow me to introduce Yasmin's mother, Miss Cathy Maxwell."

He saw skepticism on Faiza's face. She had not been particularly close to her daughter-in-law Sherifa, Yasmin's birth mother. Even so, to the Al-Haroums, Cathy was no mother at all, just an outsider who ranked scarcely higher than a nanny.

"I beg to remind you," he said, "that without Miss Maxwell, our dear Yasmin might have languished in a series of foster homes. She would have had no one to love her, to tuck her in at night, to teach her. She is lucky to have a mother and grandmother who have opened their home and their hearts to her and kept her safe."

To his relief, heads began to nod. Faiza herself set the tone by stepping forward and embracing Cathy, who shyly hugged her back. "Thank you for being so good to Yasmin."

The tension broke as he lowered the little girl to the ground and she ran to Sara. The Al-Haroums gathered around, smiling and talking. Even Fasad, who usually wore an expression somewhere between a scowl and a grimace, beamed at the scene.

"At last, hope is at hand." He stroked his short beard and regarded Dar approvingly from beneath a red-and-white-checked headdress. "There is fierce fighting in my native town. Only last night a rocket hit a school, although happily it was empty. We must have peace, my friend, and you have made this possible."

"I have made something possible, but I am not yet sure what," Dar said, keeping his face averted from Cathy.

Before Fasad could respond, Faiza clapped her hands.

"Lunch!" she cried. "The children must be hungry, and there are many good things to eat!"

The youngsters shouted their approval. Holding hands with Yasmin, Sara and Mona turned and raced toward the brightly colored tent in front of the hacienda. The boys pelted after them.

"It's like a circus!" Yasmin's voice floated back as they ducked into the big top.

Before Dar could reach her, Cathy, too, headed in that direction, flanked by Faiza's daughters—Sabah, who was heavy with her fourth child, and Maha, who was regaling them with a story about her experiences at university. It was good to let the young women get acquainted on their own, he decided, and stepped aside.

Letting the others go ahead, Dar placed an international call on his cell phone. Within seconds, he was speaking to Ezzat.

"We have arrived on Los Olivos," Dar informed his cousin. "If I may ask, have you heard anything from the Three-Eyed Woman?"

"The Elders cannot find her," said the emir.

"She is missing?" Zahira suffered from minor infirmities and rarely traveled outside the capital city of Haribat. "Could she be in hospital?"

"No. She has been feeling very well," Ezzat said in his slightly nasal tenor voice. "Sometimes she goes into the desert to seek the spirits. Her attendant has also vanished, so probably he has accompanied her."

This was a development Dar hadn't foreseen. He had no intention of going through with a wedding without Cathy's consent, but if Zahira were unable to reinterpret the prophecy, or could not even be found, it made matters very touchy indeed.

Chapter Six

The luncheon banquet was spread on a cloth laid atop elegant Persian carpets, on the floor of the tent. This, Maha explained to Cathy, was a traditional manner of serving a feast.

"We have many dishes from our country but also from yours," the young woman said, tossing back the heavy French braid in which she had gathered her raven hair. "For Yasmin's sake, and yours. I like them, too."

Cathy wondered why Dar had not chosen to marry such an obviously suitable woman as Maha, who was educated in the West but also a part of his own culture. Like Yasmin, she came from the Al-Haroum family, so a union with her might also offer hope for peace, and she was certainly beautiful.

But such a marriage wouldn't fulfill the prophecy, Cathy remembered. Besides, neither appeared to take any notice of the other, and for reasons she didn't care to explore, she was glad.

The whole family sat cross-legged on cushions to eat. Cathy was impressed with their grace. She tried to imitate the way even Sabah, who must be seven or eight months pregnant, folded herself into position.

She recalled reading that it was traditional in Arabic

families for the men to eat first. Apparently her information was inaccurate, or else the family chose not to observe such formalities.

True to Maha's word, Cathy discovered French fries and chicken nuggets among the dishes. Even so, she was glad to see that Yasmin, snuggled between two cousins, was willing to taste the tabbouleh and hummus, although the little girl made faces at the tangy flavors.

Cathy nibbled at everything but found, as she had feared, that she lacked an appetite. It wasn't a result of their bouncy flight or the unfamiliar food, however, but of sheer nerves.

Except for Dar, these people didn't see her as Yasmin's mother, or at least Faiza didn't; that much was obvious. The grandmother might even assume that the child had come home to stay. But surely she didn't believe Cathy would simply give up her daughter, did she?

Still, the Al-Haroums were being very courteous. The conversation was conducted mostly in English, probably for her benefit and Yasmin's. The talk was quite lively, and soon Cathy forgot her reservations.

Having lived for so long with just her mother, she was intrigued to note how much more complex life could be in a large group. She found herself fascinated by the subtle interactions among family members.

Next to Dar sat the patriarch, Fasad, with his son Khalid, on his left. Khalid, who wore a beard and an impatient expression, was in his early twenties and already married, according to Maha. His wife, a shy woman named Hanan, sat near Faiza and spent most of her time fussing over their three-year-old daughter.

Khalid frequently leaned forward to make comments, to which his father paid little attention. The young man struck her as earnest but a bit brash. Cathy supposed he must be trying to fill the empty shoes left by his older brother, Yasmin's father, Ali, and finding it difficult.

Fasad himself seemed in a good mood. He had a large, expressive face, with crinkled eyes and broad cheekbones above a short beard. When he smiled, he reminded Cathy of an Arabian version of Santa Claus.

Her gaze kept returning to Dar. He wore a remote expression and paid little attention to his food, nodding politely whenever the other men spoke but uttering only a few comments himself. She'd noticed him making a phone call earlier, and hoped nothing was wrong.

"You make many observations." Sabah turned back from helping serve Salman, her youngest son. Her other youngsters, Ahmed and Sara, were giggling with Yasmin. Sabah's husband, Cathy had been told, had remained in Marakite, handling some family business. "I am curious to know what you think of us."

"We must seem very strange to you," added Maha, who sat on the other side of their guest.

"Not strange at all." Cathy blushed, and hoped no one else had noticed her scrutinizing the men. "I just like to watch the dynamics between people. How they relate to each other."

"The pecking order," said Maha. "It is very clear in this case, no? Especially our brother Khalid. He is at the bottom. Always."

"I know nothing about pecking orders," her sister responded tartly. "I have not been to university. But I do know when a woman looks at a man a certain way. You are taken with Sheikh Bahram, no?"

Cathy was in the middle of biting into something heavily spiced with horseradish. That must have been why she burst into a fit of coughing.

Maha pounded her on the back and glared at Sabah. "People in America do not comment on such things!"

"What things?" asked her sister.

"Who a person is looking at!" said Maha. "Especially when a woman regards a man!"

"They do not discuss this?" The older sister pushed away a corner of her head scarf. "Why not?"

"Well, it's considered personal," Cathy said. "Not that I'm offended or anything."

"Personal?" repeated Sabah.

"Private!" said her sister. "So what if a woman likes a man? Maybe she does not want anyone to know, so no one asks her!"

"That is ridiculous." Sabah shifted position, readjusting her large midsection. "In America, people go nearly naked on the beach and they appear on television to discuss their sexual habits, but they are too refined to mention that a woman is looking at a man?"

Cathy couldn't help laughing. It did seem foolish, viewed in that light.

Then she caught Dar's eye. For the first time since they entered the tent, he smiled. She got the impression he was glad to see her having a good time with Yasmin's aunts.

The truth was that, having grown up as an only child, she'd always envied people with large families. Furthermore, in Sabah and Maha, she saw some of the same qualities that she loved in Yasmin—intelligence, curiosity and warmth.

She wasn't so sure how she felt about Faiza, or how the older woman felt about her, either. The grandmother sat near the children, drinking in the sight of Yasmin, but from time to time she observed Cathy with an unreadable expression.

Surely Faiza must have noticed the exchange of glances between Cathy and Dar. She hoped no one would make too much of it.

The Al-Haroums were Yasmin's other family, and so Cathy knew she would be linked to them, in one way or another, for life. Dar was another matter.

He wasn't part of their family. Technically, he and the emir were at war with the Al-Haroums, although she gathered both sides would make peace as soon as they could win the consent of Fasad's fiery and independent-minded followers.

Once a way was found to end the war, she doubted Sheikh Kedar Bahram would find time for visiting a small tourist town like Laguna Beach. According to the inquiries Mary had made, Dar headed Marakite's multi-billion-dollar pharmaceuticals manufacturing and export business as well as serving as his country's minister of trade and foreign affairs.

Cathy tried to ignore a twist of disappointment at the thought of never seeing him again. But he looked so remote, sitting there in his black-banded headdress, which Maha mentioned was called a kaffiyeh. How could she even imagine the two of them had anything in common?

At last lunch was finished. Servants came to take away the dishes, and, after Sabah took her leave, Maha escorted Cathy and Yasmin into the hacienda.

The Spanish-style structure, with its open courtyards and arched doorways, felt comfortably Southern Californian to Cathy. As they strolled across a tile floor past a vase filled with calla lilies, she recalled that Spanish architecture had been influenced by the Moors of North Africa, who had occupied Spain during the Middle Ages.

Here, in this comfortable house, the worlds of East and West came together on common ground. In more ways than one, she reflected, feeling her daughter's hand squeeze hers.

"It is a large house but we are many people," Maha said as she led them into a sunny room. A blanket woven of pinks and oranges flamed across the double bed. "I hope you do not mind sharing a room with your daughter."

"It's fine. In a strange place, she'll sleep better with me anyway," Cathy said. As if on cue, Yasmin wandered toward the bed and flopped onto it. "Thank you for being so kind."

Impulsively Maha caught her hands. "I know this situation is difficult for you. I do not know how you will resolve this prophecy business. The important thing is to end the war."

She started to say more, but stopped as if she weren't quite sure how to put it, then wished Cathy a happy siesta. "My bedroom is next door, so if there is anything you need, just knock." Despite the fact that she wore Western-style slacks and a blouse, Maha glided away as mysteriously as if wreathed in veils.

Cathy explored her room and the adjoining bath while Yasmin lay curled around one of her new bears. The decor had a semitropical feel, with bamboo-style blinds and a fanfold door on the closet. She was surprised to see that servants had not only brought their suitcases from the plane but also arranged the clothes on hangers and in the wicker bureau.

One could get used to luxury, Cathy supposed. But she was accustomed to providing accommodations for others, not enjoying them herself, and the situation made her a little uneasy.

Overhead, a ceiling fan whirred lazily. The drone had

lulled Yasmin to sleep by the time Cathy returned to gaze down at her.

The little girl's skin glowed in the filtered light, her cheeks velvet soft, her small mouth curving. The unfamiliar surroundings hadn't fazed her, but then, Yasmin had always been a self-possessed child.

How well do I know her and the woman that she'll become? Cathy wondered. *Do I have the right to keep her with me, when she could have an extended family and luxuries I can never provide? When she's grown up, will she agree that I made the right decision?*

It was a troubling line of thought, and Cathy suspected she could think more clearly outdoors. She felt no inclination to rest, and since everyone else seemed to have withdrawn for the midday nap, she decided it wouldn't disturb them if she went for a walk.

She changed from her suit to a long casual skirt and an embroidered blouse. They seemed more suitable to life in a hacienda.

Yasmin should be safe enough here. To make sure, Cathy tapped at the next door before she went out. Maha, who was sitting at a desk writing thank-you notes for graduation gifts, said she would be more than happy to keep an eye on the child.

"You might want to walk down by the beach," she said, and gave directions. "The tidal pools are most interesting."

After thanking her, Cathy went down the corridor and through a courtyard where a fountain splashed musically. She made her way past the kitchen, where the staff was still cleaning up lunch, and out a back door onto a porch.

There she stopped in amazement. She hadn't realized, on approaching from the front, that the hacienda sat so close to the ocean.

Before her, steps led down a rocky slope to a slab of beach sandwiched between boulders. Beyond it, the sea dozed in the sunlight, undisturbed by surfers or people on Jet Skis in this remote location.

Seagulls strutted boldly toward Cathy. From one of the boulders, a pelican leered as if demanding payment to let her pass.

"Sorry, no food," she told the birds. "I'll bet the staff feeds you, huh? You'll have to wait till they come out."

One of the gulls mewled at her, a high-pitched plaintive sound. The pelican turned its attention toward the sea.

To her right, across a long stretch of water, Cathy could see the jagged edge of coastline that marked the mainland. They must be about twenty miles offshore near Santa Barbara, she guessed, but from this distance she couldn't make out any landmarks. To her left lay only unbroken waves, all the way to Japan.

This really was a very private island, with an air of wild loneliness. Even the scent of brine seemed different here than in Laguna.

Then Cathy heard the hum of a motor approaching from around the rocks. Who dared to break the solitude?

Into sight purred a small boat, piloted by a man in a jade green T-shirt and jeans, his dark hair stirring in the breeze. Not until he shaded his eyes and then waved did Cathy realize it was Dar.

She waved back and waited indecisively as he approached. After seeing him among so many people at lunch, she felt suddenly shy.

"Hello!" He eased the boat into the shallows and leapt out, tugging it just far enough onto the sand to anchor it. "I did not expect to see you here."

Cathy hugged herself against the light breeze. "I needed to clear my head after lunch."

"So did I." He looked so different from the impassive white-swathed sheikh who had sat beside Fasad Al-Haroum, that Cathy had to keep reminding herself it was the same man.

In the sunlight, his brown eyes seemed brighter and his smile softer. The T-shirt clung to his sculpted torso, tracing well-developed muscles and displaying broad, straight shoulders.

The faded jeans molded to his hips and thighs, above a midcalf-length pair of wading boots. His contours were firm and manly, and Cathy had to fight the urge to luxuriate in the sight of him.

"Were you sailing anywhere in particular?" she asked.

"Just cruising." Dar eyed her speculatively. "I don't suppose you dive?"

"I've never tried it," she admitted.

"Then you cannot enter the magic city, but you can see it from the outskirts," he murmured enigmatically, and reached to help her down the steps.

It never occurred to Cathy not to stretch out her hand and let him take it. The man was offering to show her something rare and hidden.

What she found herself most wanting to see, the rare and hidden parts of himself, were not to be granted, of course, but she supposed she could view them from the outskirts, as well.

Her sandals barely touched the beach before he released her hand, grasped her about the waist and lifted her into the boat. To do that, he had to brace himself, and the shift of position jostled her against him.

For one searing moment, Cathy was aware of her breasts brushing Dar's powerful arm and her cheek touching his shoulder. Through the T-shirt she inhaled his spicy maleness mixed with a hint of exertion.

She heard his quick indrawn breath, and knew he, too, felt the shimmer of unplanned intimacy. If he had been American, perhaps he would have pursued the embrace, but instead he eased her into the boat, made certain she was safely seated and then released her.

"You're still a gentleman, even without your robes," she teased, to break the awkwardness.

Dar averted his face as he pushed the boat into the water, climbed aboard and started the motor. "I apologize for my casual dress. I did not expect company, although it is most welcome."

"I'm used to men who wear clothes like that," Cathy said, but couldn't resist adding, "although they don't usually fill them out quite so well."

Dar shot her a startled look, and she wondered if she'd gone too far. Then the corners of his mouth quirked. "You have not seemed a flirtatious woman until now."

She *did* feel flirtatious, Cathy realized as they putted away from the beach in an arcing path. The sheikh's unexpected appearance and the way he had swept her from the island combined to create a sense of being freed from the usual restraints.

"I suppose I *was* flirting," she said. "It's just that, in a way, you seem safe."

"Safe?" One eyebrow arched.

She didn't understand this urge to confide in him, but it was Cathy's nature to be direct. "I got burned about five years ago. My fiancé let me help put him through medical school and then dumped me."

"And you do not think I would do that?" said Dar. "You are right. I have no desire to go to medical school."

Cathy chuckled. "I didn't mean it that way. What I meant was, well, for a while I was mad at the world. Then when Yasmin came into my life, I dedicated myself to her. I learned that I was strong enough to make a life for the two of us, and that's the way I like things."

They angled around an outcropping and Cathy realized that, far from heading out to sea, Dar was taking her to another part of the island. The water must be rocky in places, which was why he'd swung some distance from shore.

"I don't think I follow your logic," he admitted. "How does this make me safe?"

For one heartbeat, she wasn't sure herself what she'd meant by that. Then, suddenly, she recognized a small truth about herself that had been tapping at her consciousness all day.

"I *do* find you attractive," she said. "And unusual and interesting. But you and I have no future together. I *know* you're going to leave. So I don't have to worry about getting too involved and getting hurt."

"A curious attitude." Dar's mouth pursed as he considered what she had said. He sat on a narrow bench in the back of the boat, his legs stretched close to hers but not touching. "You prefer a man whom you know will abandon you."

"But knowing in advance that the relationship is temporary protects me," Cathy pointed out.

"You have your feelings so well under control?"

Not my physical feelings, she thought, but saw no need to say so. She didn't see how he could miss the way her nerve endings tingled every time he leaned toward her, or the way she focused on his strong, tanned hand as it adjusted the rudder.

"Not always," she conceded. "But at least I know what the limits are."

"Are you sure?"

Whatever Cathy might have replied was forgotten as they swept around one more rocky barrier and into a sheltered bay. This was not the sea she knew, even from a lifetime of living near it.

In this inlet, the water undulated with giant feathers of green and gold, layer after layer of them descending into unseen depths. Tiny fish darted through the underwater plumage, catching glitters of sunshine and then vanishing.

For a while, Cathy could only sit and stare. Then she asked, "What is this?"

"An enchanted city." Dar silenced the motor, and they sat suspended above delicate splendor. "In prosaic terms, it is called a kelp forest."

"I've never seen anything like it."

"It is even more beautiful from underneath." Although he was studying the water, Cathy felt as if his watchful alertness focused on her. "Someday perhaps we will come here to dive..." He let the words trail off, too honest to make promises.

She would like to learn to dive with him. She would like to do a lot of things with him.

If only they could be just two people getting to know each other, without complications. How ironic that she had finally met a man who might be able to make her forget the past, only to have to accept that their relationship could have no future.

"Do you dive here often?" she asked.

"Once in a while, when I need a break."

"I'm surprised you find the time, what with being foreign minister and heading up your tribe," she said.

"These days, the title of sheikh is purely honorary," he admitted. "I relinquished the leadership of my tribe when I decided my path lay with Ezzat."

"So, in a way, you've burned your bridges," she observed.

Trailing one hand in the water, Dar fingered a rubbery pod of seaweed. "I cannot divide my loyalties. For my cousin to make me his adviser, he must be able to rely upon me absolutely. It is a matter of honor."

"In a way that sounds old-fashioned, but I admire you for it," Cathy said.

"There is nothing to admire. I could not live without honor," Dar said. "Now let us talk of less serious matters."

"The kelp forest." Gingerly she touched the seaweed. A small wave lapped over her hand, and she withdrew it quickly. "The water's cold! This place looks so tropical."

"But it is not," Dar said. "As a result, you will not find such a wide array of fish as you might in Hawaii, but the island is popular with squid. They hatch little eggs down there—white clouds of them."

"I know abalone live in this area, because it's served at restaurants." Cathy dried her hand on her skirt. "They're kind of like snails, aren't they?"

His lazy laughter sang across the ripples of the inlet. "You Americans are so squeamish, I am surprised you eat them."

"I don't." She blushed as she realized how provincial that sounded. "I mean, I never have, but I might."

To his credit, Dar didn't tease her further. "I have met an octopus in its garden, down there," he said. "Also angel sharks. They are small and look a bit like rays."

"I hope they didn't try to eat you," she said.

"They, too, are squeamish." He slanted her a mischievous look. "They did not think I would taste as good as the fish."

"Do you?" she asked.

The question hung like a challenge above the boat. Well, it *was* a challenge, Cathy admitted reluctantly, even though she couldn't imagine why she had issued it.

"I cannot disappoint a lady. I must let you decide for yourself," said Dar, and leaned forward. One hand touched her shoulder, his light grip burning through the fabric as his mouth met hers.

She felt the whole man in the kiss, his tautness and his tenderness and the way he wanted her. Cathy rested her hand on his knee, and his breathing accelerated.

They were still barely touching, except for their mouths. Just the taste of his lips was enough, with their alluring pressure, and then she felt the flick of his tongue.

If a volcano had heated the water around them, it could not have produced a greater rush of steam than the one that shot through her. Dar must have felt it, too, for he pulled her onto his lap, one arm encircling her and holding her against him.

Through the thin fabric of her blouse, his chest brushed her breasts. The nipples strained to be touched, and her core turned molten.

She wanted him to caress her, and yield to her, and lower her into the boat and make love to her. She wanted everything, and knew she dared take very little.

"Dar," she whispered as their mouths separated. "I—wasn't thinking."

"Who can think under these circumstances?" he muttered.

"Not me," she said.

"Do you still believe I am safe?"

"I'm the one who's dangerous," she admitted. "To myself, anyway."

His finger traced her cheek. "You hide nothing from me. It is refreshing, Cathy, but it also forces me to take responsibility."

"And you'd rather not?"

A sound issued from him that was half a chuckle and half a groan. "Not at the moment."

She rested her head against his shoulder and wished they could sit here forever. A breeze brought the scent of the ocean, briny and eternal. The sun soothed its warmth across them, but they hardly needed it.

Around the boat, currents fluffed the seaweed fronds. The golds and greens reminded Cathy of a Renaissance painting, timeless and subtle. At this moment, she might have believed that mermaids lived there.

But she could not believe that love conquered all. Nor was she sure that what the two of them felt was love, especially not Dar. He was all male, and while she gathered he was nothing if not discreet, that didn't make him impervious to purely physical attraction.

Stiffening her resolve, she shifted to the other bench. "I guess we should be getting back."

Dar glanced at his watch. "It has been longer than I realized. The others will be awake by now."

His shoulders flexed as he stretched, giving Cathy a splendid view of his lean body in the clinging T-shirt and jeans. In some other lifetime, she hoped she could touch every inch of him, from the angle of his jaw to his most private places. But it would not happen in this one.

After a lingering glance at the enchanted city in the water, he started the engine. It roared in Cathy's ears.

They trailed back the way they'd come. Traveling in this direction, she could see the far-off mainland, and marveled that the realm of freeways and fast-food franchises lay so close.

What had just passed between her and Dar? she wondered. Did he think less of her for it?

Not judging by the thoughtful expression on his face, she supposed. It would take time to untangle her reactions, and even then, she doubted she could sort things out to her satisfaction.

She ought to take Yasmin and leave as soon as she could politely do so. The Al-Haroums would be welcome to visit her in Laguna Beach, but she didn't dare risk staying much longer on this island with Dar.

Another time, she might not be able to muster the restraint that she'd exercised today, and neither might he. The results could be disastrous.

"Do not worry," he said as if following her thoughts. "I will find some pretext to fly to Los Angeles in the morning so I will not interfere with your peace of mind. Please, enjoy your visit for a little longer. It is important to everyone."

Without Dar, the place would seem painfully empty. But, Cathy reflected, she'd been given two weeks of paid leave, virtually under orders to spend it with the Al-Haroums. "I suppose that might work."

They came around the last outcropping. To Cathy's astonishment, the beach and the rocky surroundings were peppered with people. Several gazed seaward, while others were calling and spreading along the shore as if looking for someone.

Her heart lurched. Yasmin! Could she be missing?

But no, there was her daughter at the hacienda level, scampering across the porch with her cousins. Someone had dressed the little girl in a lacy gown layered with pink-and-white flounces.

A shout went up as people caught sight of the boat, and on the beach Fasad signaled to them. His flowing white robe gleamed in the sunlight, finer and silkier than the one he'd worn at lunch.

Others gathered on the stones to await their arrival. They, too, had put on elegant garments.

Why was everyone so dressed up? Why had they been searching, apparently, for her and Dar? Perhaps, she thought, Maha had feared Cathy might have drowned, but that didn't explain the fancy clothes.

She glanced at Dar. He scowled at the water, and made no attempt to wave back at Fasad. Whatever was happening, he didn't like it.

Neither, she could see, did Maha. The young woman stood apart from the others, arms folded, her face a study in dismay. A little distance away waited Faiza, in a scarf and gown that sparkled with gold threads. Her face was, as usual, impassive.

"What's going on?" Cathy asked.

Before Dar could reply, Khalid strode out from beside his father and waved the boat ashore. "Why have you been gone so long?" he demanded. "Dar, you must dress at once. It is time for the wedding."

"What wedding?" Cathy said.

Above her on the porch, Yasmin twirled in her frothy new dress, and the truth hit home. The Al-Haroums intended to carry out the prophecy, and they intended to do it now.

Chapter Seven

Dar fought back a flare of anger. He had made it clear to Fasad that nothing was to be done about the wedding without Cathy's consent.

But it would do no good to publicly rebuke his future in-laws, and it might cause irreparable harm. Furthermore, he suspected there must have been some new development in Marakite to cause this precipitous change of plans.

As he turned to help Cathy from the boat, Dar found himself reluctant to meet her eyes. He wished he could assure her that he would not betray her trust in allowing him to bring Yasmin to the island, but how could he promise anything until he talked to Ezzat?

It was impossible to be objective where Cathy was concerned, Dar conceded silently as he lifted her onto the sand. What had passed between them was so baffling yet so powerful, it had turned his usually incisive mind into a kelp forest.

"What's going on?" she repeated. "Dar, they can't—"

"The situation is obvious," announced Khalid, as if she had been addressing him. "We are prepared to celebrate the nuptials. There is no reason for delay."

"There's a very good reason!" Cathy snapped. "My daughter is three years old! She's also an American citizen, and under the laws of my country, this wedding is not only invalid, it would be considered a crime!"

"We are not in your country," returned Fasad's son, who managed to look young and pompous even in his robes and kaffiyeh. "Los Olivos belongs to one of my countrymen. Under the laws of Marakite, the ceremony is valid!"

"I won't allow it!" Cathy snapped. Dar could feel her rage, and knew he must find a means to allay it without antagonizing the Al-Haroum family. Everyone was watching, except for the children playing up on the porch.

To his surprise, Faiza spoke before he got the chance. "My son, it is not our place to give orders to Sheikh Bahram. Perhaps we should allow your father to explain the situation."

"Yes. Let us all go inside." To his credit, Fasad nodded to Cathy and included her in the party. Dar knew the older sheikh believed his granddaughter belonged to her parents' family, not to this American, but was wise enough not to make an issue of it.

They ascended the rocky slope, Dar forcing himself not to take Cathy's arm even when she slipped a little. It was vital that no one believe him so besotted with the woman that he could not think clearly, or he would lose an important edge in their discussions.

Over the years, Dar had intervened in many touchy situations—involving his own country, and as a negotiator between neighboring lands. In some ways, this was the most volatile dilemma he had ever faced.

Cathy was not a diplomat seeking advantage, nor a partisan promoting a cause. She was a mother who saw her child's future hanging in the balance. And he was a man just beginning to discover what it meant when one woman became special to him above all others.

He desperately needed time to think, to breathe, to come to terms with these new feelings. Why, oh why, had the Three-Eyed Woman chosen this time to disappear from Haribat?

When they reached the house, Fasad said, "We cannot have a quiet discussion with so many people present. Kedar, I would speak privately with you and Miss Maxwell." He must have caught a warning glance from Faiza, because he quickly added, "My wife will join us also."

Khalid stalked away, too well-bred to argue but clearly angry at being relegated to the status of the women and children. Sabah's husband had not made the journey to Los Olivos, so the young man retreated alone while his wife and sisters shepherded the children away.

Things would have been very different had Yasmin's father been alive, Dar reflected as he followed Fasad. Educated in Paris, Ali had shown promise of developing into a statesman, something his younger brother might never be.

Dar took a moment to exchange his muddy boots for sandals, to slip a clean robe over his jeans and T-shirt, and to put on a kaffiyeh. Then he joined the others in a sun-washed sitting room, its high ceiling crisscrossed by dark beams.

The space was lined with pewlike benches brightened by embroidered cushions. Except for a closed cabinet in one corner, the only other furnishing was a low table in the center, across which a colorful woven cloth had been tossed. A patterned area carpet offset the hardness of the tile floor.

"Please make yourself comfortable," Fasad said when

he entered. Dar bowed and sat a short distance from Cathy.

Servants scurried in to set a coffee service on the table, then departed. Faiza filled tiny cups with the thick, strong espresso, and Cathy politely accepted hers although Dar doubted it was to her liking.

"One of my generals telephoned a short time ago," Fasad said without preamble. "A terrible thing has happened. The most hotheaded of the tribal leaders, a man named Mojahid, has seized the Citadel of the Elders."

Fear gripped Dar. "The Elders—were any of them harmed?"

Fasad shook his head. "No, no. They escaped, all twelve, but some of the staff were trapped inside. The Elders have secluded themselves in the Grand Mosque to pray for a peaceful outcome."

"Mojahid has made threats?" Dar waited anxiously for the response.

Outrage flashed across Fasad's face. "He says that he will blow up the Citadel unless the emir relinquishes power to me."

"He cannot destroy the Citadel!" Dar said. "It is unthinkable."

Cathy leaned forward. "I'm sorry to ask such a foolish question, but what *is* the Citadel of the Elders?"

Faiza frowned, but Fasad answered patiently. "It is a medieval fortress in the center of Haribat, near the emir's palace."

"The Citadel holds special meaning for our people." That was an understatement, Dar knew. He must do his best to help Cathy understand. "It was behind its walls, five hundred years ago, that our leaders successfully defended the city against marauding tribes and enabled Marakite to become a nation."

"In the center is a well blessed by the spirits," added Faiza. "People who drink from it may experience miraculous cures."

"The Council of Elders convenes in the Citadel," Dar said. "Also, it houses our national art gallery. Marakite's collection is a source of great pride. There are many irreplaceable works."

"Not all of them are so valuable," muttered Fasad. "Some of those modern paintings... The rebels can have them with my gratitude!"

"But what do these people hope to gain?" Cathy asked. "Surely if they blow up the Citadel, everyone would turn against them."

Faiza clutched her hands to her chest. "To destroy it would be to strike a dagger through the heart of Marakite!"

"Even in civil war, the Citadel unites us in spirit," Dar said grimly. "With it gone, tribe would turn against tribe. Some would blame the emir for failing to save it. Others would blame each other for prolonging the war. Ancient rivalries would be revived and Marakite could easily descend into chaos."

"In such a situation, a maniac like Mojahid might be able to seize power," said Fasad. "We cannot give in to him, yet neither must we allow the destruction of the Citadel."

"That's why you want this marriage to take place now?" Cathy's face reflected conflicting emotions. "You think they would give up the building and end the war just because a grown man marries a three-year-old?"

"This wild man, this Mojahid, he claims that the spirits have spoken to him and commanded this action," Fasad told her. "But everyone knows that the spirits speak directly to the Three-Eyed Woman. If Mojahid refused to honor her prophecy, if he failed to make peace even after the marriage, everyone would know he is lying.''

"This is insane!" Cathy blurted out.

"Are not all beliefs insane to those who do not share them?" The elder sheikh spread his hands expressively.

These events made Dar's situation, and Cathy's, extremely delicate. "It is even more important now that we find the Three-Eyed Woman." Dar voiced his thoughts aloud. "But she has disappeared."

"Find her?" said Faiza. "To what end?"

"To consult the spirits now that circumstances have changed, and learn whether the prophecy might have altered." Dar knew the Al-Haroums didn't agree that Cathy was Yasmin's mother, but by law it was so. "The child is no longer without a parent."

"Yasmin also had parents when the prophecy was made," Fasad pointed out.

"But not an American one. This makes the child a citizen of a foreign country." He knew he was grasping at straws, and he realized the others must sense it, as well. "Perhaps..."

"Perhaps the spirits would prefer that Sheikh Bahram marry some other member of our family, someone who truly belongs to Marakite!" Faiza finished for him. To his surprise, she appeared pleased at the prospect.

"It is what the Americans would call a long shot, I believe," said Fasad. "But an interesting idea."

"It makes sense," his wife insisted. "Here is Maha finished with her education and lacking a husband. She is of the right age. Why should the spirits not choose her?"

"Why did the prophecy not choose her four years ago?" countered Fasad. "The astrological signs were present at Yasmin's birth, not Maha's."

"Nevertheless, a substitute might be acceptable," Faiza said. "And Maha *is* Yasmin's aunt."

Dar's chest tightened. A marriage to a child would be a token; but if he wed Maha, she would become his real wife. He liked and respected the young woman, but he did not feel for her what he had experienced with Cathy today.

Still, if Zahira, the Three-Eyed Woman, said it must be so, then it must. But would she?

"In any event, Zahira cannot be found," he said. "She has disappeared from Haribat."

Fasad and Faiza exchanged glances. The sheikh gave a slight nod of permission.

"It is because she has come with us," Faiza said. "Zahira is my old friend. She wished to see America and to celebrate Maha's graduation, but, sadly, her legs and feet have been swollen since the plane ride and she has kept to her room."

"She is here?" Dar repeated. "We must consult her at once."

Then he noticed the dazed expression on Cathy's face. Was she overwhelmed by all the new developments, or was it possible she, too, regretted the possibility of his marriage to Maha?

It made no difference. The future of Marakite hung in the balance.

"Perhaps we should get the latest news first." Cathy's voice came out dry, and she coughed before proceeding. "To find out if anything has changed in Haribat."

"Very wise," said Fasad. "Faiza, will you go to Zahira and see if she is well enough to prophesy? Meanwhile, we will turn on the TV."

"Yes, of course." Her expression unreadable as always, his wife whisked from the room.

Fasad strolled to the cabinet and opened it, revealing a television set. He returned with the remote control and clicked it on.

Thanks to a satellite dish on the roof, the reception was crystal clear. After a few changes of channel, they arrived at the news.

The situation must be headline news worldwide, because the first image they saw was a scan of the familiar square at the heart of Haribat.

At one end rose the palace, a compound surrounded by high, ornate walls decorated with patterned mosaics and punctuated by spires. Behind it could be seen the hills of the upper city, a motley mixture of onion-domed mosques, mud-brick apartment buildings and a few steel-and-glass structures.

Along much of the square, Dar knew, lay boothlike shops open to the air. But the camera was aimed just east of the palace, at the thick, sheer walls of the ancient stone fortress.

Tanks blocked much of the Citadel from view and kept passersby at bay. Several women in black knelt on the sidelines, keening and protesting that their ailing loved ones needed to drink from the sacred well.

The camera zeroed in on a young blond man in a white safari suit, who stood as close to the military lines as a glowering sergeant would allow.

"Just minutes ago, the captors released the last of the staff members who serve the Council of Elders," he announced. "The building is now empty except for the rebels. However, the international community is outraged at the threat to destroy a national landmark and priceless works of art, including a rare portrait by Leonardo da Vinci and a decorated medieval manuscript containing holy writings."

"He does not mention that painting of a woman with her nose in the center of her forehead and an eye sticking from her chin," grumbled Fasad. "Perhaps they could blow that one up before we stop them."

"Emir Ezzat Al-Aziz refuses to consider the demand that he step down," the reporter continued. "No word has been received from Fasad Al-Haroum, whom the rebels wish to place on the throne. He is believed to be out of the country and to have no connection with this situation."

"They have got that part right," Fasad said.

The sergeant signaled to the reporter to move, and the telecast shifted back to the studio for a report on an unrelated oil summit. Fasad clicked to a soccer game between Brazil and France.

"Ah," said the older sheikh. "This is the kind of battle I enjoy."

A short time later, Faiza returned, with Khalid on her heels. "Zahira invites us to join her in her chamber. She is distressed to learn of the news and will do her best to help."

Dar arose, trying to remain impassive although he knew his future was to be decided. Whatever the Three-Eyed Woman ordained, his allegiance to Ezzat required him to comply.

CATHY KEPT THINKING that any minute she would wake up and find herself at home in Laguna Beach, with Yasmin asleep in the other room.

This afternoon's boat ride with Dar still sizzled through her senses, an experience too rich and resonant to be absorbed quickly. Then, without a moment to catch her breath, had come this bewildering business of the Citadel.

How could a situation halfway around the globe involve her and her daughter? It was absurd that Yasmin should have any role to play in the fate of a foreign nation, and yet apparently she did.

Her instincts as a mother urged Cathy to take the child home and have nothing further to do with Marakite or the Al-Haroums. But even if she had a way to leave the island by herself, she knew she couldn't.

Yasmin had not been abandoned by her mother. She had been handed over by a nanny who had no right to relinquish her. If Cathy were to have any hope of keeping her daughter, she must treat these newfound grandparents and their beliefs with respect.

And what of her feelings for Dar? What of the unaccustomed rush of jealousy that had shot through her at the suggestion that he might wed Maha? She couldn't begin to figure out what to make of it.

Following Fasad and Faiza, Cathy walked stiffly down one corridor after another, into another wing of the house. At every step, she could feel Dar's presence behind her, but she didn't dare turn to meet his gaze.

They were no longer just a man and a woman. They had become players in a much larger drama.

Cathy trailed the Al-Haroums through an arched entryway. Its covering, a brocade curtain, was lifted aside by a young man with delicate features and heavy-lidded eyes.

He wore three earrings in each lobe, an ornately engraved collar and tinkling wristbands and anklets. His clothing consisted of a gauzy shirt and velvet pants gathered at the ankle.

"Thank you," Cathy said as she went through.

"I am Basilyr," he replied, as if that were an appropriate substitute for "You're welcome." It seemed to her that he dismissed her casual skirt and blouse as beneath notice, but examined her wedge haircut with some interest.

As soon as she stepped inside, Cathy's sinuses threatened to clog. Smoke from an incense burner veiled the room, in which the furnishings were obscured beneath swathes of fabric shot with metallic threads.

Strings of golden beads draped an inner doorway and cascaded from the arched tops of the windows, over pull-down shades that blocked the sunlight. The only illumination sifted from a large table lamp with a gold-tasseled ruby-colored shade.

The decor put Cathy in mind of a nineteenth-century San Francisco bordello.

Gazing around, she saw Dar enter, and noticed that he drew an admiring gaze from the attendant. Behind him, Khalid glowered at Basilyr, who sniffed disdainfully and rustled across the room, then vanished through an inner door.

"He will help Zahira prepare to prophesy," Faiza explained. "He has been with her for many years, like a son."

"He is unworthy to serve the Three-Eyed Woman," Khalid grumbled. "The man has not even served in the military!"

"In which military should he serve, the emir's or ours?" his mother returned. "The wise woman is above politics."

The outer drape stirred behind Khalid, and Maha peered in, her expression diffident. "What brings you here?" demanded her father.

She ducked her head apologetically. "One of the servants said that Mother sent for me."

"This may concern her," said Faiza. "It all depends on what Zahira prophesies, does it not?"

"Such as what?" Maha no longer seemed the dutiful Eastern daughter but an American college graduate with a mind of her own. "Mama, are you up to something?"

Faiza shrugged. "It is out of my hands."

"She thinks to promote a match between you and Sheikh Bahram," said Khalid.

His mother glared at him. "I promote nothing. The spirits will guide the oracle."

"The spirits should guide her to replace that peculiar creature who attends her," complained Khalid.

Beads rattled angrily in the interior doorway, and Basilyr emerged. He shot Khalid a narrow-eyed glare and then turned to take the plump hand of his employer.

From the inner room undulated the Three-Eyed Woman. Although her height was not great, she possessed impressive mass, all of it sinuous and supple. Beneath pale blue robes, she moved like a dancer from the *Arabian Nights.*

Black eyes flashed across the people gathered in the room. Although the lower half of the woman's face was hidden beneath a demiveil, Cathy thought she detected curiosity and a hint of triumph in Zahira at once more assuming a position of power.

"Make way! Make way!" Basilyr shooed them aside, showing no more deference to Fasad or Dar than to anyone else. "Can't you see her feet are hurting? Let her through!"

Zahira did not move as if her feet hurt; Cathy had never seen a heavy woman with more grace. But now that Basilyr mentioned it, there *was* a certain puffiness around the ankles.

"So!" As the prophetess sank onto a cushioned chair,

Cathy observed a dark dot painted in the center of her forehead, between the eyebrows. This must represent the third eye, the one within. "Why have you summoned me?"

Dar bowed. "Your Excellency, I am Sheikh Kedar Bahram, cousin to the emir. Nearly four years ago, you prophesied..."

"Yes, yes." Zahira waved her hand impatiently, setting her bracelet jangling. "I know all that. The child's reappearance, the American adoption. I have ears, you know. This is the mother, here?" Her dark gaze raked over Cathy.

"There is great urgency," interjected Khalid. "The rebels have taken the Citadel!"

"The Three-Eyed Woman is aware of all things," said Basilyr. "She watches CNN."

"She can speak for herself!" retorted Khalid.

Zahira fixed the sheikh's son with a stern look. "You are impetuous and speak out of turn. You have what the Westerners call spunk." Her eyes danced with mischief as she added, "I hate spunk."

Everyone in the room stared at her.

"It is a line from 'The Mary Tyler Moore Show'!" cried the Three-Eyed Woman. "Have you not seen it? On 'Nick at Nite'! It is funny, no?"

"Zahira, please," said Faiza. "We have come to beg you to prophesy."

"About freeing the Citadel and ending this war?" The prophetess heaved a sigh. "It is not a new prophecy that is required, but for the old one to be fulfilled. The marriage of Yasmin has not yet taken place."

Cathy felt a cold void open within her. If Zahira insisted that they go ahead with the wedding, how could she stop it?

"But other problems may occur if we go forward with this plan," Dar said in a low, steely voice. "The child is now an American citizen, and such a marriage violates American law."

Zahira spread her hands in a gesture of helplessness. "That is not the concern of the spirits."

"Sheikh Bahram has suggested that they should be consulted again," Fasad said. "In light of the fact that the child is now adopted."

"I cannot see how that would affect the prophecy." The woman folded her arms and sat back, awaiting further debate. It struck Cathy that Zahira wanted to be cajoled. It was, apparently, the only tribute she demanded.

"You told me the spirits wished for you to accompany us on this trip," Faiza said.

For the first time, uncertainty softened the woman's expression. "It is true. But that was not related. I thought it must have something to do with Maha."

"Perhaps it does," said Faiza.

If she dropped a hint any harder, it would bounce, Cathy thought. She could see Maha's lips clamp together angrily, and had to acknowledge her own wave of dismay. The slight jump of a muscle in Dar's cheek revealed his displeasure, or perhaps, merely, impatience.

But their feelings didn't matter. Only Yasmin mattered.

"Very well," Zahira said at last. "Basilyr!" She clapped her hands, which was unnecessary, since her attendant was already hurrying to fetch a globe-shaped brass container set on three legs.

"Everything is prepared." The young man knelt to set the globe on a low table in front of his mistress. He removed the top half of the ball, revealing a deep censer filled with herbs. Then he padded into the interior room, and returned with a golden goblet containing a dark liquid.

"Ah." Contentment settled across Zahira's broad face. Lifting her veil, she sipped the fluid, nodded to herself and then, with her fingertips, flicked some drops of it into the censer. "Basilyr! The flame!"

"Yes, yes, Excellency." From a hidden pocket, the young man retrieved a book of matches. He struck one and tossed it into the bowl.

A thick cloud arose, choking off what was left of the oxygen in the room. Or so it seemed to Cathy, who had to retreat into the hallway to catch her breath.

Dar came out. "You are ill?"

Coughing, she glanced up and saw real concern in his face. "No. I'm just—not used to—" She coughed again.

"If you can bear it, you should come inside." He touched her hair lightly. "This concerns you, as much as anyone."

The contact sent longing twisting through Cathy. At this moment, she wanted the man to take her in his arms and kiss her, to hold her close and fuse the two of them.

But she could not—would not—give in to these feelings. She had known all along that an unbridgeable gulf lay between them.

That was, as she'd said, why she had allowed herself to get close to Dar, knowing that retreat was not only possible but inevitable. The only hope she had of freedom for her daughter was for Zahira to announce that he must marry Maha.

"I think I can stand it," she said.

He held the curtain, and she slipped through. Inside, the first gusts of smoke had subsided, and the air was a bit less dense. Zahira, who leaned over the burning herbs inhaling the fumes, began to slump. Basilyr yanked the censer away so his mistress wouldn't burn herself.

Dar laid a hand on Cathy's arm. "It's all right," he whispered. "She's going into a trance."

Everyone watched intensely as Zahira slept, her head resting on the table. The only sounds were the collective rasp of breathing and a shiver of golden beads in the doorway.

Long minutes passed before the Three-Eyed Woman raised her head again. With Basilyr's help, she sat back in the chair, removed the veil, and sipped some fresh-brewed tea. Her expression was unfocused, and she did not speak for several minutes.

At last she said in a monotone, "You were right, Sheikh Bahram. The spirits did wish to speak to me. The prophecy has been altered."

Chapter Eight

The room was so still that it seemed everyone had stopped breathing. Cathy didn't think she could have torn herself away if the building had been on fire.

"Changed in what way?" Fasad asked at last.

Zahira sputtered up a bit of tea, and Basilyr patted her between the shoulder blades. "Can you not see she is shaken? Such a long journey, and then she has not been well!"

"Should we fetch a doctor?" asked the older sheikh.

"Excellency?" The young man addressed his mistress. "Should we?"

"No, no." After another slurp of tea, Zahira straightened, recovering a semblance of her former self-possession. "It is rare for a prophecy to be changed. But I cannot deny what has been revealed to me."

"It is to be Maha?" Faiza asked. "That is who the spirits wish to see married?"

"Mother!" cried the girl.

"Not Maha," said the Three-Eyed Woman, and her gaze turned to Cathy.

The moment those dark eyes fixed on her, Cathy knew what the prophetess was going to say. But it was almost as unthinkable as allowing Yasmin to be wed.

"The spirits still wish Yasmin to become a part of the emir's family," Zahira continued. "That has not changed."

"Uh-oh." Maha obviously saw what was coming, too. No one else spoke, not even the usually hotheaded Khalid.

"Now the child has a mother who is unwed." The Three-Eyed Woman began fanning herself with her hand. From a nearby shelf, Basilyr retrieved a small battery-operated fan and aimed it at his mistress. "The spirits wish the designated prince of the emir's family to marry this American woman. Then Yasmin will be his daughter."

"Why can't he just adopt her?" protested Faiza.

Zahira leaned back, her pale forehead flecked with sweat. "That is not what the spirits have ordered."

"What of the curse?" demanded Khalid. "My brother and his wife died because they opposed the marriage of their daughter. What about this American woman? If she refuses, will she die?"

"Khalid!" gasped Maha.

"It is a legitimate question," said her father.

Zahira shook her head. "The woman is not one of us. A nonbeliever cannot be punished for refusing to accept the prophecy."

"So she can walk out of here if she wishes, and take my niece with her?" stormed the young man. "This stranger, this meddler, can force us to continue this civil war until there is nothing left of our country?"

"Khalid!" Dar spoke at last, in a dangerously level voice. "Miss Maxwell has done nothing to deserve such a rebuke."

"It is not she who started the war," added Fasad. "It was I, in my foolishness."

"We reject this prophecy!" cried Khalid. "We will go back to the old one. Let the marriage between Yasmin and Sheikh Bahram take place!"

The Three-Eyed Woman tapped her fingers on the table. "The prophecy has been changed. It cannot be changed back."

Everyone looked at Cathy. She could barely sort out their expressions, although at least Maha's was sympathetic. As for Dar, his impassive face revealed nothing.

"You're telling me that I'm supposed to agree to an arranged marriage?" To Cathy, her voice sounded quavery and breathless.

"It is done all the time," said Fasad. "As long as both parties consent."

"Not in my country it isn't." The very idea struck Cathy as medieval, and yet these people took it with utmost seriousness.

And no wonder, given the situation in Marakite. But it seemed incredible that the future of the country might hinge on whether an assistant hotel manager from Laguna Beach agreed to marry a man who might have stepped from a fairy tale.

The others awaited her response. Even Basilyr regarded Cathy with an interest that, this time, extended beyond her hairstyle.

"You don't know for sure that the rebels would release the Citadel just because Dar and I got married, do you?" she said.

"The spirits have declared it so," snapped Khalid. "Do you doubt them?"

His mother's face brightened. "A change of circumstances has caused the prophecy to be altered. If Miss Maxwell refuses the marriage, that will present yet another alteration. Perhaps then…"

"Mother, you're grasping at straws!" cried Maha.

Fasad lifted a hand to silence his squabbling family. "Beloved wife, our daughter would not agree to this match in any event, so you must give it up in your heart. However, before we can proceed, we must know whether Sheikh Bahram would consent to wed the American. He has not yet spoken."

Dar's troubled gaze met Cathy's. Was the prospect so distressing to him? she wondered.

But that was unfair. Surely he had many concerns, not the least of which must be that she came from a foreign culture, and that they barely knew each other.

After a slight hesitation, Dar said, "Of course I will obey the spirits. It is important for Miss Maxwell to understand that the marriage would be a matter of form only. The spirits want the two houses joined—they take no interest beyond that. Am I correct in this assumption, Excellency?"

Zahira didn't look entirely pleased. "That is true. Still, such a handsome couple."

"The spirits are never capricious," added Basilyr.

Maha laid a hand on Cathy's wrist. "You don't have to do it. You heard what Zahira said. There is no punishment."

"Not for me personally, perhaps, but..." Cathy clasped her hands together, torn by a rush of emotions.

The Marakites' tradition of relying upon an oracle might be alien to her, but how could she dismiss it out of hand? Cathy believed that on rare occasions divine intervention did occur. How could she be certain it wasn't happening now?

From the moment baby Yasmin had been thrust into her arms, she had felt that fate intended them to be together. That belief had sustained her while she struggled so hard and at such cost to adopt the child. Perhaps all along, her destiny had been to fulfill this prophecy and prevent further bloodshed.

But how could she accept an arranged marriage? Even the slightest glance at Dar made her sharply aware of the man within the robes. He would do his best to remain a husband in name only, but how long could a hot-blooded man be expected to hold himself in check?

Until she met him, Cathy had been happy with her life, with Yasmin and her mother and the cozy informality of Laguna Beach. The pain of loving a man, of giving the best of herself and then being discarded without a backward glance, had finally begun to fade.

From the moment Dar appeared in the hotel driveway, he had turned her comfortable world upside down. Now he was threatening to make that situation permanent. After what had happened between them earlier today, she knew the marriage could never be a simple matter of documents and distances.

"I can't do it," she said.

"Then on your head will be a thousand deaths!" cried Khalid.

This was too much even for Fasad. "Leave us!" he roared. "Those deaths will be on my head, not hers!"

His eyes narrowing into slits, Khalid stalked from the room. Judging by the disgusted expression on Maha's face, she was fighting the impulse to stick out her tongue after her brother.

Cathy's gaze met Dar's. "I can't," she repeated.

"This is too much, all at once." He touched her elbow, and gently guided her toward the exit. "You will think more clearly at home, where you can consult with your mother."

Around the room, heads nodded. This was a step that the family-centered Al-Haroums could understand.

"You're going to take us home?" she asked in a rush of relief.

"There is no reason for Yasmin to leave Los Olivos," said Faiza.

"Of course she must go." Maha had apparently decided to take Cathy's part. "Even the spirits recognize the adoption."

"That is true," Fasad said thoughtfully.

Faiza said nothing more, but Cathy could see she was not happy with this turn of events. It was understandable that, to a woman who lived in sheltered surroundings, relationships took on paramount importance. She only hoped Yasmin's grandmother would not come to view her as an enemy.

Dar escorted Cathy back to her room. His nearness anchored her, but he didn't speak, perhaps because they were within earshot of servants.

At the doorway, he said in a low voice, "I will have Yasmin sent to you, so you can both prepare for dinner. It is getting dark and I think it safest if we stay until morning."

"Dar," she said. "How do you feel about all this? I know you would marry anyone if the good of your country required it, but surely you must have an opinion."

He stood motionless, considering her question. The headdress partially obscured his face and she could read nothing there, but then, years of diplomatic training must have taught him to control his reactions.

"I do not know how I feel," he said at last. "Perhaps we both need time to think." With a bow, he departed.

Cathy could still see the warmth on his face that afternoon as they sat suspended above the kelp forest. He had been ready to take her anywhere, to show her anything. Had he possessed a magic carpet, she had no doubt he would have whisked her away to some private realm.

But more than anyone she had ever known, Dar was a man of many layers, some far beyond her experience. Cathy might never fully understand him, and she might never fully trust him, either.

To marry Sheikh Kedar Bahram would be like tossing her heart into the ocean. Who could tell what lay hidden beneath the illusive beauty of shimmering fronds?

DAR HAD NOT EVEN REACHED his room before his cell phone rang. No one ever called him except in an emergency, and he answered it at once.

There was no assistant's voice to say "Hold for the emir." Instead, Ezzat himself spoke. It was the first time he had placed such a call directly.

"You have heard of the Citadel situation?" he asked. On receiving Dar's acknowledgment, he said, "I know these matters are complex, my cousin, but we need for your marriage with Yasmin to take place as soon as possible."

"We have found the Three-Eyed Woman." Dar told him of the change in the prophecy and the ensuing conversation.

"So the American woman refuses?"

He struggled to frame a completely honest answer. He wasn't certain that Cathy had rejected all possibility of a marriage. Rather, he had heard in her statement confusion and alarm. "She needs time."

"We may not have time." Weariness echoed through Ezzat's mild tone. "It seems there was an international exhibition on display at the museum and the rebels refuse to release these works, although they are not the property of Marakite. The American ambassador is sitting in one of my reception rooms, and the French ambassador in another.''

"Because of a few paintings?'' Dar said.

The emir gave a frustrated sigh. "It is something called the Pride of Nations Show. Each of a dozen countries has loaned works of special significance. Can you believe Mojahid's timing? Last month's traveling exhibit was military clothing worn during World War I—mostly smelly boots and Lawrence of Arabia's old underwear!''

"But surely these ambassadors must understand how difficult our situation is," Dar protested.

"Do they?" said Ezzat. "The United Nations has asked if we will accept a rescue mission. For an art show, if you can believe that! I think it is only an excuse to intervene in our civil war. We cannot, absolutely cannot, allow foreign troops on our soil.''

"You are right." Whatever his personal concerns, Dar knew he must function now as the emir's closest counselor and as Marakite's minister of foreign affairs. "We must take steps to forestall this.''

"What action would you recommend?" asked his cousin.

"First, I will arrange for Zahira and her attendant to fly to Haribat immediately," he said, grateful that the Al-Haroums kept two jets and flight crews at hand. "She and the Council of Elders must meet with the rebels and ensure that they will abide by the prophecy and lay down their arms if it is fulfilled.''

"You think this American woman will change her mind?" Ezzat asked hopefully.

"At least we should be able to hold off the UN for a while," Dar said. "Also, I will request that Sheikh Al-

Haroum formally ask these rebels to withdraw. After all, they claim to be his followers.''

"This Mojahid follows no one but his own arrogance,'' growled Ezzat. "At times like this, I wish I were a warrior. I would settle for being a great diplomat, but I am not that, either. Sometimes I wonder what I truly am.''

"You are a wise man who was born to lead by diplomacy and to bring us justice.'' Dar had grown up hard and tough at the head of a desert tribe, but he held deep admiration for his scholarly cousin. "You must try not to worry excessively.''

The emir uttered a low chuckle. "That is not so easy, my friend. Leila is so furious at the rebels, I think she would burst in with a machine gun and shoot them all if I did not restrain her.''

"Your wife is too intelligent for that. And she knows it would not serve you well.'' The emir's wife had a degree in political science and a keen interest in the affairs of government.

Her father, the president of a neighboring country, had been assassinated by a traitor when she was in her teens, and he knew that Leila's first priority was always the safety of her husband. "She will give you wise counsel.''

"She told me to call you,'' said Ezzat.

"You see?''

They both laughed. "I will stall the ambassadors,'' the emir said. "But my friend, we cannot afford to fail.''

"I know. Peace be with you.''

After hanging up, Dar tried to collect his thoughts. From now on, he could not allow himself to think of Cathy as a special woman who fascinated and excited him, but as the object of delicate negotiations.

For the good of Marakite and of his emir, he must win her consent to marry.

CATHY DIDN'T SLEEP more than an hour or so that night. Yasmin kept her up late, chattering about her newfound cousins. But mostly, Cathy's mind kept replaying the scene in Zahira's room.

How could she believe in a prophecy issued by mysterious and perhaps imaginary spirits? On the other hand, how could she *not* believe that she had an obligation to help the people of Marakite?

The slim hope that the rebels would withdraw overnight vanished when she joined the others in a sunroom where a long table had been set up for breakfast. On a big-screen TV, she could see the central square in Haribat filled with tanks and troops.

"A rumor is circulating that bombs have been planted throughout the Citadel," the reporter was saying as Cathy slipped into a seat. "Tension is mounting as night approaches...."

"Halfway around the world, it's evening now," Maha told the children, who were squirming and making faces at each other across the table.

"Can I have some pancakes?" Yasmin pointed at a plate making its way down the table. "Where's the peanut butter?"

"Most people don't put peanut butter on their pancakes." Cathy could feel herself blushing. Her family's peculiar dining habits were not something she felt comfortable revealing to other people.

"Peanut butter?" said Sabah. "What is that?"

Mercifully someone turned off the TV as Maha answered her sister's question. A few minutes later, Dar arrived to announce that the small plane was ready to take Cathy and Yasmin home.

"The jet is also prepared," he told Fasad. "Thank you for agreeing to send Zahira home immediately."

The older man spread his hands. "Of course. And, as you asked, I have telephoned Mojahid, but he will not listen to me, at least, not until he has met personally with the Three-Eyed Woman."

"I have heard talk of this man." Dar stood stiffly. The white severity of his robe and headdress emphasized the taut planes of his face. "There are rumors that he thinks of putting himself on the throne."

"He knows the other factions would not support him, but I dare not reject him openly." Fasad released a long breath. "What a nest of vipers I have stirred up!"

Cathy scarcely tasted her meal. As soon as Yasmin finished eating, they collected their suitcases and left.

The flight home passed quickly, perhaps because she was so busy with her thoughts. Even Yasmin seemed subdued, staring toward the mainland without comment.

Cathy wondered how Dar planned to proceed. Yesterday he had said that he didn't know his own mind. But today he was all business.

Had he given up on her? But he couldn't, not with so much at stake.

She closed her eyes against a flash of sunlight and wondered how her ordinary life could have been thrust into the center stage of world events, and where it would end.

Two limousines met them at John Wayne Airport. "I am sorry that I must be absent for a short time," Dar said. "A number of our citizens who live in Los Angeles have asked to meet with me and express their concerns.

It would give offense if I refused. This driver will take you home, and I will talk with you later.''

Instinctively Cathy pressed his hand. "You've been wonderful.''

His wry smile was like a warm breeze. "Not wonderful enough, it seems.''

"This isn't about you and me,'' she said. "You told me yourself that we are talking about formalities.''

"Formalities that nevertheless involve our persons,'' he reminded her. "Consult with your mother. I have faith in her judgment.''

After giving Yasmin a hug, he strode to his waiting limo. Reluctantly Cathy entered the other one.

They were en route to Laguna when Yasmin turned in her seat and said, "Is Dar going to be my daddy?''

Cathy remembered that Yasmin had asked more or less the same question on the flight to Los Olivos. "You mean can you call him Daddy? Well, sweetie...''

"No,'' said Yasmin earnestly. "My cousin Sara says he's going to marry you and be my daddy for real.''

Even though she knew it might not be a good idea, Cathy heard herself asking, "Would you like that?''

"He dresses funny,'' the little girl said. "But I like him a lot. Okay, you can marry him.''

In spite of her tension, Cathy laughed. "Just like that?''

"Sara and Mona think it's a good idea,'' she said. "Ahmed said *I* should marry Dar. Isn't that dumb? Little kids don't get married.''

"No, they don't.'' They were passing through Laguna Canyon, approaching the seaside resort.

"I told him it was stupid.'' Yasmin folded her arms and settled back in her seat.

And so we've traded one set of problems for another, Cathy mused. *I guess that's progress of a sort.*

The limousine had barely halted in front of her house when Mary came out. Cathy had called last night and sketched the situation. Still, that didn't explain her mother's fluttery gestures and the nervous way she caught Yasmin's hand.

"You'd better come inside," Mary said, and led the way.

Once Yasmin was settled in her room, busily renaming her dolls after her cousins, the two women adjourned to the living room.

"I just had a visit from the undersecretary of state," Mary said.

Cathy blinked, trying to make sense of what her mother was saying. "Somebody from Marakite came here?"

"Not Marakite! Washington." In spite of herself, Mary chuckled. "You should have seen all those cars jammed into our street! Actually, the undersecretary was on his way back from Singapore when the president asked him to stop here."

"The president?" Cathy felt foolish, repeating her mother's words, but she could scarcely believe it.

"Along with the Citadel, the rebels captured a traveling art exhibit with several important American works," her mother explained. "The undersecretary mentioned a portrait of George Washington. Closer to the president's heart, there is a painting of his great-grandmother as a child, holding her stuffed bear. She sat for James Whistler—you know, the one who painted *Whistler's Mother.*"

"But why should anyone connect this with me?" Cathy asked in dismay.

"The president personally contacted Emir Al-Aziz and

got the whole story." Mary ran a hand through her meticulously coiffed silver hair. "The cat's out of the bag, honey. The emir told him about this prophecy business. Our government couldn't have endorsed a marriage with a three-year-old, but you're a different matter."

"Wonderful," Cathy grumbled. "Mom, do you think I should marry Dar?"

"Do you love him?"

"That isn't the issue."

"Isn't it?"

"He said himself, it would be in name only," Cathy told her.

"How unromantic." Too agitated to sit still, her mother began pacing. "I had higher expectations of that man."

"Mom, just because he dresses like Rudolph Valentino in *The Sheik* doesn't mean he's going to sweep me off to his tent in the desert and ravish me!"

"Why not?" asked her mother. "Don't you think he's cute?"

Cathy tried to glare at her, but couldn't quite summon the indignation. "Oh, Mom! Dar told me he trusted your advice, and here you are sounding like a teenager!"

Mary stopped by the window, her face patched with areas of light and shadow. "I lost the love of my life a long time ago. Then I had to watch you get hurt, and try to cope with the fallout. Cathy, I know women can be strong and make their own way in the world. But that doesn't mean it's always the road to happiness."

"And an arranged marriage would be?" she blurted. "Mom, this guy comes from a culture where they practically worship an old woman who quotes from 'The Mary Tyler Moore Show.'"

"That was always one of my favorite programs," her

mother said. "Oh, Cathy, you have to make this decision for yourself. Just don't reject Dar because Ralph was such a creep. Or because you're afraid of the unknown, either. Sometimes you have to take a chance."

"Dar hasn't even said he *wants* to marry me," Cathy said. "What kind of relationship could we have? I would go on living here, he'd be jetting around the world..."

"You sound as if you miss him already," said her mother.

The painful part, Cathy realized, was that it was true. But she knew the antidote: hard work. As soon as possible, maybe even today, she should return to the hotel.

"I'd better call Bert," she said, and stood up.

"I don't think you fully grasp..." Mary began, when the phone rang.

"Maybe that's him now." Or perhaps Dar, Cathy thought, and wished she didn't feel such a spurt of hope.

In the kitchen, she said "Hello?" into the receiver.

"Miss Catherine Maxwell?" came a man's baritone voice.

"Yes?"

"This is Lowell Rivers of Radio News Today and we're on the air!" he said. "Is it true that the fate of Marakite rests on whether you agree to an arranged marriage?"

Mary entered just as Cathy slammed down the phone. "Reporters?"

"Live on the air!" she said. "Can you believe the nerve?"

Her mother clicked on the answering machine. "From now on, we'll monitor our calls."

The phone jangled so many times over the next hour that they turned off the ringer, too. But all day, voice after voice left messages on the machine, demanding that she return calls to newspapers and newsmagazines and radio and TV stations.

On the news, the Three-Eyed Woman, whom the Western media called the prophetess, arrived in Marakite and was whisked to the Citadel to meet with the rebel leader Mojahid. She and a half-dozen men who constituted the Council of Elders emerged half an hour later.

Mojahid, one of the Elders announced, had agreed to abide by the prophecy and make peace if the marriage took place. One of the paintings from the national museum collection was released as a sign of good faith.

It was a Cubist work of a woman with her nose in the middle of her forehead and an eyeball sprouting from her chin.

After that, the phone calls resumed with even greater intensity. Cathy tried to distract herself by going through her mail, but couldn't take much interest in advertisements and bills.

The only item of interest was a reminder that her fifth college reunion would be held that weekend. It would feature special theater and dance performances on campus.

College. It felt as if she'd attended it in some other lifetime, Cathy thought. How uncomplicated her life had been then, and how much she missed that sense of youthful freedom.

Early that evening she was still weighing what to do, when a limousine pulled up in front of the house and Dar emerged.

Chapter Nine

Mary reached the door first. "Thank goodness you're here," she said, ushering Dar inside. "The press has been ringing our phone off the hook."

His wry gaze met Cathy's. "You have my sympathy. I almost did not escape after the meeting in Los Angeles, with so many news vans blocking the street."

Thin worry lines etched his forehead, and she knew that despite the light tone, he took this matter very seriously. Yet he still had found time to buy a bouquet of roses and daisies.

"That was very thoughtful," she said as he presented it.

"A small romantic gesture in a most unromantic situation," Dar confessed. Their hands touched as she accepted the flowers, and neither felt in any hurry to pull away.

"I'll put them in a vase," said Mary, and whisked the flowers off to the kitchen. A moment later she called, "I think I'll start dinner. Why don't you two sit and talk?"

Dar waited until Cathy was seated, then took a chair opposite her. "Where is Yasmin?"

"Her best friend invited her over to play." The family

lived on the next block. "I thought it might be wise to keep her life as normal as possible."

"Very wise indeed," said Dar.

"Where's the Secret Service?" she asked.

"Under the circumstances, I was able to persuade them that their intrusiveness might harm my cause with you. They have agreed to keep a discreet distance." He leaned back, but his muscles remained taut. "You know, I have been thinking."

"So have I."

"Have you reached a conclusion, or may I present my argument?" he asked.

"Argue away," she said.

"This is not how I would choose to make a proposal." He folded his hands on his knees, atop the white robe, and studied her. "However, under the circumstances, I shall make my points logically and not emotionally. First, you yourself stated that you had no interest in marrying. Therefore, a union with me would not prevent you from living as you would otherwise have chosen."

"Except for the reporters," Cathy pointed out. "I hadn't counted on those."

He smiled wearily. "I have enough experience to tell you that once the crisis abates and you become yesterday's news, they will look elsewhere."

"I hope so." Cathy wondered if it was the shadowy effect of his headdress that made Dar appear so remote, or if he were simply overburdened by his responsibilities. She knew so little about him really.

"Second, of course, a generous financial arrangement would be made, for you and for Yasmin," he went on.

Cathy held up one hand. "Dar, please stop. I can't make a decision this way. Our situation is anything but logical, and money certainly isn't the issue."

"Then tell me what I can do to help you decide," he said.

"What makes you think you can help?"

The sheikh glanced toward the kitchen. "Surely you have already consulted your mother, but still you are uncertain. I am the other person in the equation. If I cannot assist you, who can? Perhaps we need to spend a little time together."

"I thought everyone was in a big crushing hurry for me to make up my mind," Cathy said.

Lamplight brightened Dar's sharp features as his face turned toward her. "It is unlikely Mojahid will take action precipitously. He will blow up the Citadel only if he becomes convinced no progress is possible. I do not think a day or so will make the difference."

A wave of relief ran through her. Deep inside, Cathy knew she couldn't agree to this marriage, but she wasn't ready to stand up to the entire world. She wasn't even sure she was ready to stand up to Dar.

Her refusal would put him in a difficult position. It would also bring a new barrage of attention and perhaps hostility. She needed time to gather strength, and she wanted to enlist Dar's support.

Her gaze fell on the trifold brochure with the schedule for tomorrow's reunion. She *did* want to go. She felt a strong yearning to return, if only for a little while, to that more carefree period of her life.

If she could make Dar see how vast was the gulf between them, perhaps he would help her deal with the press and with people like Khalid. And, in a way that she didn't care to examine too closely, she yearned to spend a little more time with him before circumstances tore them apart.

Cathy handed him the brochure. "Come with me," she said.

Dar angled the paper to catch the lamplight. "Your college reunion is tomorrow?" He studied the paper for a moment and then handed it back. "Yes, I would like to come. I would enjoy learning more about you, Cathy."

"I'll pick you up in front of the hotel at one." Before he could protest, she said, "We're taking my car. Tomorrow you're on my territory."

Dar got to his feet and made a slight bow. "I place myself in your hands."

As he left, Cathy told herself that, tomorrow, he would indeed learn more about her. Enough to understand why, the next time they said goodbye, it would be forever.

DAR WAS SURPRISED to find, only an hour north of Laguna Beach, a small college town that reminded him of his own college days in Cambridge, Massachusetts. That was, with the exception of a scattering of palm trees.

Funky coffee shops, art galleries and bookstores edged the streets. Students and faculty, some of them wearing the long hair and tie-dyed clothing of an earlier era, strolled along the sidewalks, and several meandered across the street in defiance of stoplights and crosswalks.

A few minutes later, as she drove on to the green, rolling campus, Cathy's expression grew calmer and her breathing steadied. Dar sensed that she was taking courage from these surroundings.

Last night, he had surmised that her invitation to accompany her was a prelude to refusing his proposal. He guessed it fell under the heading of "letting him down easy."

If so, he understood her position. From his experience

in the West, he knew that by its standards his demands posed an infringement on her personal freedom.

But as a man of the East, he saw that, although Cathy had not chosen this path for her life, fate had chosen it for her. The moment she adopted Yasmin, her future had become inextricably entwined with that of Marakite.

His country wavered on the brink of peace, or of being plunged into an ever-widening civil war that might rip it apart. Was she really willing to let that happen?

Dar had seen strength in Cathy, but it might have been corrupted by a popular culture that glorified self-indulgence. Today, he supposed, would reveal whether she possessed true generosity of spirit.

They parked in a lot marked Class Reunions. After getting out, they followed a series of signs toward the student center.

Dar was surprised to see so many other people heading the same way, including some much older than Cathy. But then, he realized, other classes must be marking their twentieth, thirtieth, fortieth and perhaps even fiftieth anniversaries.

As they strolled between two- and three-story stucco buildings, Cathy surveyed her surroundings with a faraway expression. Once she waved to someone on another walkway, but he couldn't see who it was.

"I did not attend my fifth reunion," Dar murmured. "If they notified me, the letter must have gone missing. Perhaps I will make it to my tenth to see if anyone remembers me."

"Of course they'll remember you!" Cathy shot him a startled gaze. "How could they forget?"

He gestured at the sport coat, open-throated shirt and casual slacks he wore. "I dressed much like this, or even more casually. They did not see me as a sheikh at Harvard.''

"You're not the sort of person to blend into a crowd, in any case." She tipped up her chin, regarding him as if he were a skyscraper. "Your height, for one thing."

"There were plenty of tall men at Harvard," he protested. "And certainly better looking ones than I."

"I'll bet the girls didn't think so." Her mouth pursed mischievously. "I'll bet they chased you all over campus."

It was true that he had attracted a fair amount of female attention, but it seemed immodest to say so. "Young people are always noticing each other. But what about you? What sort of person were you, in college?"

"Boring," she said.

"Boring?" Dar quirked an eyebrow. "That is difficult to believe."

A couple of lavender petals from a jacaranda tree blew into Cathy's hair and clung there like fairy jewels. "When I didn't have my nose in my books, I was working."

"You earned your own way through college?" Dar couldn't hide a note of approval. It confirmed his impression that Cathy was the sort of disciplined person who would make sacrifices when necessary.

"Not entirely. I won a scholarship and Mom had saved as much as she could." They skirted a construction zone where the skeleton of a new addition jutted from an older building. "I worked summers at first, and then I started working part-time at the hotel to help pay for Ralph's medical school. It really ran me ragged."

"Ah, the infamous fiancé." For some reason, Dar had found himself unwilling to speculate about her former relationship, but now the subject could not be avoided.

"It never occurred to you to make your assistance in the form of a loan?"

"A loan? Of course not!" She brushed at her hair, dislodging the jacaranda petals. They floated down and stuck briefly to her linen suit before drifting away. "We were supposed to be building a future together. I never dreamed he would dump me as soon as he got his M.D."

Ahead of them loomed the student center, a rounded glass-and-concrete building. Toward it funneled a throng of people.

"Do you believe Ralph was sincere in his intentions and later changed his mind?" Dar asked. "Or was he a trickster from the start?"

Cathy's grip tightened on the strap of her shoulder bag. "I think initially he meant to marry me. But then, when he began having doubts, he lacked the character to be honest with me."

"Or to discontinue taking your money," Dar pointed out. "I don't suppose he ever offered to pay it back?"

"He—he mumbled something about it when he announced he would be serving his internship back East and needed time to think things over," she said. "I was still hoping our relationship would work out, so of course I told him not to worry about it."

Sadness glistened in her eyes, and Dar wished he hadn't asked so many questions. But everything he learned made him understand Cathy better, and admire her more.

Inside the student center, they found a huge skylit dining hall set aside for the alumni. Banners on the high-tech steel rafters showed the different graduating classes where to assemble.

A couple of women started shrieking when they saw

Cathy. Dar hung back and let her hurry ahead to greet her friends.

This was her special day. Although his instincts urged him to push for her consent, such tactics could only backfire.

If he were to win Cathy, Dar knew, he must bide his time and watch for his chance.

AMID CRIES of "You haven't changed a bit!" and "I can't believe we're all here!", Cathy hugged her pals.

Some of them, like her former roommates Millie and Rosita, had kept in touch. Millie had a well-paying job as a computer programmer, while Rosita was rising rapidly as an insurance executive.

Then there were Joe and Bari, art students-turned-teachers who had married right after graduation, and Nadia, a dancer struggling to succeed in Los Angeles. Except for Christmas cards, Cathy had had little contact with them and was eager to catch up on their lives.

But even as she exchanged exclamations, she retained an awareness of Dar, waiting on the sidelines. Although he said nothing, he radiated a powerful sense of presence.

She had expected him to feel uncomfortable in the laid-back atmosphere of the campus. Perhaps, too, she had been hoping that the contrast would reinforce her decision to turn him down.

Yet he appeared perfectly at ease. She should have expected that since, after all, he'd attended an American college. But, more importantly, he had a patient, respectful attitude toward everything and everyone that came across his path, which gave him the knack of making himself at home anywhere.

A master diplomat. Until now, she had never fully appreciated the qualities it took to achieve that distinction.

She had also never considered how difficult it would be to resist him.

"Is that really you we've been hearing about on the news?" Rosita asked. "That stuff in Marakite?"

"We didn't think you'd come!" added Millie. "A sheikh wants to marry you? How romantic!"

Nadia glanced toward Dar. "Is he—is this—?"

"Yes. Come on and I'll introduce you." Cathy presented her friends to Dar. Their faces shone with fascination as he shook hands and paid undivided attention to each in turn.

"Wow!" whispered Millie afterward. "He makes you feel like you're the only person on the planet."

"He's so handsome!" added Rosita. "And exotic. Have you two, I mean, you know, uh, done it yet?"

"Done it?" Cathy repeated. "Rosita!"

"You can't blame her for asking." Millie gave her a conspiratorial grin. "I'll bet the whole world is wondering!"

The whole world was wondering *that?* Cathy felt her cheeks flame.

She was grateful when the head of the alumni association stood up to speak and the room quieted. After a few minutes, Cathy managed to concentrate on the welcoming speech and a reminder of the day's events. There was a wide selection of offerings, from seminars to performances, as well as a dinner here in the student center.

The president of the college added a few words about the institution's building fund. Cathy wished she could afford to contribute, but at the moment, it was out of the question.

When the formalities ended, she reviewed the brochure with Dar. He insisted that he didn't care which events they attended, so they went along with her friends.

The afternoon passed in a blur. To Cathy's surprise, people she didn't recognize approached her, many with questions or comments about Marakite. Although she'd managed to avoid the TV cameras, apparently someone had found a photograph of her and broadcast it, and a lot of people recognized her.

Her face grew stiff from smiling and her neck ached from nodding. It was a relief when Dar began shielding her from inquiries by claiming she had a headache. At that point, it was true.

After dinner, her friends planned to attend a dance performance. Cathy would have skipped it, but Nadia's younger sister was a featured soloist.

"Don't worry," Dar said in a low voice as they left the dining hall and walked through the rapidly cooling air. Twilight bathed the campus in sepia tones. "I'll run interference, if you wish."

"I certainly do." Cathy rubbed the muscles that connected her neck to her shoulder. "I never thought about how exhausting it is to be a celebrity."

What she didn't say was how disappointed she felt at realizing she couldn't escape. The events halfway around the world not only involved her and Dar and the Al-Haroums, they affected even her college reunion.

Would she ever feel truly free again? But wouldn't it be even worse to marry Dar and give up her freedom entirely?

A marriage of convenience. Such things were common in some places, and she supposed it could work if both parties agreed on the terms. But what if Dar changed his mind and wanted more?

The three hundred seats in the performance hall were so sharply raked that, as she navigated into her seat, Cathy half feared she might lose her balance and fall.

Dar caught her arm, and the momentary panic passed. No one else seemed worried about the steep pitch, not Rosita and Millie beside her nor Joe, Bari and Nadia, who sat directly in front.

She buried herself in her program, and was relieved to see that tonight's production was a tribute to Broadway. Although Cathy sometimes enjoyed long classical ballets like *Sleeping Beauty,* she was in no mood for one tonight.

The theater darkened, and suddenly music crashed through the air, startling her. The program was beginning with a bang, in this case, with music from *West Side Story.*

Nadia's sister starred in the second dance, the waltz from *Carousel.* Her pixielike lightness made her stand out, and Cathy applauded with enthusiasm.

Someone must have cranked up the air-conditioning, because as soon as she stopped clapping, she felt cold air seep through her light suit. Noticing her shivers, Dar slipped off his sport coat and draped it over her.

"You don't have to do that," she protested, although she didn't really want to give it up.

"I could not be comfortable if you are not," he murmured.

Perhaps it was the warmth settling around her or the effects of a long day and a full meal, but a pleasant sleepiness crept over Cathy. She wasn't ready to doze off, but her head felt so heavy, she leaned it against Dar's shoulder.

Next to her, Rosita made a clicking noise with her tongue, an expression of friendly teasing. Cathy chose to ignore it. Let her friends be amused. She felt entirely too mellow to care.

Dar slipped one arm around her as the music began

for the third piece. It was the theme from *The Phantom of the Opera.*

The words of the song whispered across the theater with eerie seductiveness. On the stage, dark figures wove their way through columns of hazy light. Cathy nestled closer to Dar, both relishing and shivering at the strange allure of the music.

He felt solid and warm. Not just physically, but at a deeper level. Whenever she was with him, Cathy realized, she felt sheltered by the force of his character, and by his iron sense of honor. She had never felt this safe with Ralph, and for good reason.

As the music summoned her to experience the unknown, she conceded silently that she would trust Dar with her life. She also, reluctantly, faced the fact that, if she were ever to be truly free again, she might have to.

DAR HATED TO BREAK the spell that the dance concert had woven around them. Feeling Cathy's head drift onto his shoulder in the theater had been like having a wild bird alight on his open hand. He had scarcely dared to breathe for fear of startling her.

Afterward, in silence, she negotiated her car through the sleepy streets of the college town, then blended into the currents of the freeway. Like stars from the far side of the galaxy, cold impersonal headlights swarmed around them.

He dared delay no longer. "We must speak of the future."

Cathy stiffened but said nothing.

Arguments ticked through Dar's brain, sensible and, he knew, useless. The erectness of her back spoke volumes. "You have already reached some conclusion, have you not?"

"I have."

"And?"

She moved into an exit lane, preparing to switch freeways. "Even though we're attracted to each other, we would be completely mismatched as husband and wife. You understand Western ways, and I respect your culture, but that isn't enough."

Dar's heart sank. He had known, rationally, that he should expect this type of response, but he had hoped, indeed begun to count upon, better. In any case, he could not afford to give in easily.

"As you say, there is some feeling between us," he said. "I believe it is what people call chemistry. Many marriages begin with that, and grow from there."

Silhouetted against passing lights, Cathy shook her head. "Actually, this—this—chemistry makes a marriage even more difficult."

"Most people would not think so."

"Then they wouldn't be seeing the whole picture." A tight voice betrayed her tension. "It would be hard to keep our distance. But if we try to have a real marriage, sooner or later we'll rip each other apart."

At first, her words puzzled Dar, since what he had proposed was merely a marriage of convenience. But Cathy must have sensed that he wanted more, and he saw no point in denying it. "How can you be so certain we are incompatible?"

"After my fiasco with Ralph, I did a lot of research into what makes a marriage tick." Cathy steered along a ramp to another freeway. "It takes shared values, and openness, a willingness to compromise, and enough time to build a private world together."

At such close range, her feminine scent percolated through Dar's blood. He could feel the intensity of her mood, could almost reach out and touch her thoughts. He had never felt so attuned to a woman. "We can have all of those things. It would require effort and a certain flexibility, perhaps, but it is possible."

"Flexibility on whose part?" Her hands clamped onto the steering wheel. "You have your responsibilities and expectations, and I don't think they could possibly mesh with what I would need from a marriage."

"This, then, is your answer?" he asked regretfully.

"I'm not finished." She squared her shoulders. "What I'm saying is, the only way we could get married is if it's temporary. A few weeks or a month, just until this rebellion is settled."

Dar could scarcely believe he had heard her correctly. "You are saying you will marry me?"

"Yes. But only on a short-term basis." After a moment, she added, "I do want to help your country. And I'm thinking of Yasmin. If I reject the prophecy, the Al-Haroums will probably seek custody. Maybe that's selfish—"

"It is not selfish for a mother to hold fast to her child." Her decision was both honorable and sensible, Dar thought. It was exactly what he had hoped for. Why, then, did he feel this pang of disappointment?

"You don't think they'll push for custody anyway, do you?" Cathy asked worriedly.

"No," Dar said. "Once I become the child's stepfather, even if we divorce, it is unlikely they will pursue the issue so long as you allow visits."

"Of course I will!" Cathy said. "Then do you agree to my condition?"

Dar would prefer to woo this woman until he made her see that they could indeed have a true marriage. But his duty required haste.

"I accept," he said. "I will ask my staff to research the legal requirements for a quick marriage."

"I called the county clerk's office on Friday, just out of curiosity," she said. "All we have to do is fill out a few papers, show our identification and pay a small fee. They don't even require blood tests. We can do it Monday."

He blinked in surprise. Sheikh Kedar Bahram was not used to being one-upped, but, in this case, Cathy's efficiency pleased him. "Very well." He tried to keep his tone businesslike, to match hers. "I will notify the emir, and of course the Al-Haroums. They may wish to attend."

"I don't suppose we should tell them it's temporary, should we?" Cathy said. "It would be a disaster if word reached the rebels."

"Already you are thinking like a diplomat." Then, although it pained him to say it, Dar added, "After the wedding, you may return home to Laguna Beach if you wish. Because of the unstable situation in Marakite, we will explain that you and Yasmin are remaining in the United States for the time being."

"That's what I had in mind," she said.

It will be almost like not getting married at all, Dar thought bleakly.

He had always expected to make a politically suitable union. He had even been willing to wed a child if the good of his country depended on it. But he had never expected to marry a woman he truly cared for, and be forced to live as if they were strangers.

Whatever it cost him as a man, however, Dar must act first as a patriot.

With a great effort of will, he turned to gaze out the

window at the shifting patterns of the nighttime landscape. But for the rest of the drive, he felt Cathy's presence beside him like a pillar of fire, scorching him with his own desire.

Chapter Ten

The previous Christmas, Cathy had impulsively bought a long white skirt and a jacket embroidered with glittery gold thread to wear to the hotel employees' dinner-dance. Now it would have to substitute for a wedding gown.

It came with a lightweight golden shawl, which could double as a scarf. A wedding was one occasion on which head coverings were as appropriate for American women as for Middle Eastern ones.

Mary, resourceful as always, provided an heirloom diamond ring, since there would be no time to purchase and fit a new one. It was already the right size and, she assured her daughter, there was no hurry about getting it back.

Her tone implied that, should Cathy change her mind about the temporary nature of the match, that would be perfectly fine.

On Monday morning, when her daughter's hands were so fluttery she could scarcely apply makeup, Mary fixed Cathy's hair and touched up a scuff mark on her gold pumps. Then she went to get Yasmin ready.

I've got the dress, Cathy told herself as Dar's gleaming limousine pulled up in front of her house. *I've got the man. Now all I need is the nerve.*

That was the hard part, she admitted silently. She could scarcely bring herself to look at Dar, dashing in his white robes, as he escorted her to the luxury car. She was marrying a man she barely knew, joining a wealthy and powerful family, and cementing her central position in a world crisis, all at the same time.

When Mary in a pink suit and Yasmin in her flouncy dress joined them in the limo, Cathy felt her breathing begin to calm. That lasted for about thirty seconds, until Dar took his seat beside her.

His robes were made of silk so intricately woven, it was almost sheer. He eased into place, smoothing the fabric so it didn't bunch or tear. Despite his practiced finesse, there was a barely restrained impatience to his movements that indicated such finery was not his preferred garb.

In the shake of his head as he tossed back an errant fold of the kaffiyeh, she glimpsed the desert warrior he had once been, the teenager who had taken control of his tribe and won the respect of his powerful cousin Ezzat. Some of that wildness still lurked beneath the civilized surface.

How on earth did she think she could tame him, even for a short while? Their agreement might be for a marriage in name only, but in the eyes of the world, and certainly of his people, they would be husband and wife, Cathy thought with a twist of panic.

Deliberately she focused on how she'd felt Saturday night at the dance concert, with her head resting on Dar's shoulder. Safe. Trusting.

She needed to hold on to those feelings now.

Mary made casual conversation with Dar, and entertained Yasmin by pointing out a newly remodeled shopping mall as they passed. Thank goodness for her mother's assistance, because right now Cathy didn't have a clue what to say to this man beside her. And if she couldn't talk to him now, what on earth was she going to say later, when they were married?

But she wouldn't exactly be facing him over the breakfast table, Cathy reminded herself. Dar had informed her last night that he would fly to Marakite immediately after the wedding to help resolve the situation at the Citadel.

The hotel corporation had generously extended her leave, but once the news media turned their attention elsewhere, Cathy planned to resume her job. It was her intention to proceed as if this union had never taken place.

They turned off the freeway and, a few minutes later, arrived at the redbrick courthouse. In front, passersby paused to gawk at the cluster of exotic-looking men and women in foreign dress. It was hard for Cathy to believe that this family was waiting for her.

Had it really been only a week ago that she'd come to the newer courthouse across the street to finalize Yasmin's adoption? How simple everything had seemed then!

"Nervous?" Mary asked.

"Petrified."

Dar took her arm. "I will hold you up."

"What does 'petrified' mean?" asked Yasmin.

"It means it's a good thing Dar's going to hold me up," Cathy told her.

The sense of stepping into the midst of strangers vanished when the Al-Harooms gathered around to greet them. In the short time that she'd known the family, she realized, each person had become distinct and memorable.

There was Fasad, bowing gallantly as Dar introduced

him to Mary. Beside him, Faiza took Yasmin's hand and nodded approval at her lacy dress, which had been a gift from the Al-Haroums.

Khalid eyed Cathy with a ferocity that made her wonder, if she'd refused the marriage, whether he would have taken it upon himself to hunt her down and force her to become Dar's bride. His wife, Hanan, hesitated behind him, peering out curiously whenever she thought no one would notice.

Maha caught Cathy's hands warmly, her eyes brimming with sympathetic concern. Only her sister Sabah seemed at ease, smiling as she folded her hands atop her round belly.

"I always wondered who would bring Sheikh Bahram to the altar," she told Cathy as they strolled into the courthouse. Dar's attention, fortunately, was engaged in accepting best wishes from a friendly bystander. "Of course, there was Yasmin and the prophecy, but I knew someday he would choose a real woman."

"He wasn't the one who chose me," Cathy pointed out. "It was Zahira."

"It was the spirits," Maha corrected.

"They must have seen you looking at him," Sabah said. "Even though we are not supposed to mention it."

In spite of her anxiety, Cathy laughed. Dar turned, one eyebrow rising in an unspoken question. "Just girl talk," she told him.

"We will be sisters now," Maha said. "Or will we?"

"We are your daughter's aunts," Sabah pointed out. "What else could we be?"

"I've always wanted sisters, and now I have two." Noticing Hanan nearby, Cathy amended, "Three." Khalid's wife lowered her eyes, but looked pleased.

There were papers to fill out and a short wait to get

the marriage license, and then the county clerk himself came out to perform the ceremony. He welcomed them with genuine warmth.

Cathy recited her vows in a daze. Her entire body tingled at the awareness of Dar standing beside her, holding her arm, claiming her for his own.

It isn't real. It's just a show.

"I don't know what the customs are in your homeland, sir, but at this point most grooms kiss the bride," the clerk said when they finished.

"I always honor the customs of my host country," Dar replied gravely. Cathy could have sworn she saw a twinkle in his eye as he turned toward her.

She ought to object. He had promised there would be no close contact and here they were, barely married for a minute, and he was already bending over her.

On the other hand, he *would* be leaving that very afternoon in the Al-Haroums' private jet, and heaven knew when she would see him again....

His mouth closed over hers, silencing her internal debate. The kiss was brief but thorough. *Masterful,* she thought dazedly. Like a desert warrior claiming his woman, and marking her as off-limits to any other man.

He drew back, and Cathy had to struggle to catch her breath. Had it been her imagination, or had something more than a kiss passed between them?

Dar studied her with hooded eyes, his lips still parted. Then he gave a short nod, and turned to scoop up Yasmin.

"Are you my daddy now?" she cried.

"Indeed he is," said Fasad.

"The spirits must be pleased." Khalid regarded them with cold satisfaction. "Let us hope the rebels are equally content."

"Come." Dar finished shaking hands all around and turned to Cathy. "Let us flee before the press discovers we are here."

She put her hand in his firm, square one, and realized she still hadn't recovered from their kiss. The painful part was that, just for a moment, she had enjoyed the sensation of belonging to him.

But he isn't really yours, she reminded herself. *You'd better keep your feet on the ground, because sooner or later, you're going to have to fend for yourself.*

Dar belonged first to Marakite and to his cousin the emir, not to her. There was no question where his loyalty lay, and never would be.

They emerged from the courthouse into a blinding wash of sunlight and the deafening noise of lenses clicking and reporters shouting.

The entire front of the courthouse was covered with cameras and people, spilling down the steps and across the sidewalk. The news grapevine must have been working overtime.

Thank goodness Dar knew how to handle the press, Cathy reflected as he raised his arms for silence. Standing at the top of the steps, with his robes and his impressive height, he awed the crowd.

"Please, I would like to make a statement," he said into the resulting hush. "I am Sheikh Kedar Bahram, minister of trade and foreign affairs for the Emirate of Marakite. I have just had the great honor to be married to Miss Catherine Maxwell of Laguna Beach."

Tape recorders and Minicams whirred. "Is this because of that prophecy business?" a reporter yelled.

A woman shouted, "How will this affect the occupation of the Citadel?" And a man called, "What does this mean for you, Miss Maxwell? Are you renouncing your American citizenship?''

Again, Dar raised his hands. When the din subsided, he said, ''We are honoring the prophecy, and we have the word of rebel leader Mojahid that he will yield to a higher power.'' He waved Fasad to join him. ''Please, may I introduce Sheikh Fasad Al-Haroum. From this day forward, I consider him as my honorary father-in-law.''

Fasad drew himself to his full height, a few inches shorter than Dar. ''Yes, yes,'' he said. ''I am hopeful that peace negotiations will follow, now that our families are united.''

''Where's the little girl?'' called a voice. ''What about her?''

Yasmin squeezed under Cathy's arm and pressed against her mother. ''I'm right here and I like Dar even better than my new Elmo!''

Smiles and a few laughs greeted this announcement, but the press were not easily distracted from the thread of their story. ''Do you plan to make your home in Haribat, Miss Maxwell?'' asked a woman.

''Not right away,'' Cathy said. ''Until—until things stabilize, we thought it would be less disruptive for Yasmin if she and I remained with my mother.''

Fasad frowned. Behind him, Faiza uttered a sharp cough. Cathy was glad she couldn't see Khalid's reaction.

To her surprise, a buzz went up from the reporters. When one man finally made himself heard above the rest, he was saying, ''But the rebel leader insists on meeting you both. And the little girl, too.''

''Excuse me? What is this?'' Dar asked.

''It came across the Associated Press wire half an hour ago,'' the man said. ''This Mojahid character gave a news conference and said he must see the bridal couple for himself."

"He wants the prophetess to be there, too," someone added.

"And Sheikh Al-Haroum and his son," called a third reporter.

Cathy could feel Dar stiffen. Impulsively she stood on tiptoe and whispered in his ear, "I'll go."

She tried not to think about what that would mean. The whole reason for the marriage had been to bring peace to his country, and she couldn't back down now.

He ducked his head and murmured, "Thank you, Cathy. This demand—I do not like it. I do not trust this man. But we have little choice."

To the reporters, who were waiting with uncharacteristic patience for the response, Dar said, "I think this is the first press conference in which I have received as much information as I have given."

"What about you, Miss Maxwell—I mean, Mrs. Bahram? Are you going to Haribat?" a woman called.

"That's up to my husband," Cathy replied. "If he needs me, I'll go."

This time, as she turned toward her mother, she did glimpse Khalid's reaction. In the twist of his mouth, she read reluctant approval.

Mary, however, didn't look pleased, and Cathy couldn't blame her. They would just have to make the best of it.

With any luck, she wouldn't stay in Marakite for long.

DAR AWOKE TO THE HUM of the jet engine. He shifted position and nearly rolled off the bed, a converted seat that was too short and too narrow for him.

On an identical berth nearby, Cathy lay curled beneath

a quilt, short blond hair in disarray around her sleep-softened face. He could hardly believe she was here.

Although he had admired her spirit from the moment they met, each day she revealed new facets to her character. She had no obligation to make this journey to a strange land, yet she hadn't even hesitated.

It was ironic. He was beginning to realize that, had he searched the world, he doubted he could have found a woman better suited to be his wife, despite the cultural differences. But Cathy was not really his. They had made an agreement, and he must abide by it.

Feeling uneasy, as he had ever since Mojahid demanded to meet Cathy and Yasmin, Dar glanced around the interior of the private jet.

Other berths held little Yasmin with her stuffed animals and dolls; Faiza and Fasad; Khalid and Hanan; their daughter, Mona, and several servants. Rather than cram in the rest of the family, it had been decided to let the two Al-Haroum daughters, the other children and the remainder of the servants await the return of the second jet, which had taken Zahira to Marakite earlier.

For the moment, the cabin had become a safe haven, but Dar felt as if dark forces gathered outside. Sitting on his pull-out bed, he studied his new wife and hoped he would not be forced to place her in peril.

He had experienced a burst of joy when she agreed to come with him to Marakite. Even though he knew it was foolish, he had been dreading the moment of their parting, aware that they might not meet again for months, and then only to dissolve the marriage.

He wished they could have more time together, as man and woman. Time to scuba dive, or ride Arabian horses side by side, or merely walk along the beach.

Although that might never be possible, he was glad

she would have a chance to see his country. He looked forward to watching her reactions. He was learning that Cathy always had a unique perspective on the people she met, and he would value her impressions of Ezzat, Leila...even this accursed rebel leader.

An involuntary shudder ran through Dar. Why did the man insist on meeting Cathy and Yasmin? What was he planning?

Across from him, his bride stirred. Bright blue eyes blinked open, and she took a moment to get her bearings. Instinctively her gaze flew to Yasmin, and then, reassured, she shifted her attention to Dar.

"Some wedding night, huh?" she whispered.

He chuckled. "At least we were in the same room."

"Are we almost there?"

He indicated the window shades, around which showed thin slivers of fading light. It was growing late in the Middle East; they had traveled for nearly twelve hours, and had lost nearly another half day to the time difference.

"We should arrive at Haribat in an hour," he said. "I am glad you slept well, for we shall have a busy evening."

Cathy stretched sleepily. "Did I imagine it, or did we land somewhere during the flight?"

"Refueling." Even Fasad had dozed through the stop, but Dar had gone forward to make sure the pilot and copilot felt alert. He was prepared to take the controls if there were any doubt, but that hadn't been necessary. "We change our stops each time, to prevent interference."

"You mean terrorism?" She sat up, abandoning the warmth of the quilt. "I don't think I'd ever get used to living this way."

"Once we have peace, it will no longer be a problem," Dar assured her. "Although in today's world, it always pays to take precautions. For Americans, as well as Marakites."

"I suppose so." She rubbed her eyes sleepily. At this hour, her face took on the innocence of a child, Dar thought. But there was nothing immature about the feminine curves giving shape to her sleep shirt.

Quickly he moved his gaze to a safer spot, the smooth inlet of her throat. That reminded him of something he'd forgotten to do.

Reaching beneath the seat, Dar pulled out the compartmentalized case he always kept close on trips. In it were his most important documents and computer disks, a change of clothing and whatever else he might need in an emergency.

From a side pocket, he drew a small jeweler's box. "I forgot to give this to you yesterday," he said, moving to sit beside Cathy. "I had planned to present it after the wedding, but matters became hectic."

Her eyes widening in surprise, she reached out gingerly for the box. It struck Dar that Cathy was not used to being pampered by a man. She should have been expecting a gift of this nature, but clearly she had not.

"This is—" she swallowed "—very kind."

"You should not thank me until you have at least opened it." He fought down the urge to lean close and drink in her light herbal scent.

She ran a finger across the plush box once more, then pried it open. "Oh!"

Nested within lay the diamond-and-emerald necklace with matching earrings that Dar had selected at an exclusive Newport Beach jeweler's. The abstract design, suggestive of a leaf or a feather, had brought to his mind the lacy kelp at Los Olivos.

Hesitantly, as if reluctant to handle something so delicate, Cathy picked up the necklace. "It's like your magic city in the sea. Oh, Dar, I love it."

Lifting it from her hands, he reached to fasten the gold chain around her neck. Cathy turned slightly and lowered her head to accommodate him.

The blond fuzz on the back of her neck tickled his hands. The contact felt intimate and trusting, the way a wife naturally would yield to her husband as he assisted her. He tried not to read too much into her action. Trust, after all, could occur between friends as well as mates.

But he didn't want to be merely friends. After closing the clasp, Dar brushed the back of his hand along Cathy's cheek. Her lids drifted shut as she relished the caress.

His body grew taut with longing. He had promised not to provoke her, but she obviously enjoyed his touch. They were married, and by all rights they should be alone together in a nest of silken hangings.

He should be laying her back against the cushions, removing her garment and tracing his tongue between her breasts. He knew exactly how he would taste each nipple, and how his thumbs would stroke down her stomach to stir the fire below.

There had been women before in Dar's life. He knew how to please them, and they had known how to please him, too.

But what he felt for Cathy ran much deeper. And if she let herself go, he suspected that his response would overwhelm even his worldly self-control.

Nearby he heard a rustle and then a little voice said, "Mommy? Are we there yet?"

Reluctantly Dar drew back. "I hope you will wear it in joy."

"I can't wait to try on the earrings." She flashed him a smile. "These are special."

"To me also," he said.

The others began stirring, and within moments the plane was abustle. The women retreated to the dressing chamber and the men straightened their clothing and put on their robes and kaffiyehs.

Soon they would be landing in Haribat. The time for relaxing had ended.

CATHY HAD STUDIED a map the night before, so she knew that Marakite lay along the southern coast of the Arabian peninsula. It was one of a number of small nations that bordered Saudi Arabia.

At least she was appropriately dressed for her arrival, in a long, loose garment, called a thawb, that had been a gift from the Al-Haroums. Made of white fabric embroidered with patterns of black and green thread, it reminded Cathy of dresses she had seen imported from India.

As the plane swooped in from the Arabian Sea, she expected a desert landscape to unfurl below them. Instead, the land along this coastal strip turned out to be green and filled with stubby trees. Although she glimpsed mountains inland, the landscape here was flat.

The airport had two runways, a control tower and a small terminal, she noted as they made final preparations for landing. The entire facility was surrounded by a high barbed-wire fence dotted with small, fortified outposts.

"Those are guard stations," Dar said, following her gaze through the window. "Today they are all occupied."

Cathy glanced around for Yasmin. The little girl,

belted into her seat, was absorbed in playing dolls with her three-year-old cousin Mona.

Although nothing seemed amiss, it was troubling to think that she had brought her daughter to such a dangerous place. Yet somehow, with Dar beside her, Cathy felt as if nothing could harm them.

The real danger came from him, or at least from the temptation he presented. There had been a sense of intimacy in the way he fastened the necklace in place a short time earlier. His hands had trembled as if aching to explore her, and his breathing had quickened.

Her own reaction had been an almost overwhelming urge to turn and touch her mouth to his. Thank goodness Yasmin had interrupted them!

Cathy fingered the pendant at her throat. The leaflike design took her back to the private world she and Dar had shared off Los Olivos. It was reassuring, this sense of closeness, as she prepared to enter a land of strangers.

The plane landed with a light thump, then reversed engines to slow its onrush. The pressure forced them back into their seats, until at last they slowed.

They had arrived in Marakite.

Chapter Eleven

Even before the craft came to a full stop, servants began collecting luggage. Faiza and Hanan tied scarves over their hair, and Cathy followed suit, using a gold-printed white triangle that had come with her thawb.

Both of the sheikhs put through calls on their cellular phones. After a brief conversation, Dar reported that the emir awaited their arrival, and Fasad informed his wife that the Al-Haroums would be guests at the palace during the peace negotiations.

Khalid, who had paced irritably while the other men were on the phone, made a point of questioning his father privately. He wanted so desperately to be important, Cathy thought, yet Fasad brushed him off as if he were a mere boy.

Two limousines pulled onto the runway, followed by a van for the luggage and the servants. After a moment's discussion, it was decided that Yasmin and Mona would be happiest if they stayed together. They would ride with Cathy, Dar and Khalid in the first car.

As she took her seat, Cathy felt a moment's disquiet. Khalid always seemed dissatisfied with everyone and everything, and today he was particularly edgy.

On the other hand, he *was* Fasad's heir, and of course

he was Mona's father. It seemed highly unlikely he would cause any problems.

As they drove away from the runway, a half-dozen military police cars closed in. Cathy's heart thumped hollowly, even though it quickly became apparent that this was their escort.

"You are not accustomed to living this way," Dar said. "After a while, you will hardly notice."

"I'm not so sure." Cathy's memory flashed on to the previous Saturday, just a little over a week ago but before she'd ever heard of Dar or the Al-Haroums.

She and Yasmin had driven to an outdoor mall, and lingered in the plaza to eat ice cream and listen to a steel drum band. She had taken for granted the freedom to go where she liked and do as she pleased.

But the sights through the limousine window were too fascinating for Cathy to dwell on memories of home. Small stone and mud-brick houses dotted the landscape, and, far off, a farmer was plowing with a 1950s-style tractor.

In front of one house, a grumpy-looking camel plodded in a large circle, pulling a beam that operated a rough mill. A child of about ten sat near the hub, evidently providing a counterweight.

In the opposite lane of the highway, a four-wheel-drive vehicle and a Japanese car whizzed by. Paying no attention to them, a dark-skinned girl walked on a parallel trail of bare dirt, tossing pebbles to drive a herd of cattle. She wore sandals, a scarf and a robe of bright yellow and red.

Farther down the dirt trail, they passed several camels piled with baskets and bundles. One also carried a young man who swayed to Arabic music blasting from a boom box.

"You see those trees?" Khalid pointed to a clump of

thick-trunked bushes, scarcely taller than the passing camels. "That is the plant from which we derive frankincense."

"That was very valuable in ancient times, wasn't it?" Cathy said.

The young man smiled. "Of course, for things smelled very bad, and any sort of perfume was welcome! Incense was prized for religious rituals, as well."

"When he told me about Marakite, Dar mentioned something called the frankincense trail," Cathy recalled. "What was that?"

Judging by the warmth of his expression, Khalid enjoyed talking about his country's history. "It was a trade route. It ran through Arabia for nearly 2,500 miles, all the way to Jordan, and from there the incense was shipped to Egypt and Rome."

"I know about Egypt," said Yasmin. "That's where the pyramids are."

"Also Cleopatra," said Mona. Giggling, the girls returned their attention to the scenery.

"Fortunately, there are also many plants with medicinal value in Marakite," Dar added. "Our scientists have rediscovered cures known to the ancients, and developed new applications. Our pharmaceuticals industry provides the country with considerable income."

"But not as much as oil gives to our neighbors!" Khalid, his mood shifting abruptly, glared at a mud hut in the middle of a green field. "People should not have to live in such squalor."

Cathy refrained from pointing out that the Al-Harooms, with their jet planes and servants, were hardly living in poverty. Still, she couldn't resist asking, "Isn't there enough money to go around?"

"In normal times, there would be," Dar said. "The

emir and his wife have instituted a program of public works and improved education. Unfortunately, civil war has disrupted the process and drained our funds.''

''The war must be stopped.'' Khalid's fingers tapped on the inside of his door, and his voice rose to a near shout. ''This Mojahid is a menace!'' Yasmin and Mona, who were holding up stuffed animals and dolls so the toys could ''see'' out the window, turned startled gazes toward him.

The highway curved around a cluster of palm trees, and suddenly the city of Haribat rose before them. In the harshly angled light of late afternoon, the buildings clustered together on a hill that dominated the surrounding plains.

The city looked, to Cathy, like a vision from a Middle Eastern legend, except that satellite dishes protruded from almost every rooftop. She could hardly sort one structure from another, so closely were they packed.

The most common type of building was made of reddish brown bricks and rose four or five stories. Since she saw no houses close by, she guessed that at least some of them must be residences.

Lacy white minarets and onion-shaped domes punctuated the brick buildings at random intervals. A couple of modern steel-and-glass skyscrapers also thrust themselves into view.

Peering uphill toward the center of town, she made out a regular pattern of spires. ''What's that?''

''The royal palace,'' said Khalid. ''That is just across the square from the Citadel. How convenient for Mojahid, do you not think?''

For a moment, Cathy had forgotten she was anything more than a tourist. Now a tremor ran through her at the reminder of what lay ahead, and she was grateful when she felt Dar's hand close over hers.

The motorcade passed through the city's gate, a great arch inscribed with Arabic writing. "Our decorations are not the same as you will find in Europe," Dar advised. "Our traditions do not permit statues or other graven images of people or animals."

"Some countries have gone so far as to ban photographs and films," Khalid added. "However, our Council of Elders has determined that film is only a matter of light and shadow, not an actual attempt to reproduce God's works. Therefore those things are permitted here, if their subject matter does not offend."

"The gates look so ancient," Cathy observed.

"Alas, no." Khalid waved a hand dismissively. "Haribat was not established until the Middle Ages."

"Oh, is that all?" She was pleased to see the young man's expression soften at her teasing.

"By American standards, I suppose it *is* ancient," he conceded.

The limousine prowled through narrow lanes, past tiny street-level shops that stood open to passersby. Baskets, strings of beads, pocketbooks and other wares dangled so thickly from the ceilings that there was barely space for the merchants to stand.

Most of the pedestrians were men, some in robes and kaffiyehs, others in thawbs and turbans. Here and there, Cathy spotted a curved dagger tucked into a richly embroidered belt.

"Is this place like Disneyland?" Yasmin asked. "Are those costumes?"

"It is not Disneyland," Mona replied sadly. "There is no Mickey Mouse."

"My little niece, am I wearing a costume? Is your new father wearing one?" teased Khalid.

Yasmin considered. "No. You always dress like that."

"Just so," said her uncle.

Cathy spotted a few women walking together, shepherding their children. The adults were cloaked in black from head to toe.

A moment later, the car passed a cluster of schoolgirls in long gray skirts, white blouses and suspenders. Watching over them were two older women wearing thawbs and scarves.

"Women do not have to be veiled here, as they do in some countries," Dar said. "Western women sometimes go out with their hair uncovered, but it is considered immodest."

Khalid indicated Cathy's scarf. "I am glad that you honor our customs."

"We have an old saying," she answered. "When in Rome, do as the Romans do."

"It is a good philosophy," Khalid said. "But then, you are now one of us. This is your home, and it is wise to fit yourself to our ways."

It seemed dishonest not to tell him that her stay was only temporary, but Cathy knew she should not. The gentle pressure of Dar's hand on hers indicated that he shared her concern.

The streets grew wider as the limousine ascended toward the palace. Several shops bore familiar names, one of a Paris couturier and another of a Japanese athletic shoe company.

Ahead of them, the police escort set off its sirens. At the harsh sound, Cathy's chest squeezed.

"Don't be afraid," Dar said. "They are announcing our arrival."

"Cool!" cried Yasmin.

The motorcade proceeded from the street into a large square. Along two sides lay dozens of shops, all shuttered. Although twilight was falling, Cathy suspected they had been closed not because of the late hour but due to the crisis.

To their right, barricades and tanks cut off access. Above them, she could see the massive shape of the Citadel, its sheer, windowless walls joined at each corner by round, tapering bastions. The fortress's reddish color appeared to derive from a clay veneer, which had crumbled in spots to reveal gray stone beneath.

There was a squat, hulking defiance about the building as if the zeal of centuries of Marakite warriors had infused its thick walls. Surely an explosion powerful enough to destroy it would send chunks of jagged rock smashing into the palace and across the city, as well as into the soul of the nation.

A couple of camera crews ran toward the limousine, but military policemen halted them with shouts. The reporters withdrew, but not before several Minicams panned the procession.

"Did they get my doll's picture?" Yasmin asked. "Will she be on television?"

"Probably so," said Khalid. "These newspeople are such fools, they will put anything on the air."

They were almost across the square before Cathy got a clear look at the palace ahead. Her first impression was of a vast reach of arches and towers, and walls inlaid with geometric designs. Although it was solidly built, compared to the Citadel it had an almost dainty air.

Browns and golds and the unearthly green of old copper were the main colors, with here and there an accent of black and white. She guessed the building to be octagonal, with four long sides and four shorter entrance-ways, one of which faced the square.

"It's beautiful," she breathed. "Yasmin, look."

"Wow!" said her daughter. "Does the king live there?"

"He's called the emir," Cathy said. "He and his wife both live here."

"It is a business complex and a sort of grand hotel, as well, although only for honored guests," Dar added. "On the ground floor, there is space for storage and all manner of food preparation. Offices are one floor up, and above that are the living quarters, and some private offices."

Cathy tore her attention away. "Are we going to stop and see that man, Mojahid?"

"No. He has requested the meeting be held tomorrow morning." Their motorcade halted, and they waited while their police escort conferred with the palace guards.

"But why the delay?" Cathy asked. "Has he made other demands?"

"Today, he asked that the leaders of the other rebel tribes be summoned to Haribat," Khalid said.

"It may indicate that he wishes peace negotiations to begin as soon as possible after he agrees to leave the Citadel," Dar explained. "Naturally, he will expect to play a leading role."

"A terrorist?" Cathy asked. "In America, he'd be thrown in jail. But I guess it's not that simple here, is it?"

"He has many followers," Khalid agreed. "It would be disastrous to imprison him, especially if he releases the Citadel without harm."

"In fact, this situation may actually increase his prestige, if he resolves it in a statesmanlike manner," Dar said. "We must prepare for him to wield a certain power at the negotiations."

"Power?" Cathy asked. "To what purpose?"

Khalid gritted his teeth so hard, he could barely force out the words. "No doubt he expects to be awarded some position in the government. It is even possible that he may try to replace the emir, if not with my father, then with someone else of rank whom he believes he can control."

Cathy didn't understand much about politics, especially in Marakite, but she knew that Fasad and Ezzat were the leaders of the two warring sides. "I can't imagine the emir's people and the rebels agreeing on some third person to rule the country."

"Khalid is only speculating," Dar said.

"But Mojahid must have some scheme to entrench himself in power!" Khalid countered. "And it will not be through my father. Everyone knows that he is too stubborn to be manipulated."

"Who else could make a claim to the throne?" Cathy asked. "Does the emir have a brother?"

"No, but he has a cousin," Khalid said slowly. "A cousin who is now also part of the Al-Haroum family. Why not you, Dar?"

"No!" The response cut the air like the flick of a whip. The two little girls jumped in surprise.

"Dar?" Cathy said, stunned. "Someone might try to make Dar the emir?"

Khalid waved a hand appeasingly. "Of course, Sheikh Bahram does not seek this, nor would he ever let Mojahid control him, but the rebel scum does not know this. He will expect your husband to act as he would in such a situation—with ruthless ambition."

Dar stared ahead, his expression severe. "This should

not even be spoken. It is treason. I would never agree to such a thing.''

"What if the emir himself were to request it?" Khalid probed. "Would you turn him down?"

"It will not happen," Dar said flatly. "Besides, Khalid, you are also the emir's cousin."

"But you are an independent sheikh and I am not," said the younger man. "I could never rule over my father."

"And I could not rule over Ezzat."

The motorcade started forward with a jerk. There was no time for further conversation as they rolled into the palace, leaving the police escort behind.

Although she had been looking forward to meeting Ezzat Al-Aziz and his wife, Cathy could hardly concentrate as they motored into a large courtyard edged by a cloistered walkway. Her brain on automatic, she took Yasmin's hand and, following Dar's directions, exited the limousine.

Even the rich mosaics and colored fountains failed to snare her attention as she went with the others into the building. Her mind was caught in a loop, playing and replaying what she had heard.

Her marriage to Dar, and his status as Yasmin's stepfather, might have put him in line to become the emir. What if, despite his objections, it came to pass?

She hadn't signed on to be a queen, or whatever one might call the emir's wife. This was only a temporary tour of duty, not a lifelong commitment.

Resolutely Cathy forced herself to breathe more slowly. As Dar said, Khalid had only been speculating. None of this was likely to happen.

From Dar, she had gained a sense of the deep attachment between him and his cousin. He had already risked his life once to save the emir, and would not hesitate to do so again. Whatever Mojahid might be planning, he would be wise to leave Dar out of it.

They entered an ornately decorated receiving room, and she snapped out of her reverie on seeing the distinguished group waiting to greet them. Especially, she noticed a richly robed man of middle height and slim build, and the tall woman beside him.

These must be the Al-Azizes, looking like figures from a fairy tale. Feeling as if she were stepping into another dimension, Cathy let Dar lead her forward to be introduced.

She curtseyed, since it seemed to be expected, and Yasmin did the same. Ezzat gave them a friendly nod, which made his wire-rimmed glasses slide down on his nose. As he pushed them back, she thought that, even in his robe and headdress, he resembled a scholar more than a king.

His wife, by contrast, appeared regal and reserved. Leila's cheeks were too broad and her nose too pronounced for Hollywood's standards, but she had the kind of presence that transcended beauty.

In her coolly assessing gaze, Cathy read caution and watchfulness. Although Dar had described Leila as a friend, she did not appear friendly now.

Could she, too, have heard speculation about him? Or perhaps, Cathy chided herself, the woman simply assumed a formal manner while carrying out her official duties.

After the introductions were completed, Faiza whisked the two little girls away to have supper in the playroom. Yasmin didn't object to leaving her mother once it was promised that she could sleep with Mona, and Cathy decided not to argue. She needed to keep her wits about her tonight.

After the children left, the conversation buzzed in Arabic, and she waited for what might happen next. At last, Dar took her aside.

"It seems you and I are expected to dine privately in our bridal chamber," he said. "The emir understands that we have had no chance to celebrate our wedding night."

"Wedding night?" Cathy repeated, trying to absorb what he meant. The two of them were expected to share a bedroom? Without thinking, she blurted, "I hope they don't expect proof of virginity!"

"Yours or mine?" he teased.

She couldn't suppress a chuckle. Her good humor lasted while they took their leave and maneuvered through the palace, until the moment when they were left alone in a sumptuous chamber equipped with the largest bed she had ever seen.

Mary's entire house in Laguna Beach would have fit inside this room, Cathy thought as she surveyed the expanse of carpet, the pale orange walls decorated with molding, the heavy curtains at the window, and above all, the bed.

Because of the scale of the room, she couldn't be sure exactly how large the thing was, but it certainly exceeded a standard king, both in width and length. The canopy drapes had been pulled back to reveal trays of food set on the coverlet.

There were no tables in the room, only a couple of chairs and one velvet-upholstered love seat. "Do you often eat this way?"

Dar brushed a strand of hair from Cathy's temple, his touch light. "It is a wedding custom."

What other wedding customs did he intend to comply

with? she wondered as his caress turned her blood to champagne.

Dar did not appear fazed in the least. Striding over to a chair, he removed his white robe and kaffiyeh and tossed them across the back.

"We had best make a show of doing what is expected," he advised. "If you wish to change clothes, the bathroom is through there."

He indicated a small door tucked between two wooden wardrobes. Hesitantly she opened one of the cabinets and found that her clothes had already been hung inside in the short time since their arrival.

"Does the staff get around on roller skates, or what?" she asked.

A deep laugh stopped Dar in the midst of removing his suit jacket. "They are quick, aren't they?"

Staring at the array of clothes, Cathy decided she didn't feel like putting on a nightgown, especially since she'd spent most of their flight dozing. On the other hand, whoever came to collect their dishes might gossip if she spent her wedding night fully clothed.

Then she realized that the sleep shirt she'd worn on the plane was missing, no doubt taken to be laundered. "I don't have anything to sleep in," she said.

"Check the bathroom." Without a trace of self-consciousness, Dar slipped off his shoes and began unbuttoning the top of his shirt.

What was *he* going to wear? Cathy wondered, her mind flicking over a range of tantalizing possibilities. An open-chested robe...a loincloth...or...

Heat scorched her cheeks. Embarrassed by her flight of fancy, she fled into the bathroom.

It was large and old-fashioned, with orangey tiles and a large claw-footed tub, oddly juxtaposed with a new etched-glass shower stall. From a hook hung the sheerest, laciest, clingiest bit of lingerie she had ever seen, scarlet trimmed in black and suitable, in Cathy's opinion, for a biblical harlot.

Was this someone's idea of what a bride wore on her wedding night? Did those black-draped ladies on the street really toss off their robes behind closed doors to reveal underwear that knocked their husbands' eyes out?

She braced herself against the sink. So many things had happened today that she couldn't think straight, and the dried-out weariness of jet lag had begun sapping her energy.

She was hungry, too. And the only way she could eat was to sit on a King Kong-size bed with Dar.

Hunger won over modesty. Stripping off her thawb, Cathy folded it aside and examined somebody's idea of a nightgown.

Who had chosen it, she wondered? Surely a man wouldn't have been given such a delicate task, so it must have been a woman. Leila, perhaps?

Wriggling it over her head, she pulled the garment into place. It skimmed her waist and hips, and nestled snugly across her bosom, revealing almost all of her legs and more cleavage than Cathy had thought she possessed.

After a moment's hesitation, she decided to wear the earrings and necklace Dar had given her. They made her feel at least partly dressed.

In the full-length mirror, she studied herself. Somehow, during the past twenty-four hours, her eyes had become larger, her figure more alluring and her skin softer. How and when had she changed?

A casual observer might mistake her for a woman in love. A real bride, about to make love to a real bridegroom.

But I'm not. Cathy swallowed the lump in her throat and wondered if she could snatch a jacket out of the wardrobe and throw it on before Dar noticed. She doubted it.

Slowly she opened the bathroom door and wandered out. The carpet felt lush beneath her feet, and for an insane moment she half expected to stumble across a snake charmer playing seductive music.

Dar sat cross-legged on the bed, his white shirt open at the collar with the sleeves rolled up. He had changed into drawstring cotton pants and he, too, was barefoot.

For a moment, he didn't notice her, and she had a chance to drink in the unstudied masculinity of the man she had married. Her gaze trailed from his dark, rumpled hair to the sharp planes of his face, down the contours of his chest and then to the scar on the back of his hand as he straightened a tray that tipped toward him.

There was an air of wildness about her sheikh, a mixture of hardened warrior and fierce lover. He did not belong in a bed alone.

When he caught sight of Cathy, Dar blinked, and she saw his pupils widen. Despite being well schooled in controlling his reactions, he came close to gawking.

"I didn't pick it, you know," she protested as she edged closer. "Can I borrow one of your shirts?"

"I am amazed that you put it on," Dar admitted. "But why spoil the effect by covering it?"

"Who do you suppose chose this thing?" She couldn't bring herself to actually sit on the covers.

"Women in the palace take a great deal of interest in weddings and brides," he said. "It might have been a matter of great discussion."

This was even worse than she'd imagined. "You mean

a whole building full of women are sitting around picturing me in this—this—''

"And picturing me, as well," Dar pointed out. "The
speculation will be endless, but no one will say anything
to you tomorrow."

"No, they'll just stare and make me feel like an idiot."
For some reason, grumbling made Cathy feel more like
herself and, besides, she could smell delicious spices
wafting from the trays. Reluctantly she sat on the bed.
"What if we spill something?"

"Are you going to worry all night?" he teased. "Why
don't you just eat?"

*And pretend the top half of my breasts aren't exposed,
and that I can't feel the way your eyes keep raking over
me?* But Dar had discreetly shifted his attention to his
plate.

"I *am* hungry," she admitted. "And I love Middle
Eastern food." Cathy recognized only a few of the dishes
but was in no mood to quibble.

"Then let me serve you." Smoothly Dar filled a plate
for her. As he handed it over, he reached past her and
tugged on a cord. The bed curtains whispered into place,
enclosing them in a cocoon.

Pulling the covers around her legs, she nibbled at the
food and watched him from the corner of her eye. Dar
ate as if he spent every night in bed with a half-naked
woman, and, with an unexpected rush of jealousy, Cathy
wondered if he did.

It wasn't her place to ask. Besides, although he attracted feminine interest everywhere they went, Dar
didn't seem to respond to it. He was always too occupied,
smoothing the way for her, she thought, and wondered
just how far his feelings extended.

Was she more than a means to an end for him? Marrying her had certainly provided opportunities, even if he claimed not to want them.

"Dar," she said at last, "what about that emir business?"

"Khalid is young and he likes to play the what-if game," her husband replied, his tone so even that he must be restraining a strong response.

Cathy knew she should drop the subject, but she needed to share her concerns. "I think Leila takes the possibility seriously."

He stopped with a piece of pita bread halfway to his mouth. "You do?"

"She didn't seem very friendly," Cathy said. "Not the way you had described her."

"This past week has been hard on everyone. She is merely distracted." Dar ate the bread before adding, "I cannot believe she would credit such gossip."

"You said she's very protective of her husband," Cathy pointed out. "Fasad has been his enemy, and now you're a member of Fasad's family."

"Fasad is also Ezzat's uncle, and until the old emir died, they were on good terms," her husband said. "Still, I am glad for your observations. You are an intelligent woman and you detect points that I miss. I will try to reassure Leila and Ezzat of my loyalty."

Relaxing beneath his approval, Cathy finished her meal and helped clear away the trays, which they left on the love seat. Dar poured cups of strong mint tea from a samovar, and they sat side by side within the curtained bed, drinking it in companionable silence.

When they finished, he collected the empty cups and set them out of sight on the floor. Sleepily Cathy stretched.

As she caught Dar's appreciative gaze, she realized

that the arch of her back emphasized every intimate curve of her breasts and waist. She barely resisted the impulse to snatch the covers around herself like a child.

"You are a beautiful woman." The words, spoken with intensity, caught her off guard. "Not only on the surface, but inside, as well, Cathy. I would like to seduce you."

His directness startled her. More than that, she instinctively imagined the pulse points of his body aligning with hers, and felt a hot rush of desire.

In the smoky depths of Dar's eyes, she saw the battles he had fought and the enemies he had bested. When he claimed her, he would bring to that moment the pure intensity of a man from whom all weakness had been seared away.

He reached to her throat and fingered the pendant that lay there, a symbol of the closeness between them. The back of his hand brushed the swell of her breasts, and Cathy's nipples tightened.

She knew that, if they embraced, she would be able to hold nothing back. If she once began, if she became his lover, it would mean yielding to him in every way.

One thing she had learned from life was where her own weaknesses lay. Even a man as unworthy as her former fiancé had been able to mold her to his uses. How much more would she give herself to Dar?

To consummate this marriage would mean an end to the self-sufficiency for which Cathy had fought so hard. This was not her culture; it was not in her nature to follow a husband meekly, as Hanan did, nor to devote her life to serving his interests, as did Leila.

Dar was not only the most sophisticated man she had ever known, he was also the most deadly. How had she ever imagined, on that long-ago day when they rowed to the kelp forest, that he was safe?

"I can't," she whispered.

Disappointment flashed across his face and then was immediately suppressed. "I understand," he said.

Did he? she wondered. It seemed unlikely either of them could truly understand the other.

Before she could say anything further, or even figure out what she wanted to say, Dar parted the curtains. "You should sleep now."

"What about you?"

"It is my custom, when danger may be near, to sleep in my office, which adjoins Ezzat's," Dar said. "It is next door to his bedroom, and although there are guards posted, my ears may be keener than theirs."

"Or at least more trustworthy," she said.

He smiled. "Exactly. I will wait here a while longer, until the palace is quiet, and then I will go."

"Won't people gossip about your not spending the night with me?"

"We have spent enough time together to soften their doubts. And it is no shame for a man to leave his bride in times of crisis," Dar said.

"Good night, then." Cathy wished she could put her arms around him, but that would be tempting fate. Instead, she burrowed into her pillow and lay gazing at the curtains as they sifted into place behind him, leaving a small gap.

Through it, she watched as Dar sat down and, in a cool circle of lamplight, began reading a sheaf of official-looking papers. Mentally and physically, he might as well have been miles away.

Chapter Twelve

Dar awoke from a sensual dream. He and Cathy had been swimming in tropical waters and were embracing on a sunlit beach. Soft, fragrant air bathed and welcomed them.

There was nothing soft or welcoming about his lumpy cot. Directly overhead, a water stain on the office ceiling was doing a fair imitation of a Rorschach blot. He decided it resembled an imp thumbing its nose at him.

It would be unfair to blame Cathy for her demurral. His desire for her had been selfish. Dar knew he could give her pleasure, but she was not the sort of woman to take such matters lightly.

Nor did he. Dar had never expected to want a woman the way he wanted Cathy. With her perceptiveness and courage, she would make an ideal partner for his life. But she was an American woman and must have a life of her own.

The clock showed he had two hours to prepare for today's meeting with Mojahid. Swiftly Dar rolled out of bed and went to wash up.

He spent the morning consulting with Ezzat, preparing responses to any demand the rebel tribesman might make.

In the end, however, Dar would have to rely upon his own resources in representing the emir.

"You will do well," his cousin said as they walked through the palace. "I rely upon your judgment."

"For that, I am humbly grateful." This day would require all his diplomatic skills, and perhaps his fighting ones as well, although Dar devoutly hoped not.

The fact that the emir could not personally attend the meeting bothered him, even though he knew that security would not permit it even had Mojahid made the request. Still, it seemed to Dar's suspicious mind like the first step in a plan by the rebel leader to squeeze Ezzat from center stage.

Near the entrance, they found Leila helping Cathy adjust her scarf. The emir's wife nodded politely to Dar, but he realized that she was indeed more reserved than usual.

The others of their party assembled quickly: Fasad in his finest robes; Khalid, unsuccessfully trying to hide his joy at being among those chosen to attend; Zahira, with Basilyr fussing over her bejeweled gown, and little Yasmin, wearing a white-embroidered green thawb and clutching one of her new teddy bears.

Dar himself would drive the limousine. Mojahid might suspect anyone else of being an assassin sent to remove him.

As he helped Cathy into the car, Dar noticed how pale she looked. A couple of freckles, scarcely visible at most times, stood out on her cheeks.

"I'm worried about taking Yasmin," she said. "How can we be sure she'll be safe?"

Dar had been mulling the same issue, but now he was able to reassure her. "We received a request from Mojahid half an hour ago, to meet him in front of the Citadel with a reporter and cameraman from an international news service. I believe he wishes to appear as a statesman, not a terrorist.''

She nodded tensely and slid across the seat. Yasmin was already peering out the window, waving to Mona and several other children on the far side of the driveway.

When everyone was seated, Dar put the car into gear and eased out through the palace gate. They had no police escort, since the distance was so short. Besides, the car was heavily armored and equipped with bulletproof glass.

Fasad sat beside him. ''Perhaps we are on the road to peace at last.''

''An uneasy peace,'' Dar observed. ''With a snake among us.''

The older sheikh shrugged. ''There will always be ambitious and greedy men. Better one we know than one we don't suspect.''

Behind them, he heard Basilyr asking his mistress if she were comfortable. Then, with a clink of his bracelets, the young man turned to Cathy. ''You should not worry about this silly rebel person. When we met him a few days ago, he was all smiles and bowing. He would not dare to hurt Zahira.''

''I hope not,'' she said.

''Is it true that we will be on television the whole time?'' asked the Three-Eyed Woman. When Dar confirmed it, she said eagerly, ''Perhaps some producer might see me. I would be perfect for a situation comedy. Or a talk show, do you think?''

''Either one,'' Cathy murmured diplomatically.

As the limousine rolled across the square, Dar saw that the tanks and most of the barricades had been removed. A bomb squad in full protective gear stood ready to move in should the Citadel be relinquished.

Against the far perimeter of the square clustered the world press, lenses at the ready. Dar could only imagine their frustration at not having been the ones chosen to participate.

The military policemen saluted and withdrew a short distance, leaving a clear space. Dar pulled the limousine to its edge and braked.

His throat clenched. It was one thing to go into a dangerous situation as a soldier, another to bring women and a child. If Mojahid even attempted to injure them, Dar would hunt him down and kill him if it took the rest of his life.

But he could not turn back. The destruction of the Citadel would not only raze a large part of the city, it would shatter his nation's heart. The ferocity of the fighting that would ensue could plunge Marakite into barbarism.

Into the clearing moved two men in Western clothing, one carrying a Minicam that bore the initials of a news syndicate. Dar had feared Mojahid might try to disguise two of his own fighters as newsmen, but he recognized one of the men as the reporter they'd seen on the air in Los Olivos.

The Minicam trained on the limousine. Dar paid no attention to it, but he wished Cathy could be spared such exposure. He knew she would not welcome it.

He stepped away from the car and surveyed their surroundings for any sign of unexpected movement. Much as he wanted to assist Cathy, he could serve her best now by staying on the alert.

Fasad emerged from the front passenger seat, while Khalid exited through the rear door and held it for Zahira. Basilyr followed, straightening her robes officiously.

As soon as her feet touched ground, his mistress gave

the camera a smile so big, it revealed two missing teeth in the back of her mouth. "Is my left side better or my right, do you think?" she asked the reporter.

"This is the Three-Eyed Woman," Basilyr added. "Very important psychic."

The reporter shook hands with them and the Al-Haroum men. The camera panned to Cathy and then to Yasmin as they stepped from the car.

The child, her expression solemn, held the teddy bear aloft. "He wants to meet the president's great-grandmother's bear," she announced.

If anyone got their own TV show around here, it would be Yasmin, Dar reflected wryly.

At the sound of a door scraping behind him, he whirled. The front portals of the Citadel were groaning open.

Two unshaven rebels in military fatigues shoved the massive doors wide and anchored them. Neither carried a weapon, as far as he could see. Across the square, he heard the policemen snap to attention, but they kept their guns lowered.

With a casual stride, a stocky figure emerged from within the fortress. In a red-and-white-checked kaffiyeh over coarsely woven white robes, Mojahid formed a picture of civilized benevolence. He had even trimmed his usually scraggly beard.

Keeping his face toward the camera, the rebel leader shook hands first with Fasad, then with Dar, finally with Khalid. He bowed to Zahira and Cathy, then bent and shook hands with Yasmin's teddy bear.

From the cameras across the square came a chorus of clicks and whirrs. The charming image would make front pages worldwide, exactly as Mojahid intended.

So this was to be a public-relations opportunity. Dar relaxed, but only a little.

Mojahid clapped once, and his assistants ran out with folding chairs. These were swiftly arranged in a semicircle, and then the men returned with a large thermos and a dozen small cups.

The participants sat around like guests at a tea party as the scruffy guerrillas served bitter cardamom-flavored green coffee. Dar detected a hint of bewilderment in Cathy's face, but she held herself erect and nodded politely at their host.

Yasmin made a face when she smelled her coffee. At a signal from Mojahid, one of his men replaced the cup with a can of Coke. The little girl pretended to give her bear a drink, and again the cameras clicked.

"It is agreed we will speak in English, for the news media?" said Mojahid. Everyone nodded.

Articulating distinctly, he continued, "I ask only three things. First, the emir's promise than neither my followers nor I will be punished in any way."

"If the Citadel is not damaged, the emir gives his word," Dar said, as he and Ezzat had agreed.

Mojahid smiled. His teeth were so perfect that they must have been capped. "Also, I wish peace negotiations to begin immediately between the emir and the followers of Sheikh Al-Haroum. I wish to be one of those at the table."

For security reasons, all the participants would be expected to stay at the palace. "You could not bring any arms when you are the emir's guest," Dar warned.

The rebel leader bowed his head in acknowledgment. "Naturally not. I will require only two of my men to serve me, and they will not need weapons."

"Then the emir agrees, if this is acceptable to Sheikh Al-Haroum," said Dar.

Fasad's expression was guarded. He had never been comfortable with delicate diplomatic situations, and Dar knew he didn't like having his hand forced.

"I am the leader of the rebellion," the older sheikh reminded everyone. "Of course you and other tribal chiefs are welcome at the table, but you, Mojahid, will have no greater influence on me than anyone else."

It was a ticklish moment. Dar felt rather than heard Cathy take a deep breath.

"A compromise," Mojahid said at last. "You will allow me to consult with your son if I have special concerns, and he can relay them to you privately. In this manner, I will feel assured of having your ear, but there will be no appearance of favoritism."

Khalid blinked in surprise, then waited for his father's response. Dar suspected he was pleased at this chance to play a role in the negotiations, but to the young man's credit, he kept his reaction to himself.

"That would be acceptable," said Fasad.

Dar did not want Mojahid to run the whole show, so he spoke next. "Please state your third request."

"I ask the blessing of the Three-Eyed Woman as we attempt to bring peace to our land." The rebel bowed toward Zahira.

"But of course!" She stood and raised her hands heavenward. In dramatic tones, undercut slightly by the jangle of Basilyr's bracelets as he gestured her to keep her face toward the camera, she began a prayer in Arabic.

When she finished, she grinned broadly. So did Mojahid. He clapped loudly, and Dar heard a great stir behind them.

He leapt to his feet in time to see rebel soldiers swarm

from the Citadel and heap their weapons into a pile. Then Mojahid himself escorted the bomb squad into the fortress to make their inspection.

Two of the rebels brought out an antique-framed oil painting of a little girl in Victorian dress clutching a raggedy stuffed bear. Yasmin skipped forward and held up her own teddy, nose to nose.

The press, although still wary of an explosion, couldn't resist the chance to photograph this appealing scene. Soon others ventured forward to interview Zahira, who repeated her prayer in English.

At last the bomb squad leader emerged with Mojahid and gave an all-clear signal. The reporters and police broke into a cheer, and the square filled with merry chaos.

THE SOUNDS AND IMAGES blurred together in Cathy's mind: news crews racing from spot to spot, policemen and rebels shaking hands and more paintings being carted out and set on display until the square resembled one of Laguna Beach's art fairs.

But the main picture burned into her memory was of Dar, standing apart from the others, his assessing gaze leveled at the beaming Mojahid.

He did not trust the rebel, and neither did she. Not until a peace treaty had been signed and the war was officially over could Ezzat's followers afford to let down their guard.

As soon as they returned to the palace, Dar went to confirm that the other tribal leaders had accepted their invitations to come to Haribat. They must have, because everywhere Cathy looked, servants were carrying clean bedding or rearranging furniture or unloading supplies.

She spent the evening in her sitting room with Yasmin,

eating dinner on a tray and watching a videotape. Dar dropped by but could only stay a few minutes.

The next morning, Hanan and Mona joined them for a game of cards. They had progressed from Old Maid to Go Fish when Dar appeared in the doorway.

His eyes looked darker than usual, and there was a trace of stubble on his jaw. Cathy set down her cards and hurried to him. "Is everything all right?"

"So far, yes," he said. "However, we have just received word from Maha that Sabah went into labor at Los Olivos."

"But she is not due for three weeks!" cried Hanan.

"She was flown to a hospital in Los Angeles, where she has delivered a healthy son," Dar said. "Faiza and Sabah's husband, Muhammed, will go back there this evening."

Hanan's face fell. "Khalid has many pressures, and I cannot leave now. I wish I could see my new nephew."

"Soon enough you will," Dar assured her. "Hanan, may I talk with Cathy alone?"

"Yes, yes, of course." The young woman hurried the two girls off to the palace's playroom which, Cathy had discovered earlier, was a child's paradise of toys, games and indoor climbing equipment.

"What is it?" she asked.

"We made an agreement, and I feel honor-bound by it," Dar said, his eyes hooded. "You came to Haribat to help free the Citadel. Now that is done. If you wish, you and Yasmin may fly back with Faiza and Muhammed."

It took no more than an instant to realize she didn't want to go, and yet, perhaps she should. Yasmin's fourth birthday was only a few weeks off, and Mary had been looking forward to it.

"Actually, I said I would stay until a peace treaty is

signed," she admitted, "but I am kind of in everyone's way."

"Never." The sharpness of her husband's tone made her look directly into his burning gaze. "You are my most trusted observer. You can help me just by keeping your ears open. Just by being here."

"Dar, I don't know what I should do."

His arms closed around her and his dark head came down. Her lips parted instinctively, welcoming him, and then his mouth covered hers and his tongue penetrated, and she felt heat sear through his robes.

Cathy brushed her palm over his rough cheek, and angled herself tighter against him. A ragged groan tore from Dar's throat, and then he lifted his head, breathing heavily. "Please stay."

She nodded. She was afraid to speak. If she did, she might tell him she loved him, and she wasn't ready for that.

"If you wish, I can arrange for you to assist Leila," he said. "Your business experience should be invaluable."

"I'd like to, very much."

He hesitated as if he wished to kiss her again, then drew back. "Come with me."

After navigating a dizzying series of corridors and elevators, they reached an office suite. A guard bowed to Dar and admitted them.

Inside, Leila glanced up from her computer. "Yes?"

"Cathy would like to help," Dar said. "Would this be possible? She has been assistant manager of a hotel, and her skills might be useful."

Cathy felt the other woman's gaze rake over her. She remembered Dar telling her that Leila's father had been the ruler of a neighboring country and had been assassinated. No wonder the woman was cautious.

"Can you use a computer?"

"Yes, of course," Cathy said.

Leila nodded. "Thank you, Dar."

He bowed, cast a grateful look at Cathy and departed. As he went, she realized that by accepting this assignment, she had in a way committed herself to stay in Marakite, at least until the end of the peace negotiations. That suited her just fine.

She sat at the terminal next to Leila's. "What are we doing?"

"I have been monitoring the discussions on the Internet." Leaning over a keyboard with her dark hair escaping its French braid, Leila looked less formidable than usual. "The followers of Mojahid are putting their own spin on things, and we must set matters straight."

"Just tell me what you need."

Before long, Cathy was cybersurfing to a list of web sites, checking for rumors and opinions to which Leila could respond. The two of them fell into an easy rapport, and by the time they broke for lunch, Cathy felt as if she had made a new friend.

"There are few women here with a Western education," Leila confided as they ate pita sandwiches at their desks. "Also who speak good English, which is the primary language on the Internet. I have looked forward to Maha's return, but she is young and lacks your experience."

"What else can I do to help?" Cathy asked.

A smile softened Leila's regal face. "By the time the day is over, you may regret asking."

"I like keeping busy."

And busy they were. Leila oversaw the palace's press

office, Cathy discovered, and also took personal responsibility for ensuring that the peace negotiators were provided with comfortable quarters, faxes, stationery supplies and telephones.

There were meals to arrange, and the thousand other tasks involved in accommodating guests. Cathy was thankful that her hotel experience enabled her to make some useful suggestions.

In the middle of the afternoon, she went to check on Yasmin, but even though Faiza had departed, the little girl was having a ball. She had discovered some second and third cousins, and a toy store's worth of dolls and tricycles and talking storybooks and computer games.

"I will watch over her," Hanan promised. "You are doing important work."

Cathy thanked her and headed back to the office. On the way, she took several wrong turns, and each time had to ask a servant to direct her back on course.

The third time she got lost, she found herself on the floor where guests' quarters had been arranged. With a sigh, Cathy went in search of a servant.

She paused in a nook to examine a colorful mosaic of birds. A plaque in Arabic, English and French indicated that it had been removed from an archaeological dig and brought here for safekeeping.

This design was more than two thousand years old. Awed, Cathy ran her finger over the shiny stones and wondered who had created this in ancient times and what his life had been like.

The sound of masculine voices down the hall startled her. Some men had just emerged from one of the rooms. To her dismay, she realized they might not be expecting a woman to wander on to this floor, so she ducked deeper into the nook.

But not before she sneaked a peek at the men. There were two of them: Mojahid, wearing what she considered his crocodile smile, and Khalid.

Mojahid was doing most of the talking. His voice had a hypnotic quality, soothing and flattering, Cathy guessed, and wished that she understood Arabic. Even so, it was obvious he wanted to curry favor with Sheikh Al-Haroum's son.

She remembered what Maha had said at their first luncheon in Los Olivos, that Khalid was on the bottom of the pecking order. The younger son had always walked in the shadow of his dead brother. Would he seize the chance now to become important in the rebel leader's camp?

The men exchanged farewells, a door closed and she heard footsteps heading in her direction. It would be impossible to hide, so Cathy pretended to be absorbed in the mosaic.

The footsteps halted abruptly. "What are you doing here?" demanded Khalid.

"I'm lost." She gave him an apologetic smile. "I was trying to get back to Leila's office from the playroom."

"I will escort you. This is not a proper place for women." It was impossible to read his expression.

He walked her to the elevator and they descended in silence. Cathy would have to report to Dar what she had seen, and she had no doubt that Khalid knew it.

FOR THE NEXT THREE DAYS, Dar deliberately avoided being alone with Cathy. Every time she came near, he found himself so distracted, he had to struggle to return his attention to the peace process.

Nevertheless, the information she provided was valuable, and worrisome. Although Khalid sat quietly beside his father at the negotiating table, it was apparent that, offstage, he was forming a friendship with the cagey Mojahid.

Still basking in his role as liberator, the tribal leader held daily press conferences and made a point of circulating among the other sheikhs, flattering and joking with them. In negotiations, he repeatedly brought up minor points and pontificated on them at length.

Dar believed the man was intentionally delaying a settlement while he sought a way to turn the talks to his own advantage, but Fasad disagreed. Mojahid, he said, was merely a peacock who enjoyed strutting in public for as long as possible.

On the second day, when discussions appeared deadlocked, Ezzat proposed that Marakite establish a full parliamentary democracy. It quickly became evident that the participants did not want to relinquish their personal power, but at least the proposal broke the logjam and brought forth a flurry of new suggestions.

Democracy would have to wait until the country's population became better educated and its infrastructure modernized, Dar reflected. It pleased him to know that Leila and Ezzat had long ago drawn up plans to work toward those goals, and that these would be implemented as soon as the civil war ended.

On the third day, matters took a turn for the better. A preliminary draft agreement was drawn up and the meeting adjourned early so the tribal leaders could fax their supporters for comment.

Mojahid appeared satisfied with a provision naming Fasad as prime minister to the emir and providing him with an advisory council of five tribal leaders, whose positions would rotate every four years. Mojahid would serve on the first council.

That meant the palace would be stuck with him for quite a while. Still, once the war was over, the man would have little chance of restarting it.

It was time, Dar thought, for him to visit his bride. With peace soon to be upon them, she would have every right to insist on leaving. He only hoped he could persuade her otherwise.

Chapter Thirteen

"I've never seen this part of the palace before," Cathy said.

Dar had claimed her from Leila's office and swept her away to a steamy glass-roofed courtyard filled with orange and lemon trees, orchids and ferns. Brightly hued birds flashed from branch to branch, and the sultry natural scents made her wonder if the Garden of Eden might not have been very much like this.

And, possibly, located not too far away, she realized. It was hard to believe that she had come to feel so much at home in a land where people had lived since the days of Adam and Eve.

She wished she felt more like Eve now, as she strolled arm in arm with Dar. He was freshly shaved, and had changed into a snowy robe and headdress before calling on her. By comparison, Cathy felt a bit wilted in her thawb, which she'd been wearing all day.

"I wish I could jump into that." She indicated a meandering pool at the foot of a waterfall.

"This place is a bit too public for swimming," observed her husband, "but the palace has a private spa. If it is free, would you like to use it?"

"With you?" she blurted.

One eyebrow lifted. "Or alone, if you prefer."

She felt crimson steal across her cheeks. "I—don't mind if we both take a dip."

"Neither do I." Although his tone was light, she caught a glimmer of invitation in Dar's eyes.

The prospect tantalized her. In the eyes of the world, they were married. They could very properly do whatever they liked, and it was obvious their thoughts ran in the same direction.

But what would happen afterward? Cathy wondered. She loved being here, but America was her home, not Marakite. The ways of this land were still largely alien to her.

Most importantly, the deepest expectations and attitudes of her husband might be very different from the way they appeared during courtship. Dar would never deliberately deceive her, but he might take it for granted that a wife would defer to him in ways that Cathy found unacceptable.

"I couldn't..." She let the sentence trail off.

A muscle jumped in his cheek and he averted his face, but a moment later he turned back toward her. In that short time, he had mastered his disappointment.

"Then let me introduce you to an ancient custom of my tribe," he said. "When a woman has given him good counsel and assistance, the sheikh himself plies her with delicacies and waits upon her."

"In the bath?" she asked.

"Of course."

"You're making this up."

"Well, actually, I am," he admitted.

Laughter bubbled from her throat. "Really? You made the whole thing up?"

"Come and let me show you the spa." Mischief animated his face. "It is not far."

For days, Cathy had felt Dar's smoky nearness and ached for him. Soon it would be time for her to leave this country and this man. She wanted him to herself, just once more.

They didn't have to actually do anything. It would be enough to spend time together, truly alone, as they had been during their boat ride at the island.

Without giving herself time for further doubts, Cathy said, "Ready when you are."

Taking her hand, Dar pulled her through the garden. They pattered down a tiled hallway and through a gateway into a smaller version of paradise. As he locked the door behind them, Cathy surveyed the spa with wonder.

It comprised a series of curving rooms, the walls painted with vistas of a great garden and, far off, a mystical palace. Near the entrance, heated water emerged from a pipe and tumbled down a series of small rocky falls, then formed a burbling stream that meandered through the rooms.

Ferns, wild grasses and flowers overhung the banks, while natural illumination floated from a skylight. Steam brought her the scent of roses.

"All this, and it's private?" Cathy asked.

Dar pulled off his headdress and ruffled his hand through his dark hair. "Completely private," he said. "It is the custom of my people for the lady to bathe without clothing, but if you prefer, you can find something appropriate through there." He indicated a small door.

"I like your people's traditions, even if you are making them up," she admitted. "But I think I'll err on the side of caution."

"As you wish." He bowed, but not before she saw his jaunty grin.

The man was impossible, Cathy told herself as she slipped into the dressing room. Impossible and adorable and, if she weren't careful to guard her heart, irresistible.

They were not going to make love, she told herself sternly as she examined a rack of swimsuits. They were just going to have fun.

The suits looked new. They also appeared to have been selected by the same rascal who had chosen that seductive piece of lingerie for her wedding night. She could almost have suspected the outrageous Basilyr, but she doubted he had that much influence.

There were eensy weensy bikinis, and high-cut racy maillots with low cleavage. Flipping through them, Cathy finally discovered a modest design with a high neck and jungle-printed blouse-style bodice. She was even more relieved when it fit.

Snatching a towel from a rack, she ventured out. Jets had been activated, filling the room with a low rumble as the water boiled and swirled.

At first she couldn't spot Dar, and then she saw him lazing in a small bay edged by lilies. His upper arms rested on a ledge and his body was extended, floating.

In the roiling water, she couldn't tell at first whether he was wearing anything, but then she spotted a wisp of dark fabric across his hips. Cathy felt a tinge of relief, which vanished as she realized that Dar had caught her staring at the most intimate part of his body.

She forced herself to march toward him as if nothing had happened. When she came close, he said, "Don't worry, that's another one of my people's customs. The lady is allowed to ogle the sheikh."

"The lady just wanted to know if the sheikh was

dressed,'' she said tartly, depositing the towel on soft grass near the lilies.

"I see you have made a conservative selection." He eyed her swimsuit. "Come and let me introduce you to the Sultan's Surprise."

"The Sultan's Surprise?" She wasn't sure she was ready for this, but that hot water looked fabulous. Cathy stopped fighting the inevitable and slid into the pool. "Oh, that's wonderful."

Dar guided her to a low shelf. "Sit here and let me massage you."

"Absolutely." She positioned herself sideways, with her back to him.

He lifted the hair away from her neck and, before Cathy realized what he intended, brushed a kiss across her nape. Electricity tingled through every pore and follicle of her skin.

"Stop that!" she said.

"You cannot blame a fellow for trying," he murmured, and began pressing the sore points between her shoulder blades. Slowly Cathy let herself sink back until she rested against Dar's chest.

That was when she discovered what he'd meant by the Sultan's Surprise. In the water, her once-modest swimsuit had become transparent.

"Oh, my...!" She tried to stand up, slipped and landed in Dar's lap.

"Hey, do not worry about it. We are alone," he teased.

"Dar, this isn't what I intended." She swiveled toward him to protest, and then forgot what she'd meant to say.

Her hands had come up against his bare chest. Through the sculpted muscles, she could feel his heart pounding.

"Do not forget, a sheikh must serve his lady well,"

Dar said softly. "It is my task to bring you endless delight."

The low hum of the jets surrounded them. In this fragrant inlet, Cathy felt sheltered and, suddenly, not at all self-conscious about her round breasts and curving waistline visible through the suit.

Dar's hands probed her shoulders and back. When he eased down her straps, she made no objection. It was as if she were waiting breathlessly to see what he would do next.

His dark head bent as he bared one breast, then the other. His tongue traced the valley between them, then touched each nipple lightly. Scarlet flames shot into her core.

Cathy cradled his head between her hands, relishing the silky feel of his hair as his tongue made lazy circles around her breasts. This was a man who since adolescence had honed himself to conquest. Now, she thought as she sank helplessly into a sea of hot longing, he was going to master her.

And, judging by the rasp of his breathing, he was about to be conquered, as well.

She helped him pull off the rest of her suit. Before she realized it, he, too, had slipped free of his trunks, and their bare skin brushed at shifting points, tantalizing her almost past endurance.

They half floated as they embraced. Perfume wafted from trailing flowers, and she thought perhaps they really had found the Garden of Eden.

Dar's gaze slanted along her golden skin. A smile touched his lips as his finger traced the tan lines left by the California sun. "You have several different swimsuits. The shadings overlap."

"I'm surprised you notice," she said.

"I want to know all the little things about you," Dar told her gravely. "What you dream about. What songs you sing when you are alone. How you taste from this angle." His mouth grazed hers. "And this." He tilted his head and kissed her again. "Your nipples are as tight as flower buds about to burst, yet you hold yourself away from me."

Cathy hadn't been aware of it, but she was keeping several inches of water between her hips and his. "I don't want to tempt fate."

"You may not be tempting fate," said Dar, "but you are certainly tempting me."

Why was she resisting? Cathy wondered. She wanted to touch this man all over and hold him inside her. If she didn't, she would ache for him the rest of her life.

Without further thought, she reached to his knee and let her fingers trace the length of his leg, all the way up to the thigh and then inward. From Dar's mouth came a gasp of unbelievable pleasure.

For this brief moment, she had tamed him. He was hers. The realization filled Cathy with a shimmering glow.

She let the water carry her atop him, and their mouths met. But Dar was not conquered, only yielding, and now the wildness came alive again. With a swift hard movement, he caught her waist and buried himself inside her.

Joy burned through her, so intense, it wiped out past and future. There was only this moment, keen as a knife edge and splendid as fireworks. Nothing existed except Dar and his magic.

The water rolled them gently, teasing them apart. When Dar withdrew, he left a dark void, but a moment later he filled it again with his fire.

Cathy ran her hands along his shoulders and down his

back. He was almost too perfect to be anything but a figure from the *Arabian Nights*, yet there was nothing imaginary about the way he was propelling himself into her.

At last Cathy's back met the rim of the pool, and she was able to return thrust for thrust. With a hoarse cry, Dar drove into her with all his strength.

She felt his body vibrate as he lost control, and then she, too, was swept into a maelstrom of sensations. Clinging together, sobbing and laughing, they spiraled upward in a great burst of steam and brilliance until Cathy thought they must be fused forever.

Gradually she drifted back to awareness. She and Dar had come to rest among the languid fronds of a fern that reminded her, for a heart-twisting moment, of the kelp forest where they had first kissed.

She had made love with him, and it had surpassed even her dreams. Cathy couldn't think beyond that.

DAR TRIED TO GAUGE Cathy's reaction as, toweled off and dressed, they walked to her bedroom. She wore a dreamy look that he hoped meant she might choose to stay with him.

He knew better than to pursue the matter now. To press her for a commitment might break the delicate bond they had woven, before it had a chance to grow to full strength.

Her blue eyes took on a deeper hue, and the line of her cheek was softer. Dar wondered if he, too, had undergone a visible transformation. He certainly had changed inside.

When they made love, all his experience and skill had meant nothing. This once, he had been stripped to his male essence, unable to hold anything back. He had given Cathy not only his body, but his heart.

At her bedroom, they found a note from Hanan. She had taken the children pony riding at the palace stables. Afterward, she would bathe and feed them, and then Yasmin and Mona planned to have a slumber party.

"My daughter seems so happy here," Cathy said as she folded away the note.

"Not only Yasmin, I hope."

When her face tilted up to his, her eyes were shining. "Not only Yasmin."

Via intercom, Dar asked the kitchen staff to bring their dinner on a tray, and, as they had that first night, they ate on the bed. This time, there was less tension between them, but still a hint of wariness.

He knew he must win Cathy's trust as a leader wins that of his tribe. First, bravery and boldness set the tone, but afterward must come diplomacy and a meshing of patterns and purposes. It would take more than one night, or one week or one month, to accomplish.

Reluctantly his thoughts returned to duty. With so many strangers in the palace, he had redoubled his attentiveness to Ezzat's safety. At bedtime, Dar now moved his cot from his own office into his cousin's, in front of the connecting door to the emir's bedroom suite.

There was no electronic alarm system, although, during the early days of the civil war, Leila had tried installing one. Several nights later, Ezzat had awakened early and wandered into his office.

This set off the alarm and provoked a confrontation with a sentry that nearly resulted in the emir's being shot. The alarm had been removed.

Now guards of proven loyalty patrolled the corridors. There were also solid locks on the hallway doors that led into the office and into the bedroom suite. But Dar felt better when he slept at his post.

After dinner, he intended to head there. But first he listened to Cathy outlining Leila's plans for the economic rejuvenation of Marakite. He was not sure which intrigued him more—the detailed information or her enthusiasm in describing it.

Then they made love again, slowly and tenderly. Afterward, Dar lingered in Cathy's arms, basking in a deep sense of contentment.

He awoke to utter blackness. For a stunned moment, he could not imagine that he had actually fallen asleep. Then, with a deep sense of misgiving, he hurried to dress, trying not to stumble in the dark and awaken Cathy.

By his illuminated watch, it was past two o'clock. In a few hours, if all went well, the peace treaty would be signed. If Mojahid were to attack, he could not afford to wait.

Dar should never have spent the evening with Cathy, he told himself as he slipped from the room. It was an uncharacteristic lapse, and at the worst possible time.

The corridor was equipped with safety lights, and he made his way without trouble to the elevator. He neither heard nor saw anything amiss, but then, why should there be, on this floor?

One level higher, he emerged to a silence broken only by the low hum of the dim lights. Dar tried to listen above the rushing of his blood, but he heard nothing.

He paced toward the emir's quarters, fingering the key that lay in his inner pocket. At any moment, he expected to encounter one of the guards.

Even though he would be recognized, he would require the password, which Leila changed daily. Tonight it was the hard-to-pronounce name "Appomattox," in honor of the site where the American Civil War had officially ended.

The American president during that war had been assassinated. Dar did not intend for Ezzat to meet the same fate as Abraham Lincoln.

He rounded a corner and came within sight of the office. Where were the guards? Could they both have gone around the next corner, where the door to the bedroom suite lay, or had something happened to them?

Dar pressed a button on the wall intercom, which connected with the guards' headquarters downstairs. There was no buzz, not even a click. Either it was out of order, which was not unusual given the palace's haphazard wiring system, or it had been disconnected.

Standing to one side, as he had learned in his security training, Dar tested the office doorknob. It opened smoothly.

The hairs on his neck stood on end. Something was desperately wrong. The door should not be unlocked. Was he already too late to save Ezzat?

Then he heard a faint sound from within. He identified it as the rustle of a breath against loose papers. Someone was hiding behind the emir's desk, someone not accustomed to the telltale rattle of paperwork.

Mojahid's men had not been allowed to bring guns to the palace. It was possible they had smuggled some in, but unlikely that they would have taken the risk of detection. Dar suspected his opponent was armed only with a knife.

Still, a knife could kill, easily and quickly. Also silently. Had Dar slept in his usual place tonight, he might have been murdered in his sleep, without a sound.

He tried to picture the scene inside the office. The intruder must have hidden when he heard the knob turn.

He would be watching around the edge of the desk, his knife ready.

Kicking the door open, Dar raced across the room and dove beneath the desk, through the kneehole. He came up behind a squatting man, who tried to whirl. Before the assassin could get his knife into position, Dar leapt against him, caught the man's neck and twisted.

There was a painful crack. The intruder shuddered, made a dry rasping moan and crumpled. Listening carefully, Dar heard faint breathing, but he knew he had disabled the man.

After a moment's search around the floor, he found the dropped weapon—a long, curving dagger. He took it with him.

Although the bedroom suite's thick walls blocked any noise, he assumed Mojahid and his remaining accomplice must be on the other side, stalking the emir and Leila. There was no time to waste.

The inner door was locked. Cursing the delay, Dar pulled out his key. Although he had prepared all his life for such a moment, it took far too long for his slippery hands to get the lock undone.

He leapt inside, hit the floor and rolled, trying to ignore a flash of pain as he collided with a chair leg. When there was no answering movement, Dar realized the sitting room must be empty.

But he could hear noises from within the bedchamber: harsh panting and shallow gasps. By now, whoever was inside must have heard him crash into the chair. If there were two assailants, one would be heading this way.

Keeping low, Dar zigzagged across the sitting room. The inner door stood ajar, and he kicked it wide, then rolled across the threshold at an angle.

"Help!" It was Leila's voice. "Oh, please, who is there?"

"Dar," he called, coming to his feet with the knife raised. He blinked, hard, in the almost blinding light of a bedside lamp.

"It is about time!" Thank heaven, it was Ezzat's voice, trembling but resolute.

Against the edge of the bed, Dar saw the emir struggling with a larger assailant. A curved knife wavered perilously close to Ezzat's throat as the smaller man fought to hold it off.

The pair shifted, and Dar saw Mojahid's face revealed in the lamplight, his mouth twisted into a snarl. Leila circled, trying to beat the attacker with the butt of a gun, but her blows fell uselessly on his shoulders.

"Put that down!" At the angle she was holding it, if the gun discharged, it would hit her and not Mojahid.

"It's jammed!" Leila said. "It just clicks."

It probably wasn't jammed, Dar realized. It would be typical of Ezzat to have unloaded the weapon when he discovered that Leila had it. The emir believed guns were too treacherous to keep in a bedroom.

Dar's heart twisted with love for his peaceable cousin. With a roar, he lunged across the room and smashed against the rebel leader, freeing Ezzat and sending himself and Mojahid staggering into the wall.

Dar righted himself almost instantly, but so did his foe. They squared off, knives ready, both angling for any hint of an opening.

In the assassin's eyes, he saw only feral cunning. It was like staring into the soul of a demon.

The rebel slashed so hard and suddenly that Dar barely leapt back in time. A gash in his robe showed how close he had come to death.

Mojahid took advantage of his opponent's momentary awkwardness to attack again. But Dar had not really been off balance.

Honed by years of martial arts training, he rocked back on one foot and lashed out with the other. Mojahid didn't see the blow coming until it landed on his most vulnerable point, the impact intensified by his own onrush.

The man screamed and staggered, clutching his injured parts. Unwilling to stab a defenseless opponent, Dar flipped his knife to his left hand and chopped downward with his right onto the rebel leader's neck. Mojahid collapsed with a thud.

Leila would have flown at him, but Ezzat held her back. "He could still be dangerous."

Dar prodded the terrorist with his foot, but there was no response. Then he saw a trickle of blood on Mojahid's forehead and realized he must have struck the metal bed frame as he fell.

Dar scooped up the man's knife and handed it to his cousin. "He is unconscious but you should tie him with the bedsheets. The intercom has been cut. I will go down and alert the guards myself."

"We must find out what else is happening," Leila said. "Where are his two men?"

"I left one in the office. You should tie him, as well." Dar worked to bring his breathing under control. "But the other could be anywhere."

No, not anywhere, he realized. Mojahid would also have wanted to eliminate the other key man who stood between him and power, a man whom he had learned he could not manipulate.

Dar's gaze met Ezzat's. "Fasad," they both said at once.

"Lock the doors until I return or you hear from the

captain of the guards.'' The head of security was almost as dedicated to the emir as was Dar himself. ''And Ezzat, put the bullets back in the gun, will you?''

''Oh! Yes, they are in the headboard,'' said the emir.

''They're what?'' Leila squawked.

Dar raced out. Although Ezzat was safe, if Fasad died, the peace negotiations would die with him.

Chapter Fourteen

A pounding on the door woke Cathy. Sleepily she reached for Dar, but the hollow where he had lain felt cool.

The pounding came again, and this time wakefulness rushed in. Someone sounded desperate to enter. Had something happened to Yasmin?

Cathy hurried out of bed, grateful that she had put on a nightgown. She had been concerned about servants, though, not midnight intruders.

As she strode toward the door, it began to swing open. Her heart clenched and she took a step backward.

"Cathy?" Hanan peered around the door, her eyes wide in the dim light. Quickly she shepherded the two little girls into the room and closed the door, then fumbled until she got it bolted.

"What's going on?" Cathy bent to take her shivering daughter into her arms. Yasmin clutched her favorite doll, her little body stiff with anxiety. "Let's get everybody into bed to warm up."

Hanan, she saw, was wearing her bathrobe. What could have motivated her to go running around the palace in such a state?

But the young Al-Haroum woman had more important

things on her mind than modesty. "Turn on the lamp. I think Mona is hurt."

Cathy flipped it on. As soon as her eyes adjusted, she examined the smaller child.

A purplish bruise was forming on the girl's cheek. Anxiously Cathy peered into Mona's eyes, looking for signs of concussion, but it was hard to tell. "Do you feel dizzy? Does your stomach hurt?"

"Just my face," squeaked Mona.

There wasn't much that could be done for a bruise, but Cathy knew children felt better when they were fussed over. "You stay with her, Hanan. I'll be right back."

In the bathroom, she found first-aid supplies and hurried back to apply a topical antibiotic and a large Band-Aid. "What happened?"

Hanan's breathing eased as they huddled together under the covers. "Khalid awoke and said he heard a noise. He told me to stay there while he went out, but I had to check on the children."

"I was asleep," Yasmin mumbled.

"Yes, but Mona was gone." The terror of that moment echoed in Hanan's voice. "Then I heard men shouting in the hall."

So Mona's injury wasn't merely the result of a childish accident. With a sense of shock, Cathy realized how complacent she had been.

The progress toward a peace treaty might have triggered Mojahid, or perhaps someone else, to take action. Were they in grave danger? How could she have put Yasmin in such a situation?

And Dar—where had he gone? Was he injured at this very moment? Dread twisted through her. She needed to know that he was safe.

Hanan's account provided a welcome distraction. "I

realized Mona must have gone to her grandmother's bedroom. She forgot Faiza is at Los Olivos with Sabah."

"I just went down the hall," Mona whispered.

"I found her lying on the floor. She said some man pushed her into the wall." Hanan clutched her daughter. "What kind of monster would hurt a little girl just because she got in his way?"

"You said you heard men shouting," Cathy prompted.

"I think they were fighting. In Fasad's room." Hanan's tone became shrill as she relived the scene. "I do not know what has happened to Khalid."

"Is there someone we can call? Perhaps Leila?" Cathy said.

"We can try." Hanan grew calmer at the prospect. "She always knows what to do."

There was an intercom set into the wall. Cathy pulled a list of codes from the bedside table and punched in the one for the emir's bedroom before she realized that it might be presumptuous of her.

But it didn't matter, because there was no buzz at the other end. Cathy tried another number, and that didn't work, either. "The whole system must be down."

There was no mistaking the panic in Hanan's eyes. "Mojahid has taken control of the palace!"

"Or he just knew which wires to cut." Cathy refused to dwell on which might have occurred. The children were frightened enough.

"Maybe it's a blackout," said Yasmin.

"But the lamp works," Hanan pointed out.

"Let's hope the TV does, too." There was one positioned in the corner where it could be viewed from the bed. Fetching a remote control from the table, Cathy switched it on.

The news channels had no information about Marakite,

beyond rumors that a peace treaty might be near. Finally she clicked to a telecast of "Sesame Street" in Hebrew.

None of them understood the words, but the children found it amusing, and even Hanan relaxed as they watched.

Cathy hugged her knees and pretended to be absorbed. It was all she could do, for the moment.

THE DOOR to Fasad's sitting room stood open. Inside, Dar glimpsed overturned furniture and a spatter of blood on the carpet.

Cautiously he edged into the sitting room. A moment later, the inner door opened and Khalid stumbled out, his nightshirt splotched with red. A gash across one cheek oozed blood, and he wore a stunned expression.

Was it possible that he had been part of the plot? Dar wondered. With Ezzat, Fasad and Dar himself gone, Khalid would have been the most likely choice to become emir.

The young man's next words dispelled his suspicions. "My father is hurt and one of Mojahid's scum is dead," he said. "I tried to call the guards but the intercom does not work." He staggered forward.

"Sit down," Dar ordered. "Ezzat is all right. Mojahid has failed."

"Praise God," said Khalid. "My father was able to hold the man off until I arrived. I heard his shouts from my own bedroom. Luck was with us."

"Luck and courage," Dar said. "I am glad you got here in time, my friend." But the look Khalid gave him was full of anguish, as much as relief.

Until now, the young man had been filled with swagger as he strove to establish his place in the world. Tonight, Dar suspected, Khalid had found the glory he craved. But killing, even in defense of a just cause, left a scar deep within.

After making sure that the Al-Haroums were in no immediate danger from their wounds, Dar went to fetch a doctor. In the corridor, he encountered the captain of the guards.

"We discovered the intercom had been cut," the man said. "Three of my men were found drugged. Something had been put in the coffee. Everyone else has been sent to their emergency stations."

"The emir is well. Sheikh Al-Haroum and his son have been injured," Dar said. "Mojahid and one of his men are captured, and the other is dead. Were there any other signs of attack?"

"Not as far as I know, but my men are on patrol now," said the captain. "You have done good work tonight, Sheikh Bahram."

"Khalid also," Dar said. "He saved his father's life."

So the fighting appeared to be over, he thought with satisfaction. Mojahid had been foolish enough to believe he could overthrow the emir with just two accomplices.

Perhaps the plot had not been so far-fetched, after all. Had Dar not appeared unexpectedly from Cathy's room, and had Khalid not awakened in time, it might have worked.

At the thought of Cathy, Dar felt an urge to go and reassure her, but he could not leave until he made sure the Al-Haroums received proper medical treatment. "Would you have your men check on my wife and my daughter?"

"Of course!" The captain signaled to a pair of guards following on his heels. "Also, we will wake the doctor."

"I shall stay with the Al-Haroums until he arrives." During his days as a tribal leader, Dar had learned how to stem bleeding and prevent shock, if that should become necessary.

Besides, Fasad and Khalid were not only his relatives, they were also the emir's distinguished guests. Dar's diplomatic duties required him to do everything possible to ensure their well-being.

He would then need to inform each of the other peace delegates personally about tonight's events. And after that, he would have to confer with Ezzat and Leila about issuing a news release. It was going to be a long night.

Even though the guards would make sure that Cathy was well, Dar ached to hold her. But it might be some time before he could stop in to see her.

Already once tonight he had let his feelings for her interfere with his duty. He must not indulge himself that way again.

AFTER THE CHILDREN fell asleep, Cathy turned off the TV. Hanan cradled Mona, her own eyes drifting shut.

Cathy remained wide-awake. A short time earlier, a guard had come to inform them that an attempted coup had been suppressed and everyone was safe. She supposed that ought to reassure her.

But it didn't. She felt helpless and isolated, in a strange land in the midst of terrifying events.

The silence and her own restlessness forced Cathy's thoughts back over the past two weeks. From the moment Dar first appeared at the Sand and Stars, her life had been turned upside down.

She'd been riding a roller coaster, but now she'd come to a screeching halt, stuck on top of the steepest curve, afraid of what lay ahead.

"Cathy?" Hanan stirred sleepily. "Are you worried?"

"Of course," she said. "And I hate not being able to do anything. I feel so useless."

"I, too, fear for my husband. But it is a wife's place to wait, and to have faith." The other woman sighed.

"Has this happened before?" Cathy asked.

Hanan shifted her daughter gently aside and sat up. "Not like this, exactly, but sometimes Khalid must be gone for days. He and Fasad have to meet with their followers, sometimes with people who frighten me."

"And you never know if they will come back alive?"

"Never." The younger woman shuddered. "Even friends can be treacherous. Leila's father was killed by his most trusted general."

That didn't make Cathy feel any better, but she could see that this discussion was upsetting Hanan. "You should rest. I'm sure the guard was telling the truth and it's all over."

"You are so strong. I wish I could be like you."

"In some ways, I wish I could be like *you*," Cathy admitted. "You seem to accept this way of life, and I don't know if I ever can."

"It is hardly a way of life," murmured the other woman. "It is a way of death. But as you say, perhaps that has ended now. If so, we will have much to be grateful for."

"Indeed we will." But Cathy didn't feel grateful.

She kept picturing Dar as he'd made love to her earlier that evening, his eyes shining with tenderness, his body suffused with desire.

She loved him. How could she live the rest of her life fearing for his safety?

Cathy was not a Marakite woman but an American, accustomed to a sense of security. She could not go through life waiting for her man in darkened rooms with other frightened women and children.

If only Dar would come and talk to her! She knew he must be busy, but surely he could spare a few minutes. Was she of so little importance?

This situation was, in a way, what she had feared as much as physical danger. In a crisis, Dar was reverting to ways that were alien to her, relegating his wife and daughter to secondary importance.

Now, when they needed him most, they were the farthest thing from his thoughts.

Her chest tight with unshed tears, Cathy lay stiffly in bed, wishing that Dar would come. But he did not.

THE PEACE TREATY to end the civil war of Marakite was signed at noon the next day, at a table set up in the central square of Haribat.

The world press crowded around as the emir and the bandaged Sheikh Al-Haroum inked their signatures with a plumed pen, and a series of tribal leaders followed suit. Dar and Khalid came last, out of deference to their elders, but they were the heroes of the moment.

Already, poets sang their praises. Their images were flashed on worldwide television as the men who had saved their country.

Dar felt not like a victor but like a fool. Inside the palace, his wife was packing to go home.

Even after Leila informed him of Cathy's intent, he had been too busy with the final treaty preparations to go to her. And now he was so exhausted, he wasn't sure he could persuade her even to speak to him, let alone to stay.

The great diplomat of Marakite felt heavy of brain and thick of tongue. And very, very sore of heart.

He glanced at Khalid, standing straight and proud beside him. There, at least, Dar could take some satisfaction.

In one night, the young man had been tempered, like steel in a flame. He had outgrown his impetuosity and arrogance, had deepened in understanding and in humility. As time went on, he would contribute greatly to his country.

At the table, Ezzat and Fasad ceased posing for pictures and turned to shake hands with their followers. The formality of the press conference dissolved, with tribal leaders exchanging high fives and reporters vying for interviews.

Dar tried to slip away, but men kept pounding him on the back. Then the emir approached.

"So," said Ezzat, "Leila tells me you could not find a moment to see your wife last night, and she wishes to return to America. I fear this is my fault."

Dar shook his head. "Not yours, but mine. I wished to be assured of her safety, but I did not realize how concerned she would be for mine."

"Women are strange." The emir sighed. "She loves you so much that she must leave you. Who can understand them?"

"It is more than that." But Dar could not explain, even to Ezzat, what it was that had occupied so much of his time between the end of the revolt and the hastily called final peace negotiations, which had begun at 6:00 a.m.

He glanced at Khalid, and then away. A man of honor would not break a promise, not even to save his marriage.

At last Ezzat turned to address a reporter, and for one millisecond no one was paying attention to Dar. Before that could change, he spun and made his way through the crowd of peace celebrants, toward the palace.

THE SERVANTS were cheering in the corridors, and several stopped Cathy on her way to the elevator to thank her for having helped make the prophecy come true. She wished she could share their joy in full measure, but all she managed were shaky smiles.

Once she'd realized that she wanted to go home, she hadn't been able to contain her edginess. With Leila's reluctant help, Cathy had made reservations on a commercial flight that afternoon, and seen to her own packing.

It was best to depart while the peace treaty preoccupied everyone, she told herself. That should reduce the amount of gossip and spare Dar's feelings, at least somewhat.

The thought of him stabbed through her. She doubted she would ever again meet a man like her sheikh, as strong and romantic and fierce and kind. But she could not be the woman he needed to share his life.

The sooner she got Yasmin settled in the little house in Laguna and returned to her routine at the hotel, the faster these past weeks would fade into memory, like a childhood fairy tale, Cathy reflected. Of course the Al-Haroums would still wish to visit with Yasmin, but those arrangements could be made later.

And, after all, Dar had long ago agreed to a divorce. With the Citadel free and the war at an end, their original deal had been consummated.

So, as it turned out, had their marriage. Tears stung Cathy's eyes as she took the elevator to the playroom's floor.

She didn't regret one moment of the previous evening. Maybe it had simply been too perfect to last.

She strode through the corridors without taking even one wrong turn. How ironic, that she was leaving the palace just as she began to know her way around. She would miss this place, especially its sense of community.

But she missed her mother, too. And the soothing rush of the ocean, and the freedom to jump in a car and go...well, just go anywhere.

Outside the playroom, she hesitated. Yasmin still didn't know they were returning home.

Slowly Cathy opened the door. The playroom was very large, with enough space to ride tricycles in the center, although no one was doing so at the moment.

Across the right side spread a mock tree house, rope ladders, bridges and tunnels. The left side of the room housed a kingdom for teddy bears and dolls, complete with a miniature castle.

Overhead, an electric train whistled its way along a looping track. The rear wall supported cubbyholes filled with blocks and clay and books.

The place stood empty except for a young mother and a toddler playing with blocks. The woman was a cousin of Leila's, Cathy recalled. But where were Yasmin, Mona and Hanan?

Then she heard electronic sounds chortling from the game room, accessible through a rear door. Resolutely, Cathy crossed to it.

She stepped into a blinking, humming place filled with video screens and a wall-size TV. Shelves near the TV held VCRs and laser disc players, as well as karaoke and stereo equipment.

Beeps and honks emanated from the only video game currently in use. In front of the screen sat Yasmin and a man in white robes and kaffiyeh. Cathy knew even before he turned around that it was Dar.

The two were pushing buttons and laughing as cartoon characters rode a pair of magic carpets, swooping over and under comical birds and other flying creatures. When a dragon's flames devoured Yasmin's carpet, Dar zoomed beneath her and she fell harmlessly beside him.

"You saved me!" cried the little girl.

"That is a father's job," he replied seriously.

Dropping her controller, Yasmin threw her arms around him. "I'm so glad I have a daddy!"

When he turned to hug her, Dar caught sight of Cathy. Gently he said, "But more importantly, you have a mommy. She is going to take you back to see Grandma Mary today."

Cathy felt a rush of gratitude. She was glad he wasn't making this more difficult than necessary. At the same time, irrationally, she wished he wouldn't be so quick to let her go.

The shadows beneath Dar's eyes told her that he hadn't gotten any sleep. Still, some of his habitual tension had vanished, and she knew he must be rejoicing for his country.

But she read sadness, too, in the line of his mouth and the angle of his shoulders. Could that be for her?

"I tried to call your room but the intercom is still broken," Dar said as he stroked Yasmin's hair. "Leila thought you might be here."

"So I am." Cathy pulled up a chair. "Where's Hanan? I thought she and the children were watching the signing on TV."

"They were, but after I arrived, she and Mona went to greet Khalid," Dar explained. To Yasmin, he added, "Perhaps you could try a single-player game while I talk with Cathy?"

"Okay." Giving a happy bounce, the little girl turned to the screen.

She'd scarcely reacted when Dar said that Cathy was

taking her to see Grandma Mary. Probably, at this age, Yasmin didn't understand that that involved flying halfway around the world, and that they weren't coming back.

"I am sorry about last night," Dar said. "I sent a guard to check on you, but I should have come myself."

The words took a little of the sting from her hurt, but it wasn't enough. "You had your priorities."

"And you believe you were not one of them?"

"Hanan told me it's a woman's place to wait and have faith," Cathy said. "I wish for your sake that I could be like that, but I can't."

"I do not expect you to be like Hanan," Dar said.

"Last night, a lot of things came together." To Cathy's dismay, her voice was shaking, but she plowed ahead. "I guess I haven't had time to think this past week. Dar, I don't belong here. This isn't my world."

He lowered his head and she saw how very tired he was. "You must have felt alone and abandoned. I cannot tell you how much I wish I could have come to you."

"I've never been so terrified," Cathy admitted. "Every time I heard footsteps in the hall or someone shouting, I thought you might be dead. Maybe I'm just not brave enough to be your wife."

His startled gaze met hers. "Hanan told me how you reassured her and took care of Mona's injury. You were splendid."

"I'm still a nervous wreck," she said. "Dar, I need to get back to reality. For me, that means California."

He drew a deep breath. "Last night was traumatic for many people. It does not mean you lack courage, Cathy. I love you and I wish you would stay, but I will not hold you here. You are free to leave if you must."

She ached to stroke the curve of his cheek and touch

her lips to his. Every inch of Dar's skin was imprinted on hers. She knew the low sounds he made in the back of his throat, and the virile scent of him, and the rhythmic thrust of his hips against hers as passion seized them both.

But overriding everything was her need to get away, to get home, to be herself again. "I've got a plane to catch."

She stood up, and so did Dar. "I will walk you both to the limousine. I am sorry I cannot go to the airport, as well, but Ezzat needs me."

Yasmin grumbled about leaving her game, but soon the three of them were heading for a side exit from the palace. The front was still blocked by celebrants.

Leila intercepted them in a large foyer near the side door. "You mentioned earlier that you wanted to thank the staff. I have brought a few of them to meet you."

"Oh, thank you!" Instinctively Cathy threw her arms around her new friend. "I'm going to miss you!"

"And I will miss you, more than you know," said the emir's wife as she hugged Cathy.

Before she could finish telling Leila how much she had enjoyed their work together, Cathy spotted a couple of people filing shyly into the hall. She took a step back and smoothed her dress.

"This is our housekeeper, Jannat." Leila presented a heavyset woman in an embroidered scarf and thawb. "Without her, our lives would be chaos." Cathy shook hands, and the woman murmured something melodious in Arabic.

Next came the head chef, a thin Frenchman with a mustache. "I am told you know the hotel business," he said. "I am sorry we have no time to compare notes."

"Your cooking is brilliant," Cathy told him truthfully.

"I've never worked with anyone as talented as you." The man beamed.

Last, a wizened woman shuffled forward. Despite her festive multicolored clothing, she looked impossibly old, and her hands were so thin and mottled that Cathy wondered how anyone could expect her to work.

"This is Najiba," said Leila. "She is what you might call the head tailor. It is Najiba who sews and makes alterations for everyone, as well as selecting clothing for our guests should they need it."

This little old lady with the gap-toothed smile had picked out Cathy's wedding-night lingerie and the transparent swimsuit? She could hardly believe it, but then she noticed the twinkle in the woman's eyes.

"You're very clever," Cathy said. "You do your job well."

The woman patted her hand. "Come back," she said. It sounded like an order.

"Now you must hurry," Leila said. "You will barely make your flight."

Cathy bit back tears as she turned to Dar. There were so many things she wanted to say, and couldn't.

She wished she could be part of his life forever, but the differences between them were too great. Last night had proved that.

As time passed, he would surely slip deeper into his accustomed attitudes and beliefs, and she would be left feeling hurt and resentful. If she had learned anything from her painful past, Cathy thought unhappily, it was to leave before the bitter end.

"Goodbye, Dar." Her rebellious lips nearly turned his name into "darling." But not quite.

Reaching up, a confused but good-natured Yasmin

gave the tall man a hug. "Bye, Daddy," she said. "We'll be back soon!"

As she followed her daughter into the limousine, Cathy let herself gaze, one last time, at Sheikh Kedar Bahram. He stood straight in his white headdress and robes, as distant as a figure from some exotic fantasy.

The planes of his face were sharply drawn in the morning light. She could have sworn she saw a sheen of tears in his eyes, but most likely it came from exhaustion.

Then a messenger arrived to fetch him and Leila to the first meeting of the palace's new advisory council. Ezzat, Cathy saw, would waste no time beginning his nation's transformation.

The limousine purred into motion. She rode away with the sense of having left many things unfinished.

"WELL, DAR?" said Leila as they walked to the meeting. "I have never known you to give up easily."

"I cannot force her to stay." An image remained burned in his mind, of Cathy in the limousine, gazing at him with sorrow washing the brightness from her face. "Besides..." He stopped, realizing he'd already said too much.

"I am not stupid," the emir's wife told him cheekily. "I know she only agreed to a temporary marriage."

"She told you?"

"Of course not. It is obvious. She was afraid the Al-Harooms would take her daughter away," Leila said as they approached the conference center. "An American woman does not marry a strange man just because an oracle tells her to."

"And what is your advice to me now?" he asked, only half in jest.

"You do not need my advice, Kedar Bahram," she

said. Despite his closeness to Ezzat, Leila had always held herself somewhat aloof from Dar, but now she gave him a cousinly wink. "This afternoon you must sleep, and then you will be able to think straight."

He needed sleep, all right. But even had he been alert enough to speak more clearly to Cathy this morning, he doubted anything could have persuaded her to stay.

She needed time alone. Too much had happened for her, too quickly.

He would give her the space she needed. And then, Dar vowed with all the fierceness that had powered him to the leadership of a tribe when he was scarcely more than a boy, he would find a way to win her back.

Chapter Fifteen

The next week was not easy for Cathy. After her long flight, she suffered from jet lag and developed a nagging cold. In addition, Yasmin moped through the rooms, asking repeatedly when they would return to the palace.

Surely the little house in Laguna hadn't really shrunk, but it seemed tiny. Had Yasmin's toys always overflowed into every spare inch of the living room? And had Cathy's bed always been so narrow and cold?

As the days passed, she could feel her mother studying her worriedly. When she finally spilled the whole story, Mary listened with a sympathetic but troubled expression.

"Honey, this is outside my experience," her mother said when she finished. "I wish I could advise you, but I wouldn't know what to suggest."

"This is one time I just have to work things out for myself," Cathy agreed. "I can handle it, Mom."

Then she clicked on the TV to catch the latest events in Marakite. Since her return, she had watched afternoon and evening newscasts and bought two daily papers to make sure she got all the details of the government's reorganization.

It was fortunate that no one had notified the press of her return from Marakite. Cathy let the answering machine pick up calls, but there were only a few casual attempts by reporters to get comments from Mary.

Dar didn't phone. Not that she'd expected him to, but she couldn't help wondering what he was doing. Did he miss her, or was he already trying to put her out of his mind?

By the second week, Mary began making plans for Yasmin's upcoming fourth birthday, but the little girl responded with uncharacteristic grumpiness. Nothing appealed to her, not even the offer of a trip to Disneyland.

She wanted to see her cousins Mona and Sara. She missed the playroom and Dar, and why couldn't Grandma Faiza come visit her?

A few days later, Cathy returned to work. The first day back, Bert and her fellow workers approached her cautiously, but soon they fell into their old, easy relationships.

There was plenty to do, now that tourist season had arrived. Once on the job, Cathy didn't have time to dwell on what had happened, and for that she was grateful.

She worked through the next weekend, giving Bert a much-needed break. In exchange, she would receive Monday off for Yasmin's birthday. The little girl had finally settled on a trip to the San Diego Zoo, although without much enthusiasm.

On Sunday morning, an unseasonal rain fell, spoiling some of the guests' plans for sunbathing and boating, and forcing the outdoor art shows to open late. Although the sky cleared by afternoon, a steady stream of complaints reached the front desk.

"You'd think we were personally responsible for the weather," grumbled the desk clerk.

Cathy watched a family huff away. She had just finished explaining that she was very sorry but, no, California sunshine wasn't guaranteed and the hotel did not give refunds.

"They probably spent a lot of money on their vacation," she said with a shrug. "Then the kids complained all morning, and the parents needed to vent their frustration."

"You've changed," said the clerk.

"I have?"

"Little things don't bother you as much anymore," he pointed out.

Cathy realized he was right. "I guess being caught in the middle of a revolution does that to you."

"I'm surprised you haven't capitalized on your fame," said the young man. "Gone on talk shows and written a book and all that."

"Oh, please!" She couldn't imagine telling the world the intimate details of her relationship with Dar.

Cathy smiled to herself, recalling Sabah's sarcastic remark about people who bared their souls on television. Then she wondered whether the young woman had returned to Marakite yet, and how her new son was doing.

It was time—long past time, really—to send a baby gift, Cathy decided.

Impulsively she walked to the hotel's gift nook. After browsing for a few minutes, she selected a tiny Laguna Beach T-shirt and paid for it.

"That's too small for Yasmin, isn't it?" asked the saleslady as she gift wrapped the shirt.

"It's for my nephew," Cathy said absently.

"I didn't know you had one."

The words startled Cathy into realizing that she had come to think of the Al-Haroum children as her nieces and nephews. And of Sabah and Maha, Hanan and Leila as relatives, as well. "Actually, I have several."

"Ooh!" The saleslady stared out the lobby's glass front. "Who is that hunk? Quick, somebody introduce me!"

Idly Cathy followed her gaze. A man in a tailored suit was emerging from a sedan, his dark hair burnished in the sunshine.

She knew the angle of those cheekbones and the slashing intensity of those brown eyes. With a rush of longing, Cathy confronted the truth, that she'd missed Dar in every fiber of her being since she returned to Laguna.

"That's my husband," she said.

"I'm sorry!" The saleslady reddened. "I didn't mean to be offensive!"

"I'm not offended. And he *is* a hunk, isn't he?" mused Cathy.

"But—isn't he supposed to be a sheikh?" asked the woman. "I mean, he looks so normal."

Cathy couldn't help smiling. "He's in disguise. Giving the Secret Service the slip."

"Well, you're one lucky woman," said the saleslady with a sigh, and turned to help another customer.

Cathy's palms felt itchy, and she wiped them on her slacks, then picked up her package. What was Dar doing here? She hadn't heard anything on the news about his arrival, but then, he was obviously keeping a low profile.

He held the door for a couple of tourists, waiting patiently while their two children dawdled. He must have glimpsed Cathy through the glass, but he acted as if he were in no hurry.

Maybe he had come to discuss their divorce. She wasn't ready for that, she realized with a pang. Not yet.

Cathy scurried behind the front desk and tucked the T-shirt onto a shelf. Why did she feel as flustered as a schoolgirl and as eager as a bride? Why did she yearn for the sound of his voice, when she knew that whatever he had to say was likely to be painful?

Because, she thought as she tried to tear her gaze from that tall, masterful frame, she was in love with the man. And at any moment her heart might shatter into so many pieces she would never find them all again.

DAR SAW CATHY through the glass before he got out of the rental car. She was talking to a saleswoman in the hotel's gift kiosk, her short blond hair brushed back, her navy pantsuit brisk and businesslike.

Everything about her appearance signaled that she belonged here, in this setting. Maybe he had been wrong to believe he could transplant her to his culture.

But he had not come to plead his case. That could wait. He had an invitation to present.

The doorman was busy loading suitcases into a woman's trunk, so Dar held the door for a frazzled-looking young couple. Their toddlers kept pulling away, one grabbing at colorful brochures on a rack, the other rocketing toward the gift shop, and he waited while the parents rounded them up.

Having moved to the front desk, Cathy stood behind it as if it were a shield. By now, Dar knew, she must have seen him, but she pretended to be absorbed in her computer screen.

Emotions twisted through him, but he needed to play this scene coolly and pleasantly. The depth of his need for her was something he dared reveal only a little at a time. Otherwise he would lose what little chance he had to regain her trust.

At last the family departed, children in tow. Dar strolled toward the front desk.

"May I help you?" asked the clerk.

"I wish to speak with Miss Maxwell." He purposely used Cathy's maiden name. From her perspective, it should seem less possessive, less threatening.

Cathy glanced up from the computer, her expression guarded. "Hello, Dar." Her voice had a husky, vulnerable quality. "I see you finally got some sleep. You look terrific."

He resisted the urge to slick back his hair like a bashful teenager. "I slept on the plane."

"I'm surprised you would leave Marakite so soon."

"Actually, I hitched a ride," he said. "Fasad was anxious to see Sabah's baby."

"They're still at Los Olivos?" Keen interest chased away her wariness.

"She had a cesarean section, and the doctor recommended against making a long flight so soon," Dar explained.

Cathy fetched a gift-wrapped package from beneath the counter. "I just bought her a baby gift. Would you give it to Sabah for me?"

"You can deliver it yourself," he said. "I came to invite you and Yasmin to a party. And your mother, too, of course."

She hesitated, the gift in midair. "What kind of party?"

Dar gave a slight nod toward the desk clerk, who, although clicking away at his terminal, was probably listening for all he was worth. "Perhaps we could talk privately."

"I'm on duty for another hour," Cathy said. "Can you wait?"

He didn't want to waste another hour, or another minute. Dar was tired of civilized manners and fancy footwork. His instincts urged him to carry this woman away right now, if he could only come up with some pretext.

As his mind clicked over and rejected possibilities, his hands flexed and he shifted on the balls of his feet. Subtle as the movements were, they must have registered with Cathy.

"Oh, no, you don't," she said.

"Don't what?" He assumed an expression of mock innocence.

"You just got the sneakiest look on your face."

"Sneaky?" Dar drew himself up, offended and amused at the same time.

"You're not going to tell me another crazy story about your tribe's customs, are you?" she demanded.

He chuckled. "Remind me never to sit across a negotiating table from you. You know me too well."

He hadn't intended to make a double entendre, but a sudden clamping of her lips told him that Cathy was remembering exactly how well they did know each other. Then she relaxed. "Well, since the invitation includes my mother and Yasmin, I guess you should present it to all of us."

"Do I have your permission to go to your home and wait for you?" he asked. "I do not want to see Yasmin behind your back."

"Of course you can visit her. Yasmin thinks of you as her daddy." The last word came out in a little gulp, as if it hurt her to admit it.

Dar strove to keep his tone light. "I would enjoy talking with your mother, also."

"I'll see you there in a little while." Giving him a wistful smile, Cathy turned to help a tour group that was piling into the lobby.

With a bow, Dar retreated. He had taken the opening steps. Now the dance could begin.

CATHY'S REACTION to Dar's presence had been immediate, physical and devastating. It had taken all her strength not to run around the counter and hold him, press against him, melt into him.

This yearning might be the stuff of poetry, but it could also be a weakness, she told herself harshly. Self-destructive, just as her earlier relationship had been.

An image kept recurring of that dreadful night at the palace. She had a clear picture of Hanan, Yasmin and Mona huddling around her, the four of them alone and frightened, with only a pool of lamplight to hold the shadows at bay.

When she needed Dar the most, he had not come. Maybe her feelings were irrational, maybe she was being unfair, but she could never go back there.

Cathy got through the next hour on automatic pilot. When she arrived home, she didn't even recall walking the intervening blocks.

She half feared she might find a news crew, but the only sign of a visitor was Dar's sedan, discreetly parked to one side of the driveway. Otherwise, the wood-shingled cottage looked its usual quaint self.

As soon as she stepped inside, Cathy inhaled the vanilla fragrance of something freshly baked, and heard voices from the kitchen. She set down her purse, kicked off her shoes and went to investigate.

At the counter, Mary stood icing a birthday cake. Dar sat at the breakfast table, his long legs nearly blocking the narrow kitchen. Yasmin bounced gleefully around him, chattering away.

The little girl spotted Cathy first. "Can we go see the new baby? Can we, Mommy?"

"I apologize." Dar ducked his head. "I did not mean to discuss any plans without you here, Cathy, but..."

"Yasmin's been plying him with questions since he stepped through the door." Mary opened a package of sugar rosettes and applied them to the cake. "And so have I."

It was amazing how easily Dar fit in with her family, Cathy thought. Usually Mary got prickly when anyone invaded her kitchen, but she didn't seem to mind stepping around Dar's outstretched legs as she retrieved birthday candles from a drawer.

"The party is not only for baby Ali," Dar said. "Faiza would like to celebrate Yasmin's fourth birthday. Of course, I told her you might already have plans."

"We're going to the zoo," Cathy said automatically.

"I want to see my cousins!" Yasmin demanded.

"Of course you do." Cathy regarded her daughter with a mixture of tenderness and exasperation. "But that isn't a very polite way of asking, is it?"

"Can I see them?" begged her daughter. "Please, please, Mommy?"

"We could have our own celebration here tonight," Mary pointed out. "And frankly, I'd love to see the Al-Haroums again. I didn't get much chance to talk to them at the wedding, and I would love to meet the emir."

"He and his wife could not leave Haribat," Dar said. "But everyone else is there. Even Zahira. She is being taped for a TV magazine show."

The fearful part of Cathy's mind, the part that still dreamed about assassins stalking through dark corridors, demanded that she refuse. But how could she?

Ever since she'd left Marakite, she had felt as if she

were waiting for something to happen. Perhaps this was it.

A trip to Los Olivos might be exactly what she needed to tie up loose ends. She could see Maha and Sabah again, hold the new baby and make arrangements for regular contact between the Al-Haroums and Yasmin.

Then she could say goodbye to Dar and get on with her life.

"All right." Sternly Cathy forced herself to ignore a spreading sense of sadness. "We'll go."

THEY LANDED at the island airport on a day crisp with sunshine and ocean breezes. Mary made a low murmur of relief at being on the ground. "You're a marvelous pilot, Dar."

"And you are a good sport," he told her. "Like many people, you are not comfortable in a small plane, but you have not complained."

"Let's just say it's not my favorite mode of transportation." Mary nodded toward the two private jets sitting on the tarmac. "Now, that's more my style."

From her seat in the back, Cathy glanced toward the jets. Sitting just beyond them was a helicopter marked with a production company logo. "Is that the crew that's taping Zahira?"

"Yes, they wanted to capture the flavor of her homeland," Dar said as he brought the plane to a complete stop. "On a tight budget, Los Olivos was the best they could do."

Mary wasn't looking at the helicopter, but toward the hacienda. "Here comes everyone! They must be eager to see you, Yasmin."

The little girl clapped her hands and pressed her nose to the window. Cathy drew back. What did everyone think about her, now that they realized her marriage had been only temporary?

Dar helped Mary from the plane, then Yasmin and Cathy. Cathy gave a start as he grasped her arm and eased her to the ground, but he gave no sign of noticing.

Last night at the impromptu birthday party, and this morning when he came to collect them, Dar's behavior had been polite and restrained. For once, she couldn't read the underlying emotions. He didn't even seem to notice that she'd worn the necklace and earrings he'd given her for their wedding.

He moved ahead to take Mary's arm, while Yasmin pelted across the pavement. Mona and Sara welcomed her with screams and hugs. Sara's older brother Ahmed held back with the dignity of a seven-year-old, while two-year-old Salman wriggled his way into the middle of the action.

"I'm four today!" Yasmin shouted. "Hurray for me!"

Cathy scanned the people clustered around her daughter. Faiza and Fasad were maneuvering to get hugs from their granddaughter; behind them, Maha and Khalid stood with Sabah's husband, Muhammed. Sabah and Hanan must have remained in the hacienda with the baby.

Dar wasted no time in reintroducing Mary to the Al-Haroums. Faiza welcomed her more warmly than Cathy would have expected, slipping an arm around her waist and beaming at this fellow grandmother. That, at least, was encouraging.

Maha hurried forward to catch Cathy's hands. "I am so glad to see you! I was afraid you might not come."

"I've been worried that you'd all be angry at me," Cathy admitted.

"Angry? No!" The younger woman stared at her in astonishment. "Everyone is so pleased, the way you kept calm that terrible night. Hanan would have panicked without you.''

"Where is she?" Cathy asked. "With Sabah?"

"Perhaps." Maha frowned as if about to say more, but Khalid was approaching.

There was something different about the young man, Cathy noticed, a calm air of maturity she had not seen there before. He nodded to her and said, "I never had a chance to thank you for helping my wife and daughter."

"We helped each other," she said. "I was glad to have them with me."

"It is gracious of you to say so," he murmured.

"We should all make haste," called Muhammed. "Zahira wishes to include Yasmin in the taping, and I believe the crew is almost ready."

As they crossed the lawn, Cathy realized something was missing. "They've removed the tent."

"Oh, yes." Maha smoothed out a fold in her long skirt. "There are new austerity measures, now that Papa is prime minister. We must spend our money to help restore the country, not on idle pleasures."

They had come abreast of Faiza and Mary. The older Al-Haroum woman must have overheard Maha, because she added, "Still, I think your father goes too far. Here we have both a birth and a birthday to celebrate, and not even any acrobats!"

"Acrobats!" said Mary. "That would have been fun!"

Muhammed ushered them through the front courtyard and around to a garden that Cathy hadn't seen before. It was stuffed with squatty palm trees, birds of paradise and calla lilies.

Beneath an arched trellis thick with roses, Zahira sat on a stone bench while Basilyr fussed over her. The Three-Eyed Woman sported voluminous layers of pink chiffon and a matching half veil. Her eyes were smeared with too much black liner, and what could be seen of her skin had an orange tone from an excess of foundation.

A Minicam operator, a male reporter and a woman who must have been the producer hovered about, studying the light and the camera angles. When she noticed the new arrivals, the producer came to consult with Fasad, then drew Yasmin into the garden.

"Here's our prophecy child." She regarded the little girl closely. "There's a lot of shine on her face. I knew we should have brought our own makeup artist."

"Perhaps I can help." Mary angled through the crowd, and held up her oversize purse. "I'm in the cosmetics business and I always come equipped."

"Thank goodness!" said Zahira. "Basilyr makes me feel like a pancake covered with syrup! Is it necessary to wear so much goop?"

"Not in natural light." Mary glanced apologetically at Basilyr. "Do you mind if I help?"

"Actually, I will be curious to see what you do." He made a slight bow that set his jewelry clanking, while a breeze ballooned his gauzy shirt until Cathy feared he might float away.

Mary went to work swiftly and efficiently. Basilyr watched over her shoulder, so fascinated that his bracelets scarcely jangled. Even so, the producer asked him to remove them, and, with a pout, he complied.

Soon Zahira's face took on a more natural yet still exotic aspect, while Yasmin's shine vanished beneath a touch of powder. The onlookers murmured their approval.

Cathy watched the first part of the taping. The reporter asked Zahira how it felt to be a living oracle—"Better than to be a dead oracle!'' was the tart response—and questioned Yasmin about life in the palace.

But as it became obvious the taping was going to drag on, Cathy slipped through a side door into the house. Dar had been standing apart from her, but now he appeared at her side.

"Is something wrong?" He bent to speak quietly, although they weren't likely to disturb the taping at this distance.

"I'd like to see Sabah and the baby." Did he have to stand so close? Cathy wondered. She could barely resist tracing the curve of his jaw and nuzzling the pulse point in his throat.

And she loved the way his hair feathered over the top of his ears. But she must remember that he was no longer hers, this man of the desert.

"Of course." Dar escorted her through the hacienda. They passed the spice-scented kitchen, where servants scurried to prepare pans full of food.

"I guess this new austerity campaign doesn't apply to meals," Cathy couldn't resist observing.

Dar smiled. "In fact, there is a good reason for that."

"Healthy appetites?"

"Yes, certainly," he conceded as they walked. "But also, our people have known real hunger. Before our current prosperity, there were famines in Marakite. To us, the most important symbol of our achievements is to have plenty to eat."

There was so much to learn about his country, so much that was different from her own. Cathy wished she'd had more time to explore Marakite and visit its ancient sites and study its customs.

"I hope you'll instruct Yasmin in these things," she said. "She needs to know her heritage."

"I would rather instruct you." Dar shook his head as if chiding himself. "But only if you wish it. Now, here is Sabah's chamber."

He knocked lightly, then held the door as she went in. "I will tell the others where you are," he said, and retreated.

Sunlight streamed through a partly open window, playing across bright tiles and onto the double bed where Sabah lay propped against a stack of pillows. In the crook of her arm nestled a tiny baby, wrinkled and pink and utterly content.

"How sweet!" Cathy halted as little Ali opened his mouth in a yawn. "My goodness, that was so wide, he nearly swallowed himself up!"

Sabah burst into laughter. "Goodness, what an idea!"

From her purse, Cathy produced the gift she'd bought at the hotel. "It's a souvenir from my hometown."

With an expression of delight, Sabah opened it and held up the T-shirt. "It is darling. Laguna Beach—such a romantic name!"

"Oh, let me see!" From a dim corner, half-hidden by curtains, Hanan stepped forward.

Until that moment, Cathy had not realized she was in the room. The two exchanged hesitant glances and then, impulsively, threw their arms around each other.

The younger woman felt thinner, and a little shaky. There were shadows beneath her eyes, Cathy noticed when she stepped back. "Have you been ill?"

"She has become nervous," Sabah advised. "Ever since the coup attempt."

"It is foolish," Hanan said quickly. "I have this fear that someone will attack us, even though I know the danger is past."

Cathy's heart went out to her. "I've had nightmares, too."

"You? But you are so brave!"

"Not all that brave." Cathy struggled to understand the sense of dread that filled her as she recalled that night. "I guess in some ways I'm afraid to go back to the palace, myself."

"Is that why you left Kedar?" asked Sabah.

"Not exactly." But perhaps, Cathy thought in surprise, her anxiety *was* part of the reason she'd left so hastily. "I felt as if he'd abandoned me. He didn't stop by, even for a few minutes. It would have meant so much."

"I cannot believe Dar gave no thought to you," Hanan said. "Khalid was with him much of the night. I will ask him why he thinks your husband did not visit you."

"You see?" Sabah said to her sister-in-law. "Even Cathy was afraid. You have nothing to be ashamed of."

Hanan's expression warmed. "I always wish to be the perfect wife. These past two weeks, I have felt as if I were failing my husband, with my fears. But perhaps I am only normal."

"Of course you are!" Cathy said.

Sabah shifted Ali in her arms, and he responded with a burp. His expression was so cute, Cathy couldn't resist leaning down to touch the baby's cheek. She hadn't felt anything so soft since Yasmin was tiny.

"Someday you could have a baby of your own," Sabah pointed out. "A little boy, a tiny Sheikh Bahram. I think you would like that."

Cathy's breath caught in her throat. "In some ways." Quickly she turned the conversation to less personal matters.

A short while later, as Sabah prepared to feed the baby, Cathy excused herself. The fact was, she realized, that she needed time to examine the new insights she had gained from talking to Hanan.

It struck Cathy that the danger of that night must have shaken her more than she realized. Until now, it hadn't occurred to her that her urge to flee from Marakite had been a natural response to a traumatic incident, independent of her disappointment in Dar.

Finding the corridor mercifully empty, Cathy wandered to an arched opening and sat on its ledge, overlooking the central courtyard. The fountain's spray pattered across the pool, a few breezeborne droplets fanning over her cheeks.

Years ago, she had survived betrayal by the man she'd thought she loved, and had vowed never to let anyone take advantage of her again. Strength had become part of her self-image.

Perhaps, that terrifying night at the palace, she had sought someone to blame for her sense of vulnerability because it felt like a weakness. In some ways, Cathy realized, she was like Hanan, ashamed of her own fears.

Still, although her own unrecognized stress might have been a complicating factor, it did not change the basic problem. As special as he might be, Dar remained a man from another culture. What had felt like abandonment that night might very well be a warning of further problems ahead.

She was willing to concede that she had not truly examined her own reactions. But Cathy could not return to Marakite when she had so many doubts.

Wistfully she stood and prepared to join the others.

Chapter Sixteen

Dar watched with scarcely disguised impatience as Zahira went through a mock prophesying session for the benefit of the cameras. Yasmin had been excused, and had disappeared into the hacienda with her cousins.

He wished he could hear what Cathy and Sabah were talking about. He wanted even more strongly to talk to his wife, alone. It would be difficult with so many people around, but he must seize his chance today.

These past two weeks had been crammed with the excitement of rebuilding a nation. Work started early in the morning and often lasted until midnight.

As minister of trade and foreign affairs, it fell to Dar to encourage international investment without yielding too much power to outsiders. Sometimes he felt as if he were walking a tightrope.

It was also his duty to explain the reorganization to foreign diplomats, many of whom had fled during the civil war but were now descending on Haribat by the score. And, as heroes in their homeland, he and Khalid had personally visited many tribes, both loyalists and former rebels, to ensure their support.

He would not have had much time to spend with Cathy had she been at the palace, but he missed her. It was as if, beneath all the activity, a void lurked in Dar's personal world.

To win her back, he must first understand her. Why was it, he wondered, that women seemed to sense each others' feelings instinctively, while a man might struggle for all he was worth and still be left in the dark?

Today, when he'd noticed that Cathy wore the jewelry he'd given her, he had hoped it might be a sign of reconciliation. Yet every time he came near her, she drew back, subtly but unmistakably.

Life had been simpler in his ancestors' days, he told himself ruefully as the taping wound to an end. A man simply carried a woman off and then she belonged to him. But if she didn't love him, how satisfying could that be?

The TV crew began packing up. Dar watched in amusement as Basilyr waved Mary over to show her an herbal cream concoction he used to remove Zahira's makeup. The young assistant took pride in how soft it left the skin.

"You know," Mary said, "I specialize in holistic beauty preparations. I'd like to arrange a source of these herbs from your country."

"I will give you the name of a good merchant, very trustworthy," Basilyr assured her. "But you should come to Haribat and see the spice market for yourself. There are many unique herbs in Marakite."

"Perhaps I will," she said. "You've given me a lot to think about."

Zahira lifted herself heavily from the bench. "That was most grueling. Are those people gone?"

"Muhammed is escorting them to the helicopter," said Fasad. "We invited them for lunch, but they could not stay."

"Good," grunted the wisewoman. "Do you not think they ask stupid questions? 'How does it feel to be a living oracle?' My feet hurt and I am so fat I wheeze, that is how it feels. I think I will go on Oprah Winfrey's diet and take up aerobics, that is what."

"Then you can make your own exercise video!" cried Basilyr. "Like Jane Fonda!"

Zahira waved a hand dismissively. "No more TV shows! I know many people will be disappointed. I have been told I have charisma. But what I do not have is patience!"

The family members were chatting among themselves and drifting into the house. "Where is Cathy?" asked Khalid.

"She has gone to talk to Sabah and your wife," Dar said.

Absentmindedly, Khalid stroked his short beard. "That is good. Perhaps she can help Hanan feel better. I will go and see if my wife might join us for lunch." She had been eating in her room since they arrived.

A few minutes later, a servant came to announce the meal. Dar would have taken Mary's arm, but she was flanked by her new friends, Faiza and Zahira, and he didn't wish to intrude.

Already, his mother-in-law felt at home among the Al-Haroums. He hoped that would reassure Cathy, but he knew it would not be enough to change her mind.

THERE WAS NO CHANCE to talk to Dar at lunch, not that Cathy would have broached a personal subject among so many people. But in any case, she sat with the other women, caught up in the buzz of conversation.

Unlike her first meal on Los Olivos, lunch was served at a long table rather than on the floor. The children ate in an adjacent room, under the supervision of Ahmed's governess.

Fasad sat at one end of the table, debating the merits of various soccer teams with Muhammed. Khalid and Dar had their heads together, talking earnestly. Their banded kaffiyehs half obscured their faces, giving them a secretive air.

The conversation was much livelier in the women's group, especially since both Sabah and Hanan had joined them. Everyone exclaimed over the small packages of cosmetics that Mary had brought as gifts.

"Your assistant, Basilyr, has given me some new ideas," she told Zahira. "He's fascinating."

"Oh, that one!" sighed the Three-Eyed Woman. "He was a street orphan when I rescued him. Very smart young man. And ambitious, I think."

"May I make a business proposal?" asked Mary.

"But of course!" cried Zahira. "In Marakite today, even a prophetess must suffer budget cuts. So I am open to suggestion."

"I've been looking for a name for a new line of herbal products," Mary began. "It includes face creams and astringents, potpourris and teas that can be used to steam open your pores as well as to drink."

"Very unusual!" Faiza passed a plate of fresh-baked pita bread, so absorbed in the conversation that she didn't even take any for herself.

"Basilyr is going to help me find some new products from your country," Mary went on. "And he's given me an idea for a name. What do you think of Wisewoman Herbal Preparations?"

"Wisewoman?" repeated Zahira.

"I would pay you to be our spokeswoman, if you're

willing," Mary went on. "There would be some print advertisements, and perhaps a video for cable TV."

"Would anyone ask me stupid questions?"

"Certainly not," she said. "You would demonstrate the products and make a few comments, that's all."

"You should do it," Faiza advised. "It is perfect."

"Now that we have peace, there will not be as much call for prophecies," Maha pointed out.

"I agree!" cried Zahira. "Done, and done again!"

Beside Cathy, Sabah chuckled. "Your mother is very clever."

"She's wonderful," Cathy agreed. "She's been my inspiration."

Hanan happily accepted a second helping of hummus. "I am glad I came to lunch today. I would not have missed this!"

"Cathy," said Sabah. "I know it is rude to say that a woman is looking at a man. Is it also impolite to say that a man is looking at a woman?"

She knew instantly what Sabah meant. Cathy had felt Dar's gaze on her ever since she entered the room.

It was hard to sit across the room from him, attuned to his intensity and yet unable to talk to him. Even as she listened to the conversation around her, she had been aware of him at every moment.

Now she lifted her head and saw that he was regarding her directly. In his face was a spark of hope that hadn't been there before.

Had something changed? Hanan had promised to ask Khalid about that night at the palace, and the two men had been conferring throughout the meal. Did their conversation have anything to do with her?

Before she got a chance to find out, Cathy had to wait through the serving of a giant birthday cake. The children poured in, and Yasmin joyfully tore into a pile of presents, assisted by her cousins.

There were dolls and dresses, games and child-size jewelry. Cathy was pleased to see that the garments bore the bright colors and distinctive designs of Marakite. This was a part of her daughter's heritage that she wanted to encourage.

Then came another stack of gifts for Sabah and baby Ali. By the time they were all unwrapped, many of the guests and most of the children were yawning and stretching.

Nap time. But not for Cathy. She had never felt less sleepy in her life.

As everyone drifted away, she left Yasmin with her mother and Faiza. By unspoken agreement, Dar waited for her in the corridor.

Even after so much time, the sight of him in his white robes and headdress took her breath away. He was everything she craved and distrusted, handsome and alien, his high-boned face reflecting thousands of years of desert fierceness, his eyes tender and uncertain.

Cathy held out her hand and he cradled it in his large one. "Would you care for a boat ride?" he asked.

She could feel the others glancing at them with curiosity and encouragement, but she was too absorbed by Dar's nearness to care. "I'd love one."

He led her out of the hacienda, through the garden where the grass still bore the footprints of the TV crew and into a small boathouse. Dar pulled off his kaffiyeh and robes and hung them on hooks.

Their removal revealed the suit in which he'd piloted the plane. "You're going boating in that?" Cathy asked.

He glanced down ruefully. "It may be a bit formal, but there is not much I can do." He did, however, exchange his shoes for the pair of wading boots he'd worn previously.

She decided her blouse and long skirt would have to do, as well. Impulsively she kicked off her pumps so they wouldn't get wet. "Any objections to bare feet?"

"I have no objections to bare anything." With a devilish grin, Dar untied the boat and slid it down a ramp.

Cathy itched to ask what he and Khalid had discussed, but the time wasn't right. Besides, now that they were alone, she wanted the moments to stretch out with delicious languor.

When the boat reached the waterline, Dar stopped to help her inside. "Are we going to the magic city?" she asked as she sat on the middle bench.

"Would you like to?"

"Very much."

"Then we will." He climbed in and started the motor, and they arced out into the sparkling water.

There was no point in trying to talk over the thrumming noise. Leaning back, Cathy closed her eyes and lifted her face to the sunshine.

An aroma reached her, of seaweed and spices. They blended with the heat until scent and sensation became indistinguishable.

As the boat pushed forward, the ocean lifted and rocked them. Its restrained power reminded Cathy that they were skirting the edges of a vast unseen world, its depths uncharted, its secrets ancient and unexplored.

This vessel was tiny, its occupants mere specks, and yet she felt liberated rather than diminished. She and Dar were figures in a great panorama. Their passion, their fears and their driving need for each other were as elemental as the sea and the waves.

She opened her eyes to see that they were coming

around a spit of land. Although she had thought herself prepared for it, Cathy was startled by the sudden vista.

Feathery golden fronds swirled around them, parting to reveal layers of green lace that descended into inky depths. A school of fish twinkled near the surface. Among the sleek bodies of silver and black, she glimpsed luminous red-gold shapes.

Dar turned off the motor. "Those are called garibaldis," he said. "They are a protected species."

"They should be."

The engine sputtered to silence. Wavelets soughed by the boat, rocking it like a cradle. Sunshine warmed Cathy's nose and cheeks.

"Maybe we shouldn't talk," she said softly.

"Why not?" Dar watched her steadily.

"I like being near you," she admitted. "I'm afraid words will just bring back my fears. Make me face things I hate facing."

"But we must talk," he said.

"Why?"

"Because there is something I must tell you, that I could not tell you until now."

Cathy's heart got stuck between her ribs for several beats. Did this have something to do with his conversation with Khalid?

"It's about the coup attempt, isn't it?" she said.

He gave a tight nod. "You know that after I left Ezzat's quarters, I went to Fasad's."

"And found that Khalid had killed the third assassin, and he and Fasad were injured," she filled in. "Then what?"

"I stayed with them until the doctor arrived." Light refracting off the water dappled Dar's face. "When their wounds had been treated, Fasad needed to sleep.

"Khalid and I went to his room to talk, at his request. Although he had saved his father's life, he blamed himself for what happened that night. He wanted me to tell the emir because he was too ashamed to do so."

"Ashamed?" Cathy pictured Khalid's solemn, bearded face. Until recently, he had sometimes struck her as impetuous and even arrogant, but never disloyal. "Is this related to the time I saw him talking with Mojahid?"

Dar stared toward the horizon as if gazing at a memory. "In a way. As he had requested, Mojahid insisted on 'consulting' frequently with Khalid. The man was a skilled manipulator. He not only made Khalid feel important, he created a sense of...perhaps not friendship, but at least comradeship between them."

"Surely Khalid knew nothing of the assassination plans!" Cathy protested.

"No, he did not." Dar rested his elbows on his knees and made a tent of his hands. "But in Fasad's room, the assassin regarded Khalid in astonishment when he came to his father's defense."

"They expected him to condone murder?"

"It would not be the first time a son has been party to such a thing," Dar said. "You see, even if Ezzat, Fasad and I were all dead, the tribal leaders and the army still would not have accepted Mojahid as their emir."

"But they might have accepted Khalid." The pieces were falling together.

"Mojahid would not have gone ahead with the attack, had he not believed he could put Khalid on the throne and then control him," Dar explained. "So Khalid realized afterward, and I had to agree."

Cathy hadn't given much thought to what might have happened had the coup succeeded, but Dar's speculation made sense. "So Khalid blamed himself?"

"All his life, he has struggled to be as worthy and respected as his brother. Even after Ali's death, he never came close to achieving this goal." The breeze stirred Dar's hair, and its coppery highlights gleamed in the sunshine. "Now he felt that, in his foolish self-importance, he had given encouragement to the rebels and endangered us all."

Listening to him, Cathy felt a sudden sense of unreality. Conspiracy and ambition, nobility and self-sacrifice were the stuff of Shakespeare's plays, not her own humdrum life. Yet she was intimately a part of this story, or Dar would not be telling it to her.

"He said he was willing to send himself into exile, or to accept whatever punishment Ezzat chose," Dar went on. "I could not allow him to do this. It would have hurt Fasad, and frankly, I think it would be unjustified."

"He was naive," Cathy said. "That must have injured his pride, but it isn't a crime."

"Exactly." Dar smiled. "Khalid is proud and strong, but he is only twenty-four years old and has always been in his father's and brother's shadows."

"So you talked him out of it?"

He brushed a windblown leaf from his suit jacket. "It took a long time to persuade him that it was his own moral uprightness that blinded him to Mojahid's motives. And even casual friendliness on his part would have been misinterpreted, because Mojahid would assume that everyone was as greedy and ambitious as himself. None of this was Khalid's fault."

"You must have spent a long time with him," she murmured.

"Over an hour, until the emir sent for me," Dar said. "Even then, Khalid needed time to think and to forgive himself. He asked me to speak of this to no one."

"That's why you couldn't tell me." To her surprise, Cathy felt tears prick her eyes.

"I suppose it must seem old-fashioned to you, that a man would withhold such information even from his wife," Dar went on. "It is my sense of honor, Cathy. I cannot betray it."

"In my culture, we don't talk much about honor anymore," she conceded. "Of course, in my country, too, there are people who make sacrifices to do what's right, but it seems as if they're getting hard to find."

"I am such a man," Dar said. "I love you, Cathy, and I would do almost anything to win you back. But I cannot betray my soul. Fortunately, today, Khalid gave me permission to speak, and so I have."

The tears that had been threatening now slid down her cheeks. At first Cathy didn't know if they were tears of happiness or of loss, and then she realized that she hadn't lost anything. Instead, she had discovered a precious truth.

All this time, she had thought that cultural differences stood between the two of them. Such matters had to be taken seriously, of course. But now she realized that Dar's strict sense of honor, which was so much a part of his upbringing, was one of the things she loved most about him.

"I think I'm ready to go back," she said.

Disappointment tightened his face. "Already? I had hoped we could talk a little longer."

Cathy chuckled, then felt a trace of guilt when she saw his confusion. "I meant back to the palace!" she said.

His eyes, lit from within, outshone the sun. "Really? You mean this?"

She was laughing and crying at the same time. "Yes. Yes, I do. Besides, if I don't go back to Marakite, I'll never get to see my mother. She's practically moving there!''

He gathered her close. ''Oh, my Cathy. This is everything I hoped for!''

''Besides, Sabah wants us to have a little Sheikh Bahram,'' she teased as she nestled against him.

''In that case,'' he murmured, ''perhaps we should get started.''

''Here?'' She couldn't believe he meant it.

''Not precisely.'' Reluctantly he eased her back onto the bench and started the motor. ''But I know a place.''

On the far side of the cove, they halted by a strip of sand. After climbing out, Dar lifted Cathy onto the shore. Then he pulled the boat from the water.

From here, she could see no sign of human habitation. The hacienda was on the far side of the island, and the mainland blocked from view. They might as well have landed on another planet.

The trees were scrubby, little more than large bushes, but they were thick. Soft bits of moss and grass covered the sandy ground.

From a compartment in the boat, Dar fetched a blanket. ''Thank goodness for emergency supplies,'' he said. ''Now that we have been shipwrecked, we will need them.''

''I wonder if anyone's going to rescue us?'' Cathy teased. ''I hope not!''

Her heart so light she felt as if it might soar away, she helped Dar create a private nest under the bushes. They crawled inside like two children playing house.

''There is a tradition among my people,'' he joked as he lifted a burr from her hair.

''I can't wait to hear it.''

"When the sheikh and his wife are alone, they must take off their clothes."

"I think it would be better if they took off each others' clothes," Cathy said.

"Ah, yes. It seems you know my people's traditions better than I do."

She ran her hand along the fine weave of his jacket. He half turned so she could pull it off. Cathy barely restrained herself from flinging it into the bushes, instead folding it neatly aside.

"This could take a long time," Dar observed.

"Maybe you should work on my buttons while I work on yours."

"That is a very progressive idea."

She reached for his white shirt as he traced one finger along her delicate necklace, then began undoing her lacy blouse. The heat of his hands and his chest reached her, both at once, and she moved closer.

When he got her blouse open partway, Dar bent and kissed the tops of her breasts. Cathy's breath quickened and liquid silver pumped through her arteries.

His mouth found hers as she stripped away his shirt and ran her hands across his muscular chest. She rose to her knees, letting him stroke away her blouse and bra and catch her nipples with his lips, then trace each pointed breast with his tongue.

Her whole body caught fire. She never wanted Dar to stop tasting and stroking her, and yet she wanted all of him, at once.

Cathy wasn't sure how they managed to remove the rest of their clothing, but a moment later they were lying naked in the shelter of their nest. A warm breeze grazed her skin, bringing the earthy, tangy scents of nature, and she wondered if this was how Adam and Eve had felt when they first lay together.

With one hand, Dar cradled the back of her head as he leaned over to kiss her again. Their bodies stretched length for length, touching at a thousand tingling points.

Then Dar shifted position above her, and united them. She felt as if they were merging into one delirious being.

Cathy cried out softly with the joy of it, the ache and thrust and eagerness of having him within her. Even the first time they made love, she hadn't felt such a complete sense of connection.

She needed this oneness, wanted it to last for all eternity. But although Dar's movements were slow and controlled, she could hear in his raspy breathing the effort that it took to hold himself in check.

He kissed her again, almost roughly, and Cathy returned his ardor, her tongue penetrating his mouth. With a moan, he rose above her, angled her to his need and claimed her once more.

All the power and ferocity of a desert prince drove into her. Seizing his hips, Cathy propelled him to even greater intensity.

Red-hot flames erupted through her. Waves of lava rolled across her body, leaping and flowing until they forever altered her interior landscape.

The intense heat abated slowly. Cathy felt purified, as if she and Dar had been fused into something new and rare.

Slowly she became aware of the blanket beneath her, and of Dar, holding her against his chest. His hand played with the leaflike pendant that dangled from her throat.

"I love you, my wife," he said.

"I love you, too," she said. "My husband."

After a while, they got up and helped each other dress.

It took a bit of tugging and brushing to remove all the leaves and burrs.

Then he helped her into the boat. It might be a long time, Cathy reflected wistfully as the motor sprang to life, before they returned to their magic city. But she suspected plenty of enchantment lay ahead for them, wherever they went.

"Today we begin a new life," Dar called over the noise. "Today we are married in spirit as well as name."

She could only nod. He had captured her feelings perfectly.

Ahead lay a life in which she would help Dar and Leila and Ezzat to remake their country. It was exciting, to be part of something so important.

She and Dar would create their own reality, one that encompassed two cultures and two personalities. Three, including Yasmin, and perhaps someday four or five.

When they swooped past the hacienda, she saw Mary and Faiza walking on the beach. The women were still there when she and Dar returned from putting the boat away.

Mary took one look at their rumpled clothing and gave her daughter a knowing lift of the eyebrow. "It appears that peace is at hand."

"Cathy has agreed to come back with me and be my life's companion." Dar beamed at his mother-in-law. "I hope this meets with your approval."

"Very much so."

Cathy wondered if Faiza still wished that it were Maha, and not she, who would be Sheikh Bahram's mate. Then she saw that the other woman was smiling, too.

"The spirits have foreseen it," said Faiza. "Once again, they are wiser than mere humans." She held out her arms and gave Cathy a hug.

Then they all went up the steps, into the house and into the future—together.

Take 4 bestselling love stories FREE

Plus get a FREE surprise gift!

Make a Valentine's date
for the premiere of

◆ HARLEQUIN® Movies
®
starting February 14, 1998 with

Debbie Macomber's
This Matter of
Marriage

on **themovie channel tmc**

Just tune in to **The Movie Channel** the **second Saturday night** of every month at 9:00 p.m. EST to join us, and be swept away by the sheer thrill of romance brought to life. Watch for details of upcoming movies—in books, in your television viewing guide and in stores.

If you are not currently a subscriber to The Movie Channel, simply call your local cable or satellite provider for more details. Call today, and don't miss out on the romance!

themovie channel tmc
100% pure movies.
100% pure fun.

◆ HARLEQUIN®
® *Makes any time special.™*